Defibrillator Dollybird

Shane Honey

One penny from every e book and 10p from every hardback sold will be donated by the author to the

British Heart Foundation

Published by Shane Honey

For Rhoda and Stuart

Contents

The Midlands in our Twenties

Chapter 1

Frustrated by her own lack of self-control, Josie dabbed at the tears which had sprung from the corners of her eyes. Using all the resolve she could muster, she admonished herself, *I must be strong. I can do this.* With a little effort she managed to smile warmly into the chubby, cherubim face of her beautiful baby boy. With a shaky laugh she took hold of his little feet, wobbling them around in play encouraging him to gurgle with delight. Juggling with one foot at a time she attempted to place it into a soft blue baby bootie; the pair of which had been knitted especially for him by his Grandmother. Josie thought their appearance so cute, each had been decorated with two fluffy woollen bobbles, one blue, and one white, attached to the side of each bootie.

Using the back of her hand she wiped away the two escapee tears that had trickled down and over her right cheek, while simultaneously taking a big sniff in order to collect the few drips that had collected inside her nose. Irritated, she grabbed for a tissue then blew the unwelcome moisture away, helping to clear her nose and throat.

Standing up, she made a check on her appearance in the hall mirror, only to exclaim in dismay, to no one in particular, 'Oh no! Bloody mascara.' Her tears had encouraged her naturally dark lashes to shed their artificial sticky colouring, the result of which left streaks of black running over her slightly rouged cheekbone. She had taken much time with the powder, stroking upward toward the top of her ear with the small blusher brush just so, in order to emphasise her cheekbones and hopefully give the impression that her face was slimmer in shape. There was no time to re-apply either mascara or rouge, Josie, exclaimed, 'Oh bother!' whilst licking a tissue in an attempt to tidy the damage done to the precise drawing and brushing, part of the art of making up her slightly round shaped face, half an hour earlier. Her voice wavered slightly as she screwed up the tissue, putting it to one side on the hall table which had been strategically placed below the mirror, mainly as a residence for the home telephone and house keys. 'There! You cuddly little man! We're all ready for Daddy!'

As she tickled the little boy's tummy in play, his giggling increased, encouraging him to kick his plump baby legs in response to her attention.

The baby had been carefully placed into his pushchair, now parked up in the hallway just inside the front door; he had been dressed and was now ready to go out into the big world outside. His nappy change bag had been wedged under his seat into the small, net carry compartment constructed by the pushchair manufacturer specifically for the purpose.

Josie gazed at the blue and white bobbles, studying their progress as they manically jumped up and around each time her son kicked his feet into the air. For a moment her concentration considered their rough treatment, *it would be amazing if the bobbles were still attached to the booties when he returned!* A second thought crossed Josie's mind, wiping the smile from her face as it passed through. Her facial expression created a mirror image of uncertainty in the little boy's face prompting him to whine in reaction to the huge tears, once again, flowing from his Mother's eyes. *She must stop this happening every Saturday morning*, yet again she would chastise herself, *she must buck up! Pull yourself together girl!*

Josie reached out toward her son, putting both arms around him in an attempt to comfort him, she felt guilty in allowing her inner feelings to rise to the surface and upset the little boy. He could not help being so beautiful but his sandy hair and those huge brown eyes were the image of his father's. A vision of the baby's father emerged, widescreen view, inside Josie's mind. Her feelings raced at the thought of him. *Oh, he was so gorgeous!* A ripple of excitement shot through her body. Josie shook inwardly in response to its uninvited traverse; with difficulty she tried to control the resulting conflict left in consequence. She was trapped like an unwilling passenger on the rollercoaster of emotion, sprung to life with the aid of automatic ignition, every time she thought of her baby's father.

Fighting to rid herself of sentiment, while searching for a brighter viewpoint, her thoughts were abruptly interrupted as a huge shadow temporarily cut the flow of bright morning sunshine; streaming in a myriad of rainbow colours through the frosted glass shapes that made up a small semi circle window at the top of the wooden front door. The glass shapes wobbled anxiously threatening to jump free as the door now rattled in complaint at the two very distinct and heavy knocks it received. Grabbing for the crumpled tissue, Josie looked toward her son with excitement and, dabbing at her cheek once more, exclaimed, 'Gosh! Who is that knocking at the door?'

Earlier that morning, in a house situated only fifty yards farther along the street from Josie's home, Jack, waking slowly, rolled his body, from the position where he lay on his side, over and onto his back. On completion of the roll his eyes opened wide. His initial reaction was to stare in alarm at the unfamiliar ceiling looming above him. *Where the fuck am I!* Panicking slightly he conducted a quick survey of the unfamiliar objects and furniture within the strange room. Memory and recognition, flowing back into his thoughts, helped to relax and allay his fears. Jack allowed a 'Phew!' to escape through his lips. Bright, morning sunshine was struggling in an effort to push through the bedroom's flowery patterned, nylon curtains; promising a fine day awaiting those with energy replaced from sleep after the usual Friday night booze up down the local Pub. Jack's memory replayed a few scenes selected from the previous nights' fun. *The night had gone well and why not? They all worked bloody hard on that building site.*

Jack had many mates; his company was sought after by both men and women, mainly because his zest for life and fun brought out the best in most of his friends and work colleagues. Life was never dull when Jack was in the vicinity. At twenty two years old, he was the youngest foreman ever appointed, to date, by J.M McDougall, Building Construction. All of his workmates grafted well but they also, bizarrely, appeared to enjoy the work, which, being manual, had the added bonus of building and toning a young man's body. No need to visit a gym after a day's work with J.M McDougall to encourage muscle growth. Jack's body however, was just that bit bigger and better toned than his other compatriots. The reason why? Jack had been introduced to the respected art of Boxing from the tender age of ten years old.

Walking home from work one day, his Uncle had caught him scrapping in the street with another lad, whom he knew well. Uncle George had marched across to the pair of boys, arms and legs flying akimbo, grabbed them both by the scruff of their necks and said, 'If you're gonna fight, then we'll teach you both to do a proper job!'

Uncle George literally dragged them both, there and then, along to the local boxing gym. Luckily for them, he didn't have to drag them too far. From that day forward not only had Jack been taught to fight "The Gentleman's Way" but he also received an additional bonus, a sound grounding in the appreciated social skill referred to as respect. All in all a little boxing skill is also quite handy if you should get into a spot of bother and there is no bugger around to "gang up" with you....

Yes, Jack had enjoyed a good night. Sinking quite a few pints of the local Bitter over the course of the evening he, and his work accomplices, had set the pub alight with their energy and good spirits. He had certainly used up a lot of energy come the end of the night and into the early hours of the now Saturday morning.

Propping himself up on his elbow he grinned as he looked down at the sleeping girl lying in the bed beside him. Her long hair was strewn all over the pillow. Jack smiled at the lovely sandy coloured hair and began to stroke it into individual lines, trying to make the strands align with the pink and green stripe patterned pillow case. The girl awoke gently from her sound slumber in response to the wonderful massage her hair was receiving, sighing with pleasure. Such a tender and gentle way to wake up to a new day! You see Jack had been blessed with a most impressive gift; as a young man, not only did he have an aptitude for performing as much sex as he could procure, he took far greater pleasure from the whole if his partner was completely satisfied. It was his basic way of ensuring he had completed a quality job. You know that feeling you get when you look back at a wall you've just painted, with no streaks? That sense of achievement.

Notwithstanding this most accomplished asset, he was also naturally warm and gentle, nearly always paired with a huge frame in nature. The Gentle Giant that was Jack. Unsurprisingly, the local girls were keen for a piece of the action and if they could find a way to claim the whole package, even better.

The girl with the sandy hair was employed as a barmaid at one of the local pubs Jack frequented and had caught his eye, with a cheeky smile, whilst passing a full pint over the bar to him, a few months beforehand. The pint of bitter had wobbled in her hand slightly, when she attempted to deliver it to Jack, across the bar, between a couple of other customers, allowing a little of the amber coloured liquid to run over the edges and down the sides of the glass. Punters could no way complain that they didn't get a full pint.

'Shall I lick the drips?' Jack suggested, as the tasty fluid ran over the back of his hand when he grasped the glass.

She retorted saucily, 'Is your tongue long enough for the job?'

Suffice to think her query had now been answered as she had been sleeping with Jack on and off ever since, well, as often as she could claim his attention anyway. She wondered how she might entice him to make the arrangement more permanent but for now it felt like she was going to enjoy the pleasure of his lovemaking again and she grew excited at the thought, there was plenty of time before her next shift at the pub. Her body started to relax and harden in all the right places in response to his gentle enquiring fingers. Gently, he planted tender kisses around the base of her neck, drinking in her individual body perfume with each one.

He had awoken aroused, intoxicated by the heady mix of herbal shampoo, stale cigarettes, whatever soap powder, possibly Omo, that the sheets had been washed in and the lingering aroma of all night sex. Somehow, you could never get rid of the smell of cigarettes, confirming you either smoked yourself or worked in a smoke filled environment, i.e. public house or most office blocks. Oblivious to this fairly normal bouquet, she smiled in ecstasy, moaning lazily at his touch, 'Baby, I could endure this forever.' Jack's thoughts went along not un-similar lines; *if I play me cards right, I'll get me leg over again before I leave.*

On the other side of town, a short train ride away, a pretty, blonde haired baby girl was giggling restlessly while simultaneously attempting to escape while her Mother employed gentle force in order to hold her on her back; it took some effort, at times, to change her nappy. Her mother, Geanie, kept her patience with the lively child, laughing when she, at last, was able to secure her in a hold where she would submit to the new nappy encircling her bum whether she wanted it or not! 'Stay there you little minx! We can't be late for Daddy can we?'

Geanie hated the name Jean, the name she had been christened with, this Bowie version was far better. She had initiated the use of her preferred version while at school, five years ago, along with a spiky but naturally blonde hairdo in the hope of producing a "cool" look to her appearance. To her delight, the exchange had been accepted and successfully imprinted in the minds of her schoolmates within weeks, and without the need for her to dye the ends of her hair bright red or blue and gold, like the teenager she had heard about at Summerbee School in Bournemouth, who had caused enough uproar for the school Board to ban her from the premises temporarily; the story had even made it to the national newspapers.

Geanie had to stay on schedule if she was to salvage any "me" time to order to prepare her own toilette. She loved her little girl dearly but no one told you how much of a tie a baby could be. It played havoc with dating other guys but Geanie did not have to date, if she made herself alluring enough she would get him in the end; she had already given birth to his baby. He would be hers.

With her baby's preparations complete she gently laid the little girl in her cot as at six months old she could roll and end up anywhere; *I need eyes in the back of my head!*, she thought. *Now where did I leave my makeup bag?*

"Suzie" the popular, nationwide, young women's magazine, had provided a complimentary tube of black eye mascara with every copy last week. Geanie decided she would use that one in particular to emphasise her eyelashes, hopefully giving the impression they were incredibly long, or maybe she had enough time to put on the false ones? *Bugger, no way!* The procedure required eyelash glue and she had forgotten to replace the stuff when she had gone to the Chemist. The baby always needed bathing and changing supplies but she had no worries where these items were concerned, the maintenance she received regularly from the baby's father meant there was no problem there. All the same, it was difficult to appear sexy and alluring as a young Mum, without a job or being able to afford good make up. Not to worry, later on today could see a change in her circumstances.

Her parents had been kind and understanding about their Granddaughter, mainly because they assumed their daughter would be married within the near future, but Geanie realised she was a woman in her own right and had no status stuck at home with her Mum and Dad. She thought of her baby's father. Her pretty, peach and cream complexioned face started to glow with happiness and excitement. *He was so good looking and she had his baby! They could live happily ever after. All she had to do was get his full attention. Could he not see that she and the baby were all he needed? Why did he have to go fishing with his mates at every opportunity and drink in the pub every weekend?* Geanie became worried thinking about what he had said the other evening. *Would he really go abroad to work? She must persuade him to marry her before he left. Now where was that mascara?*

Meanwhile, the girl with the sandy hair had been sexually pleasured in a way no other man could perform, as far as she was concerned anyway; she sighed as she thought of her long term boyfriend, Martin, *he was so sincere, but crap at making love.* Never before, had she been left feeling so warm and contented following a session of sex. After providing her with the best breakfast, apart from Miss World's, Champagne and Strawberries, that you could possibly feast on, (Jack called his alternative breakfast Muffin with Pussy), he had literally jumped out of bed, dressed quickly, kissed her with plenty of tongue and a grin, then departed, but he would be back. She knew he would return and always welcomed him back, in her mind, only Jack possessed such a unique technique enabling to please both himself and her.

As far as Jack was concerned the more his partners became excited, the more it turned him on. And he was turning many on. They were practically queuing at his door! His mates would tease him often and one or two were slightly jealous, of course, saying he must be working for porno movies on the quiet, but Jack had never or ever wanted to watch one. He knew instinctively how to turn a woman on, and more importantly, when not to bother. Like I said, he had been given a gift. Trouble was, although he was full of enthusiasm, sharing his present with as many women who might fancy a piece; he had become rather too enthusiastic, not assigning much wisdom in its distribution of late.

*

Josie noticed the sun disappear from the hallway; instinctively she turned toward the front door and saw the shadow responsible a few seconds before the door received its gentle bashing. She quickly wiped another trickling tear from one of her eyes and ruffed up her loose, wavy brown hair in preparation. The lively, nine month old boy had jumped in surprise when the door had produced the strange banging noise. His reaction to the unexpected sound was to kick his feet about, encouraging the little fluffy balls, decorating his boots, to spring around like Mexican Jumping Beans.

Josie opened the front door to a tall, well built, handsome young man, only to gaze directly up into the big brown eyes of her husband.

The frustration in her body could not be contained. She so much wanted to hold him, to love him. There was nothing stopping her, after all he was her husband. Her heart started to melt and her whole body started to crave with desire. 'Watch out for those hormones!' her Mother had warned her. They were playing havoc with her body right now. There really is no help available for controlling hormones; they are tricky little buggers at the best of times. The sight of her handsome husband just standing there! In an instant her emotion leapt back down as the memory she tried so hard to shut out barged right through the gate bringing forth its attached pent up anger and despair. The angry frustration combined with the garbled words of hate about to escape from her mouth, contorting her pretty face from a look of sadness into rage. She spat the words at him in greeting, his warm lazy smile fuelling the furnace of burning words.

'You fucking, fucking....bastard! I suppose you'll go to get your daughter next!

Chapter 2

Geanie's parent's front door bell rang, well, to be more precise, performed. They had just installed one of the new, musical, front door bells that play a tune when a button is pressed rather than having a door knocker to knock. This imaginative style of informing the inhabitants of a home that someone is standing outside expecting attention had just been invented; the subtle marketing strategy applied to this product was to insinuate that the discerning home owner would rise, on its installation, to a slightly higher working class.

Jack, the perpetrator of the now tinkling rendition of "When Irish Eyes Are Smiling", grimaced as he was forced to listen, while waiting for attention from within, to the boring chimes thinking, *bloody rubbish!* The bell, ringing forth its melodious if rather tinny tune was, for Jack, thankfully cut short as the door opened hastily. Jack received a beaming smile, with a hint of tease in welcome, from the long eye lashed, blonde haired young woman now standing directly in front of him in the doorway. He sighed inwardly, grateful for no aggravation at the entry to this household. A smile spread across his face, partly due to the pleasant welcome but also due to the sight of his daughter laughing up at him from her pushchair; her nappy change bag had been crammed under her seat exactly like the one belonging to her brother. As Jack relaxed, crouching down to respond to her happy greeting, his eyes flicked back up to look at Geanie, his smile, firmly fixed, lit up his handsome face.

Geanie coyly informed him, 'My parents are going out tonight, so we could have the house to ourselves. Do you want to come round later? I can cook dinner for us as well if you like.'

She felt excited, spilling the words out slowly, trying to sound matter of fact. With a bit of luck he would say yes because she really needed to have sex with him again and soon. At six months old the baby was growing well but nature (in the form of Geanie's hormones) was insisting she needed more sex and possibly another baby. Geanie worked hard to look sexy and tempting to Jack, her confidence growing in receipt of the warm smile that was slowly expanding into a huge grin on his beautiful face, and those huge brown eyes... *Oh, how bloody good looking he was!*

His handsome face laughed up into hers; just as she moved toward him, taking this sign for an imminent kiss and acceptance, Jack stood up from greeting his daughter and burst into wild laughter, his huge chest expanding with mirth, 'Have you got those stupid, false eyelashes on again?, the one over your left eye is hanging off!'

Geanie recoiled in embarrassment, flinging her hands up to cover her left eye. She was about to say something catty back in an attempt to extinguish the feeling of foolishness now steadily creeping everywhere it shouldn't when her efforts with the remaining glue (found in the bathroom cupboard) were rewarded. 'Yes, I'd love to come over later', laughed Jack.

Still laughing from the sight of Geanie's failed attempt at flirtation due to the droopy false eyelash, Jack turned to the pushchair, parked behind him that he had arrived with, containing his son.

'Did you see her silly eyelashes?' he said with a laugh to the little boy, which made the little lad giggle while simultaneously jerking his arms and legs around, in response to his father's smile. The blue fluffy bobbles responded to the kicking of his feet in their usual manic way.

Jack turned his son's pushchair to face the gate, just a few feet away, and then brought his daughter's pushchair in line alongside. Holding the adjoining handles of both pushchairs together with one huge hand, Jack took a piece of builder's string from the back pocket of his jeans and tied the two handles together. He found this most simple implement worked wonders in relation to the probable directional problems that could be encountered if the pushchairs were out of alignment. Just before he set off up the street, to take his two children out for the day, he gave Geanie a long, meaningful kiss which made her wish she could shag him then and there. Her thoughts protested, *it really was asking too much for her to wait. But wait she would and in the meantime prepare him a lovely dinner. It would be cosy to be together as a family later. Perhaps tonight they could discuss their future.* Either way she would make sure they both had a brilliant sex session for dessert which she knew, with Jack, was guaranteed.

On the odd occasion, when she was desperate for sex or just his company, and her parents had gone out for the evening, she would wait for him outside the local pub with the baby in the pushchair. She would not go in. She would let Jack know she wanted to see him by asking someone going in, to ask him to come out. He would happily emerge. He knew what she wanted. She would smile and say her parents had gone out. He would never let her down.

Now, you might think the sight of a handsome twenty two year old man pushing not just one but two pushchairs, (tied in the middle with building string), complete with offspring, would put any female off. Not so, the pushchairs attracted women akin to some sort of "Babe" magnet. Jack was not an arrogant young man, he knew he was good looking and attractive to women but sometimes it could also be a pain. This became apparent when the pushchair magnet attracted the one or two (let's do it behind the bike shed, Jack) tarts that he had tried to avoid at school. He was ever the happy wanderer but loved his two children dearly and nearly every Saturday he made the effort to collect and spend time with them, even if it meant enduring the gauntlet of Josie.

*

Conveniently parking the pushchairs, complete with occupants, in the floor space reserved for suitcases, situated just behind the driver cab in the bus, another passenger got up and kindly offered Jack his seat, while he moved to another, so he could sit opposite his children. As Jack leant forward, while pulling faces in order to occupy them for the short journey into town, he wondered; *why had Josie become such a sour cow lately*?

Dismissing the thought from his mind, his attention turned back to his children and thoughts from some of their past outings with him. Jack thoroughly enjoyed their company; only the previous week he, along with a few of his mates, had sat the little boy on the pool table in a local pub, laughing to see his pleasure and gurgles of delight while they pretended he had hit the red ball with the cue. Meanwhile, the females attached to these males stood, or sat about, cooing whilst passing his daughter, to offer attention and affection, amongst them. One of these females, a brazen piece with red lips and short, straight black Mary Quant style hair, had boldly gazed straight into Jack's eyes as she passed his daughter back to him only to ask direct but in a low voice, 'Could you give me one Jack?'

Only a couple of nights ago, earlier in the week and on the quiet, he had indeed given her one, Jack assumed she had meant sex and not the whole package to include a baby. He had enough problems with the two he had already procured. Possessing a more realistic outlook than Geanie, the young woman had settled for just sex, although she too (which Jack did not realise) would have preferred the whole package. Hormones, proper little buggers they are.

Grinning while reminiscing, his thoughts wandered off on a tangent toward the barmaid with the sandy hair. *What was her bloody name again?* He should make an effort to remember. Bugger, he had told Geanie he would go to her tonight. A smile spread across his face as a simple plan entered his head.

*

Alighting from the bus he offered a 'Cheers Mate' to the driver then, pushchairs aligned; set a course through the assortment of Saturday morning shoppers toward Mothercare. Josie had given him a list of supplies that she needed for their little boy.... Geanie had provided him with a similar list. Dutifully he would comply with their requests. After all, they had the bulk of the childcare; he had no shortage of money either. Building was big business in the nineteen seventies and Jack earned around three hundred quid a week.

After their split he had allowed Josie to keep the house he had bought for them when they had married. Slightly annoyed, his thoughts returned to her, *you would think the daft cow would be grateful!* He felt it was only right as he had cheated on her with Geanie, come to think of it, there were a few others as well, but they had not produced a baby which would always be the proof that you've shagged away from home... Anyway there was no problem going into Mothercare because if he remembered rightly, *they had a nice looking assistant with blonde hair and big tits.*

With his goal in sight, a hundred yards or so further down the high street, he started to laugh. Concentrating in earnest to reach the popular children's store as his first port of call he had unconsciously joined in a duet with Linda Lewis and now found himself humming along to her 1973 release, "Rock-a-Doodle-Doo", the notes of which were flowing gaily across the street from a nearby record shop. Jack had been singing away, unawares, with the chorus which was also the title of the song. Mildly annoyed to have been musically hypnotised into joining in with what was obviously a girlie tune of nearly eight years ago; *what the fuck would his heroes, The Who, think of him!*, he entered the store, immediately catching the eye of the blonde assistant with the amply proportioned chest.

Instructed by the store manager to always be on the lookout and at the ready to encourage any shopper to part with their cash, she had no problem spotting such a handsome young man and strode toward him with a smile full of hope and serious intent, like a wasp to a recently discarded lolly pop wrapper.

'Can I help you Sir?' she said, with a smile that suggested there was more on offer than nappies and baby cream. Before Jack could answer she bent down toward the two pushchairs and made a fuss of each child in turn.

'They are beautiful babies, are they yours?'

'Yes', said Jack grinning broadly but inwardly preparing for possible slight embarrassment when their ages might be asked. The girl then posed the question which Jack had hoped he might avoid but what the hell.

'Are they twins?'

'No', said Jack.

'Oh, they look the same age.'

Here we go again thought Jack but his engaging face grinned as he replied, 'My son is nine months and my daughter six.'

The girl's facial expression confirmed she had registered the information, processing the dates in her brain. Still looking at the babies, her face changed quickly back to a smile from the slight look of apology that had raised the eyebrows on her face. She hoped her simple question had not been thought too intrusive by the handsome young man. Jack noted her reaction, relieved there had been no recoil or look of disapproval from the girl, quite the reverse in fact. She thought, *he doesn't look the type to be married, check out any rings on his left hand.* She looked to his left hand, now resting on a pushchair handle. To her delight there was no ring, a veil of playfulness started to flow over her, she once again asked if she could help him find what he was looking for. Cheekily she threw in a statement, 'We sell double pushchairs you know?'

Jack grinned at her in reply and meekly followed her into the body of the huge store.

Looking around the shop, his eyes were bombarded by primary colours, various baby and children's clothes flashing like beacons with their gay colours. The atmosphere almost felt noisy. His mind flew back nine months or so to one of the last times he had accompanied Josie to the store. He began to lose interest in his wife soon after she became pregnant, this being the main reason they married. He was never quite sure why The Pill had not worked for her and from the minute she told him she was expecting a baby she always seemed to be at her mother's house. Most days he would return from work to an empty home. *What the hell was he doing with his life? Why be lonely when he could have the company of any girl he wanted?* He couldn't think of any other reason why he shouldn't have married her at the time though. She was a lovely looking girl and, as he had managed to remain faithful for quite a few months beforehand, it appeared the right thing to do. Unfortunately his mother had been furious with the match,

'What on earth do you want to marry her for? You can do much better!'

'Actually Mum, Josie is having a baby'

'She's WHAT! You stupid, young fool. You've been caught deliberately.'

Any reflection he might ponder in relation to his wedding day would often conclude with his Mother's behaviour, encouraging him to feel anger toward her; s*he had been most rude, wearing a sour expression on her face throughout the whole day.* Never mind, he had managed to escape the reception, and her scowling face, for an hour or so along with his Dad, Uncle Wally and Best Man Jimmy, to partake of a short sojourn to Warwick Racecourse. A favourite horse of theirs was running in a race that very afternoon and they just had to place a bet. To their collective elation the horse won. Sardonically, the equine gamble Jack placed that day paid off rather handsomely, the gamble on his marital relationship however, would prove to be a non runner from the start.

Jack's thoughts returned to the present, dismissing the memories of his temporary absence from his own wedding reception, only to wander off again re-enacting the last time he had visited the store with Josie; he had gone outside for a quick fag, bored with the cooing and interest Josie was showing in baby stuff. Sighing quietly within while temporarily enjoying a few minutes relief from attending his wife, Jack had only just lit up his cigarette when he inwardly jumped, nearly dropping the stick of nicotine that had been strategically placed between his lips. Looming toward him from across the other side of the high street was an altogether troubling scene.

Striding purposefully past Woolworth, heading straight toward Mothercare were Geanie and her parents. *Christ!* He thought. *Geanie's belly was looking huge. She hadn't looked that big when he had seen her a few days ago. Josie hadn't been that big at six months, she was about that size now and ready to drop.* Jack's accusatory thoughts went straight to The Pill. As far as he was concerned whoever said it would stop women getting pregnant was having a laugh. It had not delivered the goods for the two women about to give birth to his children. *Delivered the goods?!* He choked back a laugh at the words he had haplessly allowed to enter his head.

Luckily they had not noticed him; Jack used the advantage to keep well out of their view by lurking farther along the street until they had crossed the road, having had to dodge the constant flow of two-way traffic before they could enter the store. He let out a rather loud 'Phew!' which made a couple of pedestrians grin as they passed by; that was one meeting he did not want to attend just now. As far as he knew, Geanie had not issued a general release to the public detailing the identity of her baby's father. Not that she was running a sweepstake or anything similar. Once the family were safely in the store and his fag finished, he urgently tried to locate Josie. Jack received a worrying vision of the two women happily discussing their due dates in their ignorance. *Where the fuck was she?* Jack furtively made an entrance back into the store. He hid from no man but this was different.

Making his way quickly to a gaily painted support column, he stood behind it. *No worries*, he thought as he leant to peer around the side, in the style of a Royal Marine, scanning for any sign of enemy activity within his vicinity. With relief, he spotted the Geanie party ascending the stairs to the cot department above. A surprise slap on the shoulder made him jump with guilt.

'What are you doing hiding behind here?' said Josie.

'Looking for you my sweet!' said Jack in reply.

His cheeky grin spread across the air to land and light up Josie's face. *Oh, he is so bloody gorgeous*, she thought, *and all mine!*

Asking her hastily if she had collected everything she needed, her affirmative induced Jack to instantly propel her out of the shop slightly faster than a person who can't see their feet anymore could handle. Laughing at her reprimand he was thankful to have escaped the inevitable for just a little longer.

*

Geanie was excited. She loved shopping at the best of times but selecting clothes and accessories for the baby was proving to be so much fun. She only wished Jack could have accompanied her to the store instead of her parents. *Oh! How she hated having to hide their love. To be seen out in public with him, other women would be so envious. She must have patience! Time passed quickly. They would be together soon.*

Her parents reaction to the news of the impending delivery, the arrival of which would automatically award them the title "Grandparents", had not filled them with much joy, mainly because their daughter had become pregnant with no husband to support her. Their opinion of such a fellow was extremely low, they were further cast into dismay however, when she assured them the father would be marrying her soon, she didn't want to divulge his name yet, they must trust her. In their opinion she had gravely misunderstood his intention. Anyone genuine would have come forward to meet them, they ventured, but this observation served only to encourage their much-loved child to snap a hot retort in his defence.

Her father, struggling to come to terms with the imminent adjustment to his family unit, lost his resolve one morning while watching his beloved daughter bringing the breakfast she had just eaten, straight back up into a bucket, her stomach temporarily refusing a once cherished form of nourishment. He felt useless at, what he felt, was his failure to defend his daughter. If she would only tell him the father's name, he could "call him out", so to speak. Apart from reading the occasional glossy women's magazine, Geanie was not in the habit of reading historical romance novels, leaving her at a loss to understand the conjecture of this phrase, however, it had been uttered with such dark determined passion leaving her imagination of the opinion he was disinclined to sit down with Jack and have a nice chat. However chivalrous his intention, had her father realised the size of his potential opponent he would have checked his life insurance before avenging his daughter's insult.

Geanie was, in fact, very lucky to have such understanding parents. The shame of single motherhood was still a stigma left trailing from the remains of the nineteen sixties. Geanie was oblivious to any form of social chastisement, her hormones processing only the most positive, happy thoughts. There was even one or two for Jack's wife. *Josie will be okay*, she thought, *Jack will give her maintenance and she'll find someone else. It was simple.*

She couldn't wait to dress her baby in these lovely clothes. Picking up a pair of yellow and green dungarees sporting a cartoon tree print running, in random, all over them, Geanie's mind opened up a picture of the local woods, time zone, about six months ago. She bit her lower lip gently; concerned her excited smile might automatically project her thoughts and mind's picture to the other shoppers, thereby spilling her secret.

Jack had met Geanie in the local wood. Arriving home from work one day he found a note propped up beside the tomato sauce bottle on the kitchen table, **Over Mums back about 7.00ish**.

Fuck it! He didn't want to be at home on his own; he may as well go down the pub and get something to eat there. *What could he do till it opened? Geanie, he could see Geanie!*

One quick telephone call and a short walk later, there she was, giggling as he approached her across the common ground toward the woods. She fell forward into his embrace; her body alight with tingling sensations. Risky, naughty sex was simply the best and they both enjoyed a fairly quick, hot session. As she undid her jeans, Jack put his arms around Geanie in order to lift her up. Placing her legs astride his body, with his hands behind her lower thighs, he then hoisted her up to rest across his groin, still using his hands to support her while her back rested against a wholly innocent and unsuspecting tree. Her knickers were allowed no time to vacate due to the frantic emotion smouldering between the pair of lovers. Her hand scrambled about between her legs and his lower body trying to drag the crotch of her knickers to the side, such was her desperation to let him in. He wasted no time in finding the opening to all manner of chaos and pushed hard, her excitement and joy at the wonderful feeling causing her body to jolt. Pushing all the strength from her back into her knees with the elation, any man would need strength to keep her in place; for Jack it was easy. Within just a few minutes they had completed their mutual task. As they caught their breath they were both laughing. Jack let her down gently waiting for her feet to establish a hold on terra firma before letting her go.

Adjusting his jeans, he zipped up and turned away giving her space to sort her clothes out. She pulled her jeans back up over soaking wet knickers. Yuck! Their cold wet touch made her feel uncomfortable outside but inside her body felt warm, satisfied and complete, still tingling. Jack turned back to smile at her, reaching out to take her hand; when she suddenly started to jump about in a way not totally dissimilar to his son's blue fluffy bootie balls.

'Aaah! Aaah' Geanie leaped around seeming to have lost control of her body, giving the appearance that spasmodic electric shocks were striking different parts of her limbs, making her writhe and twist, her blonde locks leaping in unison with her body. Jack paid attention immediately, concerned that something was causing her pains but not sure how to help.

'What's the matter? Geanie, what's the matter?'

Geanie frantically grappled with the zip on her jeans. *Christ!* He thought, *she's just done them up now she's manically trying to get them off again.*

Geanie managed to pull her jeans down but then threw her hands behind her, trying to twist her body around, making panicky sweeping gestures to her lower back. Suddenly, satisfied this strange behaviour had had its effect, she looked down into the sodden knickers now entangled with her jeans. The contents of her pants, aside from the remaining love juices, made her jump and shout yet again but this act now identified the root cause of the primal dance. After a few more yelps and jumps she bent down, simultaneously shaking her knickers up and down as fast as she could. Geanie dislodged a spider.

Unobtrusively minding its own business while lurking on the side of the tree, it had been scooped against its will into Geanie's tangled jeans as Jack had placed her against the tree trunk; relieved she had not been in the acute pain her behaviour had suggested, Jack let go his usual reaction and burst into laughter.

In the few weeks that followed, when Geanie told him she was pregnant, he reckoned that spider had done more for fertility than any test tube could have achieved.

Chapter 3

Jack returned his son to Josie late in the afternoon, annoyed at his inability to stop humming another rather catchy tune, "Hands up, baby, hands up", a new record release thrown at him like musical confetti from Woolworth as he passed by the store earlier in the day. What the hell would "The Who" think when they were informed of his worrying sway to the goody, goody side? He mumbled the chorus of, "Who are you?", albeit slightly out of tune, in the hope of diverting his thoughts to real music, forcing the words into his head as he approached the entrance to, what was once, his marital home.

As she opened the front door, Josie threw a frustrated, un-musical, impatient glance straight at his daughter, happily chattering away to herself in her pushchair, now detached from her brothers; builder's string safely returned to the back pocket of Jack's jeans.

Angrily, she snatched at the baby items, requested earlier in the day, that Jack now held out to her as he exclaimed, 'You want to watch that door. Those pieces of glass are coming loose. I'll get some putty and fix them sometime if you like. I'll pick him up next Saturday okay?'

'Whatever', was the only answer he received.

Josie turned to manhandle the pushchair, still containing the 'little boy, through the front door and into the house.

Jack didn't care if she was unhappy at the site of his daughter or the items he'd bought willingly, as the afternoon had seen him make an unexpected purchase which later on that evening should cost no more than a bag of crisps and a pint up the town. Yes, the girl with big tits had succumbed to the mysterious charm of the magnet pushchair and her last name, he remembered, was Butterworth. The thought of her ample charms literally buttered on a plate was success in itself. Oh yes, he loved shopping with his children.

Setting off for his parent's home, a little farther up the street, with now just the one pushchair and child, he smiled and started to hum at his success, 'Hands up, baby, hands up....fuck it!'

*

Jack often made a special visit to his Mum and Dad's house before returning his children to their respective mothers, so they could spend a little time with one or both of their grandchildren; on this occasion he also informed his Mother he would go to Geanie's for his tea. It was also time for a spot of nappy changing. Jack was quite accomplished in the art of origami using two simple items, a rectangular piece of towel and a large safety pin. His Mother had been greatly amused by his first attempts to attach a nappy to his son's backside with the aid of the ancient art of paper folding. The little lad had promptly crawled off, nappy falling slowly down his legs and around his knees as he made off toward the Telly, exploring his grandparents front room with the aid of his hands and knees. She now found it difficult to accept them both, her own shame punishing her, stealing away the enjoyment of her grandchildren. Occasionally, social guilt would prompt her to shout in anger 'Those two girls got pregnant deliberately to catch you!'

Jack felt, at times, she shouted the sentence too often. He wondered once, when his Mother was scolding him, if he should mention the spider's liabilities toward the resulting drama.

Lately, he had sought solace a few nights each week with the sandy haired barmaid. As usual he just had to live life on the edge. The barmaid lived only a short distance away, across and up the street from Josie's home.

She had recently moved into the area with her mother but had the house to herself for a while. She had explained to Jack that her mother had divorced her father but was presently away from home looking after an old relative or something, leaving the very capable sandy haired daughter, Jennifer (Jenny) Jackman in charge.

Jack was becoming fed up having to sneak into the Jackman home, always keeping a watchful eye out for Josie, the woman scorned. Jack thought that it was all becoming far too complicated. He was growing tired of the effort that had to be made to ensure constant deception. Little did he realise his life was about to become very complicated indeed.

After returning his daughter home he spent the main part of the evening with Geanie, enjoying a nice "tea" with a session of sex for "afters" (" " known as dinner and dessert if you are posh or from Bournemouth). His "entre" was the delight of bathing and putting his daughter to bed.

Geanie, a feeling of sheer satisfaction flowing throughout her body, was glowing from within as she observed the father of her child bath and care for their baby. With sadness, Geanie remembered her parents would create merry hell if they caught Jack in the house; this being the only dark thought sent to dampen the pretty picture spread before her.

Although he really enjoyed the time spent with his children Jack found their mothers, in the main, annoying; making an easy excuse he was able to leave before the evening was entirely lost. Likewise, there was always an awkward silence if her parents were at home. He found it difficult to lie to their enquiries of, 'When would his divorce be final?' He had not rushed this as he had no inclination to marry again, this being the only hope Geanie's parents nursed that was of any assistance, encouraging civility into collective general conversation between them and their granddaughter's father.

Jack remembered the day he had gone into the hospital to see Geanie and their day old daughter. He had met her father by chance in a hospital corridor, *Boy was he angry!* Offloading his furious anger and shame onto Jack, through gritted teeth he challenged, 'How dare you make our daughter pregnant and be married to someone else at the same time!'

The hitherto unknown experience of childbirth had shattered Geanie's resolve, encouraging her to give up the name of her secret lover. The fact that he was already married was no bonus to her parents on their discovery of the absent father's identity, after the long awaited naming session.

'And what are you going to do about it, you bloody bastard? Our Jean assures us you are going to marry her. Well you had better do so and quickly or you'll answer to me!'

Jack understood his fear. He also respected his anger. No man, to date, had picked a fight with Jack and walked away upright but this man deserved his respect, however, that did not mean he would bend to his will.

His excuses accepted, Jack was eager to enjoy the remainder of the evening (and best part of Saturday night). He headed back home to hastily wash and change. On arrival, he spent a few minutes chatting with his father, asking what he was about (had planned for) the next day. Jack loved his father's company. As a lad he had spent many a happy hour with him, rabbiting, shooting or discussing horse racing. They still enjoyed these pastimes together but not as much since the children had arrived.

Making his usual, furtive, undercover return from Jenny's home that morning, he had washed, shaved and changed before setting off back up the other end of the street again to collect his son. It just felt right to wash any remains of sexual activity from his body before collecting his children and especially in between sex with one woman and another.

For the second time that day Jack used the independent, plastic, shower hose attachment and was refreshed by the quick, all over body sprinkle of water while sitting in the bath; a brilliant idea for those who did not possess the funds and space for a posh shower cubicle. Completing his toilette with a good "splash it all over" of Brut (as advised by our Henry on the TV advert, who had given the great Mohammad Ali a run for his money in the boxing ring, so it must be good) and a comb scraped through his short, curly, sandy locks in haste, he shrugged on a clean pair of jeans, selected a new shirt, grabbed his wallet and made his way downstairs.

Hanging on the wall at the bottom of the stairs was a white iron, ivy and scroll patterned, oval, sixties style mirror. It received no attention from Jack as he purposefully strode past on his way out; lazily calling a leaving shout to his parents, sat watching Bruce Forsyth in The Generation Game.

'Good Game, Good Game!' he laughed, as he made off up town. Cocky git he definitely was but vain, never.

Striding toward the lively town pub he caught sight of big tits Butterworth waiting for him outside, as planned, *he must stop thinking of her last name only, what was her first name again?*

Miss Butterworth, elated with her surprise date for the all important Saturday night, welcomed him with a shy kiss and wry smile, made all the more enjoyable due to a group of her friends catching sight of her in Jack's arms at that precise moment. From the corner of her eye she noticed their surprised, envious faces.

Jack reckoned he might be in with another session of sex later but if not, he didn't care. Some men took it personally if a girl kept refusing them after a few dates or even sadder, ditched them if they never "gave it" after a while. Jack's mates called him one lucky bastard. Women just wanted to sleep with him, he didn't have to try. It never bothered him if a date just didn't want to do it. If he liked her and she was fun, then her company was good enough. There was always another wanting sex. One of his friends was bold enough to ask, 'How the hell do you do it, Jack. What have you got, you git, that's different to everyone else.'

Jack, in reply, said he never actually thought about why he was so popular with women, he was too busy shagging them.

However, the night she had lined up ready to place as one of her best dates ever, with the hope maybe of a few more in the future, totally collapsed, only to crash around her, in spectacular manner, analogous with the Trotter chandelier. Barbara (Babs) Butterworth, notwithstanding her lovely breasts, had not turned Jack on. Now you may think this strange but nature sometimes must put ones foot down. Whether shagging Jenny for breakfast and Geanie for tea, had filled Jack's appetite for the day, we will never know. Nature has never been one to give up its mysteries easily. Jack, far from agonising over the situation, was quite unconcerned; having consumed his fill gawping at Babs's amazing assets in between slurps of bitter and conducting small chat surrounding their respective jobs, he suddenly lost interest, that's all there was to it. He felt for Babs as she had indicated straight from the start of the evening that she would be delighted to become his supper; thereby, on Jacks part, completing a three course meal for that particular day. She made it clear it was "game on". Ah well, he let her down gently, as only a Gentle Giant could.

'Sorry love but I don't fancy it tonight, maybe next time?'

There would not be a next time, he just didn't fancy her. The resulting dismissal not only flattened Babs but perhaps it was her sadness and disappointment that rubbed off on him, either way, Jack had no desire for any more sex that day. After putting quite some effort into creating subjects to talk about for the rest of the evening, he eventually escorted her home, managing to at least, kiss the girl goodnight.

With one last 'Bye Jack', she shut the front door of her home on what she imagined was the most gorgeous man she had ever set eyes on; sitting at the bottom of the stairs, holding her face in both hands, she started to cry. Tears ran through her fingers and onto her knees. Her life suddenly felt empty, how could she tell her friends it had been just one date? They would surely want to know all about it on Monday. Babs now wished she had not told every one of her workmates about her hot date. For a short while her arms had held a real man but like a tide on the turn he had retreated, out of her reach.

Meanwhile, Jack had leisurely sauntered off in the direction of home with a whistle to his step, glad to escape the awkward atmosphere that had been present for most of the evening. He also felt ready for some sleep. A most unusual outcome for one of his Saturday nights!

Arriving at work on the Monday morning, Babs tried to avoid the inevitable enquiries from her friends, their enthusiasm and demands that she tell all in relation to her Saturday night date, did not help get her working week off to a flying start. She wished she could afford to call in sick.

However, Jack's week had commenced in a far pleasant manner. His

Manager sought him out within the first hour of the working day to remind him he had a week's holiday allowance he had not taken. 'Did he not want holiday?!'

As mentioned previously, Jack almost enjoyed his work and due to his weekends normally overflowing with a variety of delights such as regular sex, the need to take a holiday had not crossed through his mind of late. His usual weekly routine consisted thus:

1. Building work for the duration of each workday.
2. Frequenting a local pub on two or three of these evenings followed by a possible session of sex with one of his female admirers.
3. Collecting his children each Saturday morning, and, after allocating the day to them,
4. Probable Saturday night shagging after spending the night on the town and / or in the pub,
5. Rounded off with possible Sunday morning shagging, with the same Saturday night, female admirer.

This regular, seven day schedule was occasionally complimented by a most desired zenith,

1. Doing a bit of rough shooting in the countryside with his father and the dogs on a Sunday afternoon.

This readily available and most enjoyable collection of pastimes meant that Jack didn't see everyday life as a chore that needed to be broken from occasionally.

His Manager shook his head with a smile, *most of his workforce had booked their holiday immediately on receipt of their annual allocation*, Jack was the first employee he had come across who didn't seem to care.

'Well you're due holiday Jack, so when are you taking it?'

They both agreed the following week would be okay. A few of Jack's friends had suggested they arrange a lad's get together, for a week in Jersey, later on in the summer and he had already allocated some of his holiday allowance toward this treat but, *no bugger had organised anything yet* thought Jack, *so until anything definite has been planned I may as well use some time now.* He then remembered that the fishing season had just started. He could go fishing! How could he forget such a favourite pastime?

With his present working week passing by in the usual way, he awoke on the Saturday morning happy to find himself, once again, in Jenny's bed surrounded by well shampooed, sandy coloured hair. After returning to his parents' home in time for breakfast, he washed and changed then (builder's string in back pocket) set off on the usual round to collect his children for the day.

Josie, as usual, was angry when he arrived. Jack noticed her eyes appeared a bit red. He wondered if she might have an eye infection or something. *Come to think of it they were a bit red last week as well.*

If she wasn't so difficult to talk to these days he would have enquired if everything was okay with her. Women were unfathomable. Well, he wasn't going to waste any effort asking about her health only to have his head bitten off, so to speak, with the angry words she habitually threw at him whenever they met.

For Jack, his Saturday "children time" passed enjoyably, if in a fairly predictable way, only this weekend Geanie's parents were spending their Saturday night at home. She wanted Jack to herself for the evening but her wish was not his to command.

When was he going to finalise his Divorce?

Why couldn't they find somewhere to live *now*, then they could be together *now*?

They didn't need to wait to be together!

Geanie threw these questions at him, in the hope of receiving answers, while he collected their daughter. She couldn't place how it happened but he always seemed to leave without offering a definite answer. Frustrated with his apparent lack of concern for their eventual independent union, Geanie became spiteful and protested when he returned their daughter later in the day. Jack shrugged off her anger and walked away. *Bugger her!* He thought. The pushchair magnet had hauled in another new catch that afternoon. A nice girl he remembered from school. He made his way home for his tea and to wash and change.

Chapter 4

Sunday Morning

Sunday morning Jack awoke in another strange bedroom to another grateful, nice looking young woman.

'Want some breakfast Jack?' she offered, jumping out of bed. *Anything to keep him just a bit longer*, she thought. *My, what a lover!* The girl, forgetting she had a life of her own, set off down the narrow staircase to the small kitchen below in order to feed the supplier of her explosive orgasms; she had received not just one but three during the course of their all night lovemaking session. She was still tingling with elation, drunk from feasting on sex. Sex! No one ever mentioned it could be that good! The least she could do was feed him. Her hormones told her to feed him. That's what women did.

Generally, most girls in the nineteen seventies found a nice man (if they were lucky) and got married. Mind you, she had heard of a book written around 1975 by some woman called Fiona, a Vicar's daughter at that, who had gone around sleeping with lots of different men and collated her experiences into a book, fancy! It never crossed her mind that she could wave Jack goodbye and refresh herself ready for the next conquest. Women just did not do that! Jack, however, being a man, normally did.

He ate bacon and eggs, playfully teasing his hostess with comments relating to her cooking, when it suddenly crossed his mind he had the following week off, *perhaps I could see her again*; this thought prompted him to pay a little more attention to the provider of his breakfast, *she was quite petit and pretty, strange how he had not paid her much attention at school.* Her very black straight hair had been cut into a Mary Quant style bob, which was still popular if cut correctly. The big "afro" hairdos of the seventies were not going to work on her nor would the "big hair" that had just come into fashion for the nineteen eighty's. Jack also noticed that her eyes were a very dark brown. *She was cute and fun! When could he see this girl again?*

'Fancy going out somewhere Tuesday?'

'Yes, I'd love to Jack.'

She was delighted. Her efforts with breakfast had obviously influenced the decision for him. Tuesday could not appear fast enough for her. With a long kiss of parting bestowed upon his hostess, Jack made his way home with a swing to his gait, reminiscing over the time spent on the town the previous night.

Although he, himself, was considered quite a catch, a fair few blokes had been gazing at his pretty date throughout the evening, for Jack, this did not go unnoticed; he wondered if this interest may have been encouraged by the sight of her long slim legs, accentuated by the short denim skirt she wore. *Bet she looks fit in a pair of jeans as well,* he thought, *she certainly looks fantastic stark naked in bed!* Breaking away from his thoughts temporarily, he once again had to employ caution as he returned home, this girl, Angie, lived just around the corner from his parents. Aside from Josie and Jenny, he knew his Mother would not be overjoyed by the sight of him cavorting up and down their street, shag hopping from one end to the other.

Announcing his arrival home, Jack called 'Morning Mum, Dad, you okay?'

His Mother, her attention momentarily distracted from the newspaper, well aware he had probably spent the night with a woman somewhere, peered at him warily from over the top of her reading glasses, only to offer a cool, 'Very well thank you.'

Graciously, she deferred any attempt at an accompanying tart comment returning forthwith to scan her Sunday tabloid which, she hoped, would not contain any saucy scandal relating to her son. Unwittingly, her modest reply had provided one of many pleasant moments in what would prove to be a really fine Sunday for Jack.

After spending a most enjoyable day in his father's company, ferreting on a local farmer's land, they made their way home in the car, still discussing the tactics employed that had rounded off their outing with a nice bag of rabbits; hopefully his mother would cook one up for supper. Both Jack and his father adored rabbit stew, the way his mother dished it up was simply the best in their opinion. Jack thoroughly enjoyed the whole process, from initially catching the rabbits to eventually consuming them; with particular fondness for the social time spent with his father, laughing and play-boxing with him as they walked back to the car. Although he was a good six inches taller than his father, Jack was warned he would 'feel the back of his father's hand' if he gave him any trouble. In good spirits, he thought he might round off the day with a visit to the local pub for a pint later. After all there was no work for him tomorrow.

Monday Morning

Jack awoke to mild confusion, *Shit! Where was he? Daft sod!* The flowery patterned curtains gave up a spark of recognition. He knew those curtains well. Jenny had already got out of bed. A cup of hot, steaming tea had already been placed on the floor, beside the bed, for him. As she moved away he caught sight of her well rounded bum nearly covered by lovely long sandy hair.

'Can you get back in for five minutes?' Jack enquired of the back of her head.

'I can't be late for the pub Jack, tempting though your offer is.'

Jenny grinned as she turned back to smile at the very handsome man now left to languish in her bed. She was tempted to call in sick but could not forfeit her full weekly wage and was also supposed to be meeting up with her boyfriend later. She wished every day that that would be the one when Jack would tell her he wanted to be a "proper" boyfriend. Deep inside her mind the knowledge that Jack was never going to wholly commit kept her main thoughts with reality. No fanciful dreams for Jenny, she was a sensible girl. *Anyway,* she mused, *her main boyfriend was nice. But if only he knew how to push the pieces of her clitoris jigsaw in the correct places,* the success of which would provide her with an explosive orgasm. She knew he tried hard to please her *but he always lost a piece somewhere.* There is no bigger disappointment than attempting a complicated jigsaw only to find it has a bally piece missing when you've put all that effort in to build it.

Jack nonchalantly wandered home in a relaxed fashion as no effort was required for disguise or haste. He noticed Jeanie leaving their old marital home earlier that morning. He wished he had arranged to collect his son for the day. Never mind, he could phone Josie later and sort something out for tomorrow or the next day. Angry or not at his arrival to collect their son, Josie was always glad of some free time whenever possible and would never refuse his request for time with their child.

After spending some quiet time (his parents had already left to go to work for the day) eating breakfast, with no real plan for his holiday week in mind, Jack left the house, heading straight for the local Bookmaker, just ten minutes walk away at the end of his street, to study the form of one or two horses he fancied that were due to run in the next few days. After placing a couple of bets for the coming week he left the shop, turning right at the end of his road into the next street, continuing his walk downhill and onward into the main town. After wandering, without haste, around one or two shops of interest, making a few routine purchases on the way, he returned home by bus in order to save the twenty five minutes' walk back; only to don wellington boots then leave the house a second time to walk the family's two Lurcher dogs. In Jack's opinion they were the best kind of dog for catching rabbits.

His parents' home, set on a Local Council estate, was ideally situated; not too far to walk into town and the countryside was only five minutes in the opposite direction.

It was slightly windy heading across the first flat open field that backed onto his estate but as Jack reached the common ground which lead on to the wood (where Geanie acquired the spider in her pants), the wind met a natural barrier in the form of a well established row of Beech trees towering loftily along one side of the area. If a longer walk was required, any potential budding rambler could traverse the wood, eventually arriving adjacent to a well marked footpath that headed east, only to terminate when it reached the River Leam. Jack had strolled happily along this footpath many a time, in his father's wake, as a small boy.

He remembered the famous show jumping horse, Uncle Rex, who could often be spotted munching grass in one of the fields running adjacent to the footpath. Ending his glory days as a household name, his owner gave thanks to a wonderful equine friend by ensuring he was buried under the grass, he had once consumed with glee, when he became too old to enjoy his horsey life. No glue factory on death for Uncle Rex. At the age of six Jack had once been hoisted up onto the famous horse by his father to sit atop with his owner and rider, a jovial local farmer. The partnership had won the King George V Gold Cup for show jumping at the Horse of the Year Show in the late nineteen sixties. *Boy could that horse jump high!* Jack smiled, contemplating pleasant thoughts of the farmer who still cultivated the land, graciously bestowing permission for Jack and his father to hunt the wild rabbits that would otherwise have run amok on it over the years.

Enjoying an uneventful, peaceful walk, watching the dogs play, Jack eventually turned back to face the wind, making his way home for some food and to ponder his entertainment for that particular evening.

Tuesday Morning

The previous night Jack had unintentionally met up with two of his mates, Tom and Jim, at a local Pub; whichever local he frequented, he would normally be guaranteed the company of one or two of his friends on any random weekday evening. Chatting happily, around a selection of easy going, mainly mundane male subjects, bar for a piece about the proposed Jersey booze up, over a few games of pool, they decided to try their bravado with new barmaid, Sandra. During the evening Tom had enquired, in jest, of both Jack and Jim, 'Are Sandra's shoulders really that big or is she wearing those new fashion shoulder pad things in her jumper like most of the cast on Dynasty?'

Jim kept the laughter going, replying 'You're talking about the bumps on the front of her jumper not her shoulders surely?'

After a few more jokey comments each lad, during the course of the evening, threw her a few (what they thought were) witty lines, in the hope of reeling her in and securing a date but the game concluded in a "no competition" because Jack's line never seemed to fail. With slight exasperation it became evident to Tom and Jim that Sandra quite fancied the idea of a date with Jack.

Tom thought, *how the fuck does he do it? What the fuck did Jack have that they didn't?* Tom, if slightly annoyed at his mate's easy success, could not be mad with such a good friend. He wondered if he should ask him for some tips. *No, too embarrassing by far! He may well be a good mate but no way was he going to make himself look a complete twat by asking Agony Aunt Jack for advice.* Breaking his thought pattern he announced, 'Oh, ho, look out Jack, you'll lose your date now, Smelly Simons has just arrived on the scene, you've no chance!' The conspirators burst into a group laugh, their attention now focussed on their hapless, if unfortunate friend as he entered the pub, heading in the first instance to the bar.

Peter (Smelly) Simons was unable to use soap as part of his daily ablutions, it reacted with his skin causing a terrible rash. Nature offered the poor lad a simple choice of itchy rash or bad body odour. He chose the odour over scratching. Many products had been tried and tested but his body refused to cooperate with any liquid other than water. The unique fragrance that composed his bodily bouquet was, unsurprisingly, unappealing to the opposite sex. Along with the misfortune of narrowing his chances of finding a partner, how do you advertise for a girlfriend possessing no sense of smell?

'We shouldn't be laughing. You've got to feel sorry for the poor bastard' said Tom.

Raising his eyebrows from across the bar in the direction of the pool table, a facial greeting to the three pool players, Peter collected his pint and strode toward them to observe while they played their fourth game.

'Want to join in?' offered Jim.

Jack produced a look of dismay, the tail end of which Peter noticed.

'Look Jack, how would you like it if you had my problem? You wouldn't shag so many birds then would you?'

Jack felt a bit of a shit, 'Sorry mate but Christ, how do you cope with it?

Tom interjected, 'Come on, game on lads and whose round is it?'

'Mine', Jack looked to Peter as he turned to the bar, 'Want another?'

'No thanks Jack, this one's okay for a minute', following him to the bar he carried on, 'You know, I do try all the time to find something that smells nice but nothing works.'

'Aw sorry mate, it can't be easy I know. Pity you can't tie an air freshener to the back of your jacket!'

Peter laughed at him 'Bloody hell! I'd tie a bottle of beer to my back if I thought I'd be more popular!'

Making sure Peter didn't notice him ease his way in front, to avoid walking in his pungent wake on the short journey back to the pool table, Jack, his hands now occupied with a pint glass in each, winked back at Sandra.

*

Jack awoke to the smell of well shampooed blonde, short but curly hair, directly in front of his face. Sandra was snuggled in the "spoons" position lying directly in front of him. With a smile on his face he remembered how well she had responded to his touch only a few hours ago. His thoughts turned to leaving. It was a shame to go but he was hungry. He knew she was not going to shift from her comfortable position unless he made her, so giving a sigh and pushing back, away from her curvy body, he looked around for his jeans.

Sandra sleepily turned to look at him a loving smile on her face.

'Morning sweetie, how are you?'

Grinning in reply, Jack said he was very well indeed but he had to go.

Sandra gave a slight groan of protest as she snuggled back toward him, trying to hold on to just a few more seconds worth of handsome man.

'Will you be in the pub later?' she asked.

'Err no. I have a bit of business tonight (a picture of Angie smiled at him in his head). I'll come in later in the week.'

Wednesday Morning

Angie was starting to wonder if she might have a future with the handsome, young man who had just provided her with a second orgasm, equally as good as the one bestowed upon her last night. He had nearly provided her with three, he had turned her on so much during their, sex, sleep, sex, sleep etc. pattern which had commenced late last night only to continue into the early hours of the now, following morning; but at one stage he had given the impression he was a bit tired. *Shit! Surely she was not complaining?!*

There had only been a few boyfriends so far, of these, only two Angie had found exciting enough to let sleep with her but the sex had been rubbish even though one was really good looking. She had wondered why people raved so much about these orgasms and how good sex was. Now she knew why. She also thought that she could happily settle down to a life with this man. They had enjoyed the film they had seen in the Cinema the previous evening although Angie was upset at the ending when the character Christopher Walken played, shot himself with a revolver during a game of Russian roulette. She didn't really like war films but she was glad her Jack had not had to endure the horrors of the Vietnam War that "The Deer Hunter" portrayed.

Fuelled back up with bacon and eggs (the rest of her family had left the house for work in the local car factory) Jack set Angie's hopes and hormones climbing to nowhere definite by setting another date for the following week. Meanwhile he headed for home and his fishing rod. Feeling slightly knackered, the blame of which he laid on the amount of beer he had drunk the night before; he thought a spot of fishing on the River Avon might revive him. He walked the short distance from Angie's residence to his house and once again entered a quiet home.

*

He knew Brown Trout were in there, they were present in all of England's rivers, all year round. He peered into the river with care, scanning the surface for any signs of a fish that might be teased out. Unlike women they were not going to be caught so easily! Any movement could spook them sending them swimming for cover in panic. For spring, although warm, the weather was slightly cloudy and there had been a little rain in the night but probably not enough to colour the water helping the fish "take", what did it matter? It was peaceful sat on the river bank; a wonderful way to while away time with easy thoughts and a few fags in the balmy afternoon part sunshine.

After a few hours of patient but unsuccessful effort trying to tempt a "Brownie" to his fly, Jack heard a dog bark and turned to the sound. Who was this human walking toward him along the river bank, a dog playing at her feet? Jack recognised the canine as a Spaniel, a decent sort of a dog for hunting at that. 'Hi!' said the girl, 'Caught anything?'

She laughed at the age old phrase she had unwittingly uttered and its double entendre. Impressed, she looked up at the beautiful vision now standing very tall in front of her as she slowly approached. The Athenian like creation (well in her mind anyway) laughed back in reply 'No, no luck!' then squat down to fuss the dog, cigarette half finished, hanging out the side of his mouth.

'Nice dog! Do you use him for shooting?'

The girl, pleased that this handsome man had, by the sound of it, some knowledge of shooting, found she could converse easily on a subject they both obviously knew and enjoyed. He appeared slightly "rougher" than the sort of man she normally mixed with; she guessed she must also be a few years older than him, at twenty five, but so what. He was gorgeous and oozed virility! She thanked herself inwardly for making the decision to walk, Samson, the family dog, by the river.

Their conversation expanded and flowed into the late afternoon. So engrossed were they in their mutually enjoyed subjects of discussion, encouraged by the balmy spring weather, that after an hour or so they wondered why they had both become so thirsty and hungry. Jack enquired, did she live nearby?

'Do you fancy some food? There's a nice pub I know of not far away, The Angler's Rest, have you heard of it?' Jack was delighted with her affirmative replies to his questions; this female enjoyed and could talk about shooting, fishing, anything to do with the countryside really, ideal!

Jack rarely visited country pubs outside the town, and then only with his mates on the way back from a day's fishing if they had travelled further afield or he might partake of the odd pint with his father after a bit of rabbit shooting when they had driven to a farm some distance from home. This young woman, Sally, was very different from the town girls he was used to but she was still a woman and a very handsome one at that. Dressed in denim jeans, a skinny rib T-shirt and v-necked lightweight jumper, she had tied a lightweight coat round her waist using the sleeves, which were now accentuating her curvy figure; during their chat of discovery she had removed the jacket from around her waist and placed it on the riverbank, as a layer between the damp grass and her bottom. However, as with the town girls, Sally eventually succumbed, without even realising, to Jack's easy conversation and charm.

They made their way, without haste, to the pub, situated only two miles from the river, in Sally's car, a blue Volkswagen; they did not plan to walk back after eating their food. She explained how she had driven to that area from her parent's home specifically, in order to walk Sampson and let him play in the water; she did not however, offer to explain her earlier thought of why she felt she had made a good choice of destination.

Their impromptu afternoon-into-evening date went well. They were both very attracted to each other which helped a fair bit, their mutual respect of the country encouraged plentiful conversation even though their backgrounds were quite wide apart. Knowing she had probably attended a private school Jack enquired, 'Did you go to the same Secondary Modern as me I wonder?'

'I was unlucky, being sent to private school, feel sorry for me Jack!' she said in sarcastic but humorous manner.

Jack replied laughing, 'Thank your parents for keeping you well clear of mine!' Although not at all like his usual surroundings, Jack blended easily into the countryside and its atmosphere. After all, he had been accustomed since a small boy to walking, quite regularly, over a fair piece of it.

With Samson, a credit to his owner, his behaviour immaculate in the bar at their feet, the evening hours passed most enjoyably for them both. The food was good and Jack enjoyed the beer. He was not used to drinking "real ales" but he found the hitherto unknown taste beautiful. He made a mental note to try them a bit more often in the future.

Thursday Morning

Sally had sneaked Jack up into her bedroom on their return from the lovely country pub the evening before. Her parent's house was rather on the large side to that which Jack was normally accustomed to, with Elizabethan style timbers supporting some outside walls and beamed ceilings adorning some of the rooms within. Because of this method of building you would think that no one would hear your shouts and gasps of sexual pleasure, especially being also situated in the middle of the country.

'Bloody hell Sally, try to be quieter!'

'How can I? It's not fair', they both stifled laughter under the duvet.

Jack was amazed how silent the surrounding countryside appeared in the dead of night, he now realised why people moved there if they could afford to. The exchange of vast amounts of concrete and back to back housing, complete with the accompanying ghastly, orange street lighting, for what he assumed was noisy, roaming nocturnal wildlife, made quite some difference to his normal, city suburb, decibel levels; it was so quiet you could hear a pin drop.

Sally bit part of the duvet cover in an attempt to stifle her gasps. Her parents would surely investigate an owl shrieking the lesser known call, 'Ah! Ah. Oh my God!', rather than the gentle "Woo, Woo" generally associated with the graceful, nocturnal, feathered feeders.

At times their shared muffled laughter was hard to control, both lovers giggling, enjoying the touch and feel of each other, especially when Sally attempted to woo like an owl in jest.

Samson, due to his acute canine hearing however, knew a real owl hoot when he heard one and so, on occasion, during the early hours of the morning, felt the need to issue one or two barks in indignant protest at the very poor bird impersonations emitting from Sally's bedroom above, the noises of which flowed down the oak staircase and into the kitchen, disturbing his sleep pattern.

In the morning, after checking the oak, farm style kitchen was clear of her parents, Sally made them both a breakfast before offering Jack a lift back to his home in her car. Jack, imagining a look of accusation on the dog's face, asked Sally if she reckoned he was annoyed with their lack of regard for his sleep during the night. At ease with each other, both lovers were still laughing, conversing with interest and attention on both sides. But as far as the future was concerned Sally explained she wouldn't be around after this week as she had only been in the area visiting her parents.

'I work in London. It's okay because I rent a flat from a friend. I'm lucky to have found nice accommodation and also in a convenient location for my work.' Anytime Jack was in the capital city, let her know, she would be pleased to see him and they could always meet up again when she came to visit her parents. 'I'll let you know when I'm back for a visit if you like.'

Jack replied he would like. No pressure; there may be a next time, maybe not.

It was only a short car journey to his home, they exchanged phone numbers and kissed goodbye at the end of his street.

Jack alighted from the car, waved to her with a grin then turned to make his way home. He laughed as a flash of enlightenment suddenly appeared before him, the preceding day's events had given him the impression he had enjoyed a short holiday in the country! Ideal!

*

During the previous evening Jack had telephoned Josie from the pub in order to ask if he could collect his son that afternoon for a few hours. Slightly disappointed he remembered he could not collect his daughter at the same time because Geanie had gone away for the week visiting a friend, taking their daughter with her, so he made his way straight to Josie's house after washing and changing; on arrival he noticed she was still slightly grumpy. His enquiry of 'How are you, okay?' received only a sharp, noncommittal, 'YES, fine.'

He wondered why she was always so miserable these days.

'Are you sleeping okay? Is he being a good boy for you?'

Jack tried to say a few light hearted things in conversation hoping to receive a better response from her but these gentle enquiries received no acknowledgement; *perhaps she had developed an earache and couldn't hear everything he was asking? Yes, that would make her feel miserable.*

After shouting a 'NO' to his suggestion she might have earache, bewildered, he purposefully stared directly into her lovely but sad, brown eyes, she shifted from her study of watching him manoeuvre the pushchair out of the front door to return his baffled stare; he thought she nearly smiled but she just looked at him, he could detect no angry mood on her part, with jumbled thought but grateful for no real hassle, he thanked her eagerly then made off with the little lad in the direction of the Local Estate Park situated just behind his parent's home.

Pushing his son at a brisk pace, he glanced across to the back of Angie's house and smiled at the thought of her warm body. The street was shaped as a "U", with the houses placed around the outside, facing the houses built inside the body of the U. The Local Council Planning Department had been successful in creating a small park on the area where the road bent around into the U between the two end houses. The houses built within the actual U shape were placed back to back and if you had mind to, could study people leaving their rear entrance to exit into the lane that ran between the back gardens and open directly opposite from the park.

After spending half an hour carefully perching his son on the swing and slide in turn, moving him in an up and down or side to side fashion in order to match the apparatus as best he could; he made his way home to find his mother, ladle/baton in hand with the kitchen orchestra in full production, the aim of which; to produce a family dinner for later.

The atmosphere was always at ease with just Jack's son in the house. His mother was always far more accommodating, happy to temporarily secrete away to a top shelf, the fact that he had two children. Two grandchildren, should be every grandparent's dream but two with different mothers? His mother would never get used to the idea and it bloody annoyed him. Notwithstanding the awkward situation, the afternoon passed pleasantly. His father always enjoyed the company of his grandson in particular and was pleased to see him on his arrival home from his days' work. His mother secretly enjoyed granny time, making sure his food was well mashed as she encouraged every loving spoonful into his mouth. His hands were jerking up and down in response to Granddad's encouraging enquiries of 'Are you enjoying your tea little man?'

All too soon the embarrassing memory that Jack was not living with his son's mother came flooding back into the family home, like a rampaging river that had burst its banks, as he collected up the nappy change bag and lifted the little chap into his pushchair for the short journey back to Josie.

After both grandparents had bestowed their parting farewells, 'Bye bye, sweetheart, come and see Granny/Granddad again soon', with kisses to the little boy's chubby cheeks; the bell attached to each bootie, adorning this pair of knitted footwear, jingled his reply.

'I must tell Josie to stop putting those bloody stupid bell things on him or at least cut the bells off! People will start calling him Noddy, poor little bugger.'

'No daughter today then?' It was her only comment, said quietly.

Ignoring Josie, *why didn't she speak to me earlier when I tried?* Jack held out his hand to offer his son's maintenance money, a few days early, kissed the little lad goodbye, stated his opinion of the bell booties, turned away and made off to the local pub for the evening. Striding with intent toward whatever fun he could procure he failed to notice Josie delay her return into the house; crouching down beside her son, she held his tiny hand encouraging him to 'Wave bye, bye, to Daddy', with a sigh she turned to enter her home.

*

Thursday was always lively as Darts were played in a slightly more serious fashion than usual, against a team from a different local pub whose only aim is to thrash the locals on their own home ground; rather like football, but on a smaller scale without the running about and the acting. Entering the Bar Jack was pleased to see a good turnout for the match. His regular mates, including Tom and Jim, were in fine fettle which helped lift his own spirits higher; especially as in between talking about rugby, fishing, horse racing and various other male topics, Jack took note of the red haired wife of one of his rugby team mates darting sly glances in his direction. He was far from slow in taking up a challenge, so for the rest of the evening in between lively conversation, beer swilling and "lobbing" a few darts, he engaged a few thoughts, tactically working out where the husband was and whether this could be the reason she was in the pub with a girl friend and not her husband.

During one of the evening's many conversations Jim suddenly made a slightly hidden upturned fist gesture to Jack as part enquiry, then boldly asked 'Well, did you get lucky with Sandra?'

Tom laughed at the weak arm gesture only to offer 'Bet he did, lucky bastard! Jack grinned back a 'That's for me to know and you two prats to try and find out!'

At every opportunity, when he was sure they were not watching him, he continued his glances toward the red hair. The red hair grinned back.

Friday Morning

On Friday morning Jack awoke with Julie and a lot of red hair in his arms. His nasal capillaries detected the usual salty, sexual aroma tinged with sweet flowers. Puzzled he tried to remember where he had smelt the same flowers before. Turning his head to look toward the bedside table on Julie's side of the bed, Jack noticed a bottle of Anais Anais. He remembered spotting the same perfume in Angie's bedroom and realised his nasal senses had detected, then stimulated the memory banks in his brain, alerting him to the presence of the same flowery bouquet.

Julie's husband was away working somewhere down south. Jack never bothered with what lurked below Bristol; his understanding was that most of the inhabitants talked in strange dialect, wore whitish smocks covered in cow shit and straw, while drinking copious amounts of Cider, which almost certainly contributed to their unusual pronunciation of the English vowels.

No parents to dodge, nothing to rush off for, Julie turned to face Jack in response to the soft kiss he placed on her neck, a look of sheer rapture on her face. 'Oh, Jack, I know this sounds stupid but I've got to tell you, my husband doesn't last longer than a couple of minutes, it's so annoying. We've tried all sorts but he just gets over excited and that's it. You could say it's a four minute fuck!'

They both laughed but she went on to defend him. 'I do love him but I just don't get anything out of sex with him. Fancy coming round a bit now and again when he's not here?'

Oh joy! Thought Jack and his grin spread across his face as he replied cheekily in jest, 'I'll have to think about it.'

They both laughed as Julie swung her pillowcase at him, unintentionally sweeping another waft of sweet flowers around his head, but she was delighted and excited to think she would make love with him again. She had sort of tasted something she didn't think would be quite so delicious. She wanted more and gave no thought for any possible cost.

Throughout the night Julie had been in receipt of most of Jack's gentle and extensive lovemaking library. It was amazing the full collection was on offer considering the amount it had been on loan in the last few days.... She felt she had been loved like never before. Never before had she experienced an orgasm, amazed by her breathlessness from both the work up and the exhausting result. Her cheeks had flushed but as her body calmed, the tingling sensation subsiding, she had slept contented feeling complete. Her fingers now alighted on Jack's chest to play with the small patch of fair hair in the middle. She smiled as she moved her hand down and over his stomach.

'What else can you show me Jack; did you really show me **everything**? She grinned watching his body respond to her gentle touch.

Julie, keen to experience a second helping of all night sexual delights, hoped he might stay the Friday night as well but although he had enjoyed her company and decided that he would definitely see her again, he just could not keep away from another possible catch.

Unbeknown to Julie, her friend had slipped her own phone number into Jack's back pocket whispering 'Try my number if you fancy it handsome', during the previous evenings gaiety within the local pub.

Like a moth to the flame, Jack telephoned the number written on the crumpled paper. He spent Friday night with Julie's friend, *what was her name again? Shit! Did he actually ask it? She just wanted sex and fun.* A one night stand was fine by her.

Saturday Morning

As he made his way home on the Saturday morning it lazily occurred to Jack that he had slept with nigh on a different woman every night of his holiday. Bugger the 18-30 Sun Club! You didn't need to holiday with them to get laid! It was all here in Britain! Okay, so there was no beach in the Midlands and the weather, well everyone was still hoping a summer like 1976 would return in a couple of month's time. Six different, willing women, over seven days, you couldn't plan that could you?! Jack chuckled inwardly, *you lucky bugger!*

Chapter 5

For the next few weeks Jack kept regular. Regular with Jenny, Angie, Julie and occasionally with Geanie: when she wanted sex only and not to demand their legal union. But living in the fast lane has its risks and Jack was pushing his risk factor ever higher.

He had seriously pissed his mother off early one weekday morning after her casual glance out of the bathroom window portrayed a tell tale glimpse of her son leaving Angie's house by the back door. Jack himself was pretty brassed off indeed with her subsequent moaning about Angie, the fact that he had two children by different mothers and to top it all, Josie had seen him leaving Jenny's home one Saturday morning. She had stormed over to his house and raised the roof in front of his parents.

Arriving home only five minutes earlier he was just about to ascend the stairs to wash when he heard the front door bell ring. Unwittingly retracing his steps he opened the door to a fury thrown up into his face.

'You're shagging that Angie with the long hair!'

'Eh?'

'Don't Eh me! Not satisfied with taking the piss out of me with that two timing tart that's got your daughter, now you're shagging the rest of my street. What the fuck did I do to you to make you treat me so?!'

As she said the last sentence she burst into tears. Only able to answer in monosyllables due to the shock of her outburst, Jack offered up a rather weak 'What?'

Without any expectation of, or letting him have a few seconds to concoct, a sensible reply, Josie recovered enough to throw sticks.

'Well don't bother coming over for your son today, go get your daughter instead, like you do anyway!'

She moved slowly backward down the path as she spat the words at him, knowing full well he would not hit her but aware he would be angry if she declined him access to their son. Annoyed, but also confused at her behaviour Jack let her go, turning back and pushing the door shut behind him. *Silly cow, he heard she had recently found a boyfriend. What was her problem?*

Collecting his thoughts he once again made an attempt to ascend the stairs only to hear his Mother ask 'Are your actions starting to catch up with you Jack?' Raising his eyes to the ceiling in frustration, he felt totally fed up with the constant, angry behaviour flung into his path by disgruntled women but how could he escape a situation that appeared to increase in difficulty as time passed. He wondered whether a letter to the NSPCC might stop his mother throwing the large, square glass ashtray, their front room used as a part time ornament, at his head every time she was informed of another of Jack's misdemeanours. His thoughts flew back a couple of months to remember an encounter with a very famous "Mother" during Royal Ascot week, he felt sure she wouldn't throw heavy glass ash trays at her children.

Jack had been part of a Working Men's Club outing to the races at Royal Ascot. As you are aware he loved horse racing and signed up for the trip as soon as it had been announced. The coach booked for the outing made the journey from Warwick to Ascot uneventfully, arriving safely at the coach park to deposit its excited human cargo within walking distance of the Ascot Main Entrance. Jack, thoroughly animated, immediately set off toward the illustrious race course, such was his intensity to study the form and bet the whole of his wage earned in that particular week.

The entrance was easy to detect by the volume of people heading in its direction. As Jack reached the large, glass double doors he was virtually alone due to a temporary lull in human traffic, this meant he would cross the entrance into his horse racing wonderland unaccompanied. Reaching out with his right hand to grasp the door handle he pulled the door back toward him in order to open it. Just as his brain sent the message to *'move foot forward and enter door'* a commanding but friendly voice hailed from behind, only to state 'I hope you are holding that door for me young man?'

Jack stopped and turned his body to look back, curious to discover whether the request was made toward him or someone else, only to find himself face to face with the Queen Mother.

A pleasant grin, accompanied by 'Hello!' lit up his face; dutifully he held the door open for the gracious Regent as she breezed through. One of her two accompanying Detectives smiled and said quietly 'Well done lad!'

Not only did his day start regally, it concluded with a fistful of cash from the Bookies, the majority of which had been collected courtesy of one of the beautiful equines entered by the Queen Mother. Both Jack and the Queen Mum had winners that day.

*

A few weeks after Josie's outburst, on a cold, windy Saturday afternoon, without any prior warning, Jack's risk appetite suddenly blew its top marker leading to complete loss of control just as he finished playing a game of rugby. Summer had come to a definite end, the Midlands' cooling temperatures indicating winter was on the way. Jack loved rugby and was pleased to be part of the local team again for the new season. He noticed Julie's husband (who played in the same team) had been a bit "off" with him during the second half of the game, deliberately crashing into Jack at one point. It was no mistake and one or two of his other team mates had also noticed, raising their eyebrows in unspoken question to Jack.

Julie had terminated their relationship a few months before, 'I can't live with the guilt of betraying my husband Jack so it's got to stop.'

He had respected her decision and happily let the affair end giving no more thought about her. He wondered now what was up with the guy.

After much splashing of water and the completion of the usual male bonding, rugby team, bath time sing song; eventually dressed and drenched in Brut, most of the men headed straight to the local pub for the required, after match, drinking session. As he made his way to leave, Julie's husband signed to Jack he wished to speak with him. He was a big bloke but no bigger than Jack. As they moved aside he gently took hold of Jack's forearm; quietly but angrily he stated accusingly into Jack's face, 'You've been shagging my misses you fucking bastard!'

'Yeh, I was, but it stopped ages ago, so what?' said Jack.

The man was taken aback by the frank answer that contained no denial.

'She's my wife, you bastard!'

'Like I said, it stopped ages ago' replied Jack, totally unconcerned.

'I ought to knock your fucking lights out, bastard!'

Although he understood his anger, Jack was slowly starting to lose his temper - he had been called a bastard three times now.

'Well come on and give it a go then!'

Jack's body started to prepare for imminent fisticuffs. Automatically he adopted the boxer stance from long term experience. Ready to block his opponent's first punch, he was thrown into sheer disbelief when the big man, now standing square in front of him, broke down in tears, putting his huge hands over his eyes rather than into Jack's face. As if this wasn't surprise enough the big man suddenly confessed, tears running through his hands, 'You see I can't satisfy my wife, I'm rubbish at sex. I just get over excited. I don't last longer than a few minutes. I don't know what to do. I love her so much!'

Shagging git he might have been but Jack would never hit a man when he was down. This frank confession also sent Jack's mind flying to a land it didn't visit often, his conscience. Perplexed and unsure of what to do or say, his mind still dizzy from the sight of the broken man's sobbing, Jack came out with the inspirational, 'Look mate, I don't know what to say.'

The land of conscience was being run all over, wildly; Jack felt absolutely stupid. Then, to top it all, the big man delivered a punch line stronger than any fist Jack could remember from his schoolboy boxing.

'Julie said you are so good at sex, you make her feel like a real woman.'

He held out for a few more seconds then asked, 'Can you show me how to do the same?'

Seconds out! One, Two, Three, Four! Jack had been knocked down a couple of times during his boxing days but had always made it back on his feet by the Fifth. Incredulous! What the fuck was he supposed to say to the man!

I find touching your 'misses' here makes her wet. She likes it better in this position. Don't try that, she doesn't like it. No, Jack realised any help would not be well received using that approach.

The two men looked steadily at each other. Each man possessed enough intelligence to realise, that with a touch of diplomacy, a lot could be saved here. 'Shall we go have a pint and talk about it?' said Jack.

*

That particular Saturday morning Jack had walked into the town without either of his children (both of them were suffering with colds) and while collecting a few items of shopping he had met a very sexy looking woman. He could easily attract the opposite sex without the aid of the pushchair magnet. She was well older than Jack, in her forties, but quite stunning. What did age matter? Each caught the glance of the other and liked what they saw. The age and confidence of the older woman was a match for the younger man's experience. He felt fortune must be smiling down on him as his parents were not at home that weekend, having made a rare trip away for a week's holiday down South, so, after walking around a few shops together and spending some time to become more acquainted over a coffee, Jack took the opportunity to invite her back to his parents house. She had brazenly teased him by stating they would not be able to be alone at her place and she could tell he was going to make her moan with delight. Jack's face spread into the usual grin. He liked older women. They laid down the rules up front. He also asked her first name. Laughing she replied 'I'm called Hilary.'

Chapter 6

Jack, initially, found it difficult to form individual words, his brain appeared to have stuck in neutral, thereby leaving him totally incapable of constructing any sort of sentence, the shock had also rendered him slightly stiff lipped which in itself was quite a novelty, but Julie's husband had meant what he said. He was listening intently to the advice Jack offered, allotting each piece careful thought. At one stage Jack thought it was going a bit too far when the big man got up from his seat and went over to the bar to procure a pen from the barmaid in order to note a couple snippets of advice on the back of a beer mat. The mental stress of dealing with a new and demanding situation made Jack feel uncomfortable and yearn for escape but with most of his suggestions; on how to stop getting over excited and induce a sex session to last longer, taken on board, the two men parted as friends. *Absolutely Bizarre!*, thought Jack.

With his solitary stint as a sex therapist ending just in time, he caught sight of his date, and probable shag for the rest of the evening, walking into the pub which was a welcome relief. He made his way over to her with a relaxed but broad grin on his face.

At the sight of Jack greeting the attractive, slim, older woman, the rest of the rugby crowd issued a sort of group welcome cheer 'Wey Hey!' Jack's a lad!' Delighted with the unexpected attention, from at least half of the players of the local rugby team, on her entrance to the pub, Hilary laughed at Jack, asking for a Rum and Coke please, while sexily raising her eyebrows at him , in reply to his offer of 'What can I get you?'

*

Jack's weekend had gone well. A human volcano had erupted straight into his face after the rugby match but any possible ash clouds or lava flow had been promptly dispersed due to a diplomatic outlook from both sides, enabling the elimination any long term damage, literally from the start.

Saturday night had been fantastic with another satisfied woman in tow. Jack liked Hilary; they hadn't spoken much about themselves really. Their attention with each other was pure lust. Lust made for great sex, especially with an older woman. Jack had difficulty in stopping his mind's replay of Hilary's pleasure. He re ran through her soft murmurs of delight as he stroked her sand coloured, straight, shoulder length hair, easy to run your fingers through and the way she went *'Ummm.'*

Shit! He was becoming excited thinking about her.

He stopped to light a fag before he reached Jenny's house. The cigarette should take his mind off Hilary's rapturous moaning. He needed his wits about him to get into Jenny's home without Josie spotting him. Jack intended asking Jenny if she fancied a drink at the local with him that very evening, he might even spend the night with her if she fancied a cuddle and to wake up with him the next morning (Monday); what a nice way to start the working week!

The Earth, still moving slowly into winter, kindly provided a natural cloak of darkness to conceal his progress toward the other end of his parent's street. Arriving at the front door Jack knocked quietly. It galled him to be quiet but was preferable in the long run. Josie would cause a scene if at all possible; thank goodness they were nearly divorced now.

The lovely, long, sandy hair flowed to the side of her face and over her left shoulder as Jenny looked around the side of the door, her face quizzical. Once the visage of her lover was confirmed she smiled broadly and opened the door wider for Jack to pass through. The front door shut behind them as Jack turned to embrace her. After planting a lingering kiss on her lips he let Jenny speak. Her words flowing, as innocent as a new born babe, placed the penultimate decoration on Jack's xmas/crimbo tree.

'Oh Jack, you must meet my Mum...Hilary.'

Jenny signed him to look toward the stairs. Jack's eyes widened from the shock of recognition building slowly within him. A slight streak of panic ran up his back. Descending the stairs to stand directly in front of him was one of the best sex sessions he had had lately, Hilary Jackman.

Chapter 7

Fuck! Was there going to be a scene? Did Jenny know he had shagged her mother? Shit! Did Hilary know he had been shagging her daughter? Idiot! He should have guessed; their hair was the same colour for Pete's sake! How was he supposed to know? And why had she not said when he took her home to his place on Saturday evening that she only lived a little way up the street from him?

Dumb struck; he started to laugh for want of nothing better to do. Speech had been temporarily taken off the menu of his mind skills.

The experience of the older woman took control. 'Hi Jack, taking my daughter out for the evening?'

His mind would now agree with anything suggested, anything to escape this madness. Still laughing, the sound of which resembled, disturbingly, a genetic cross between an American backwater dunce and Deputy Dawg, he frantically forced his jaw to form a caveman style reply 'Bu, bu, yeh, yeh.'

He wondered, *did Hilary sound angry when she asked if he was taking her daughter out?*

His brain was a merry-go-round, unable to pay attention; with no idea where this charade was going, *anything could happen. It could get ugly.*

An unusual referee, to disperse a possible mother / daughter / threesome fight arrived in the form of the final decoration that would topple Jack's crimbo tree. Heavy knocks sounded on the Jackman front door.

Jenny, slightly perplexed by Jack's behaviour, turned back to open the door. The long sandy hair repeated its earlier performance. Jack kept his eyes and thoughts on Hilary. *Was the slight smile on her face an indication of amusement or anger? Never turn your back on a wild animal it could pounce. What the fuck was he supposed to do now? Get out, and quick!*

'Oh! What do you want?' said Jenny, around the part open door to an unseen person, standing somewhat impatiently on the Jackman front doorstep. A young male voice angrily replied to Jenny's flippant greeting.

'You said you were my girlfriend but you've been shagging that fucking Jack!' Jenny caught the accusation thrown at her with ease then prepared her return parry without regard to the small but attentive audience standing behind her. 'Well he's a much better lover than you! He knows what to do and he's good at it!'

As Hilary patiently let her daughter run away with her unfeeling replies a wry smile started to harden the look on her face, not dissimilar to concrete really, and she steadied her gaze toward Jack.

Is it my imagination or are her eyes appearing to narrow and transform into deep amber colour? Oh come on! This is totally unfair. Shall I tell her I didn't know they were mother and daughter?

Would it have stopped Jack if he had known? No. But that wasn't the point. Hilary gave the impression she would spring at him imminently, claws extended, far from the sexy way that she had jumped on Jack the last Saturday evening, stark naked.

'Look, how the hell was I to know?'

It was his best effort but it brought forth a reaction from a different participant to the lively melee.

'Is that bastard in there now?' shouted the angry young voice.

Jenny's 'Bugger off' was translated by the angry young voice as, *'please come in why don't you.'*

The boyfriend, Martin, barged inside, pushing open the door. Give it to the lad, as he was no means big, he started to shout his disgruntled feelings directly toward Jack. Slightly more worried by the thought of a possible feline attack in the form of Hilary, still frozen faced at the base of the stairs, Jack stepped back one pace to keep the cat on his left hand side. His right hand, responding to its boxer mode instruction, clenched into a fist as it shot toward the lad's head. It hit home just under his jaw, bang on target, along with the words 'Oh fuck off!' 'Fuck the lot of it!'

Both Hilary and Jenny jumped back as far as they could to vacate any space the two angry young men might commandeer as a war zone but the lad had not seen the punch coming, blinded as he was by his fury. The force knocked him back against the wall where he then slid down to the floor, his legs crumpling beneath him. The temporary stunned silence gave Jack his escape route.

'That's it' was all Jack could be bothered to say as he stepped over the lad's legs, in order to make his exit through the front door without a backward glance to the two women. Tomorrow he would tell his boss, yes, if the offer still stood, he would like to work for their company in the Philippines.

The following morning, immediately on his arrival at work, while still possessed of sober thought due to a quiet night's sleep, Jack headed straight into the Site Manager's office.

Within an hour the arrangements had been completed but Jack informed no one, not even his parents that he had decided to work for his company at their site in the Philippines. J.M. McDougall was a global company who treated their employees well. When the chance arose, Management would send employees to one of the company's other sites (whether home or abroad) in order to broaden their experience and knowledge of the construction business. Jack's Site Manager had asked him if he would be interested to work in the Philippines some months ago. He could think of no reason to decline but had asked for time to consider, 'No pressure Jack, you don't have to go but if you fancy a change of scene it will add to your experience'

However, the impromptu charade, performed just inside Jenny Jackman's hallway the previous evening, had encouraged Jack to finalise his decision. Luckily, the 'lads' Jersey holiday had eventually been booked and the date chosen was well before Jack would leave the UK. He thought it would be a good way to spend some time with his mates before flying out to work in an entirely different country.

The paperwork explained how he would be based at the Asian site, on a four week on, two off, contract. He would fly home to the UK every four weeks which meant he would still keep regular contact with his children and the piece of builder's string could still be kept to hand in the back pocket of one of his pairs of jeans. Arrangements had to be completed a fair way in advance so he wouldn't leave for the Philippines until the following spring which meant he would be around for Christmas.

Chapter 8

Winter began to lose its icy grip on the land. The UK Weather people were worried it would send a batch of snow in a last ditch attempt to stamp its superiority over the Earth like 1978. No cause for worry, spring was steadily fighting its way up through the hard, compacted ground. March limbered up, made its appearance and within a few weeks of April taking over, Jack and his workmates flew off to Jersey from Southampton, as flights from Coventry Airport were already fully booked by the time the lad's allotted administration team (Jeff and Alan) woke up and made the booking for the whole party.

The week in Jersey was a typical lad's holiday. They paid no attention to the lovely spring flowers spreading riotous colour across an island famed for its flower fighting and potatoes. Most of the "gang" employed the art of sitting around drinking, hoping to attract a female while lounging outside various pubs and soaking up the warm temperate climate.

They teased Jack with good humour when he began to chat up an older woman the very first afternoon the party arrived; the group had taken over a local pub's beautiful garden and added a dash of their own brand of bonhomie. She became his first conquest of the week, explaining that she too was on holiday and hoping to have fun and enjoy herself.

Deliberately detaching from the rest of the shoal temporarily, they walked and talked, eventually returning to partake of dinner together at the same pub. Patio dining during the evening still required a coat so they gave the colourful garden surroundings a miss to enjoy their food inside where the temperature was decidedly warmer in the early spring evening. The relaxed atmosphere, good food, excitement and general absurdity of the surroundings lead to an urgent desire for both Jack and his escort to round off the whole classy menu with sex.

Desperate for somewhere to sleep with her (to reach her hotel required a taxi and they couldn't wait that long) Jack told his hotel room mate, Fred, to shut his ears that night as he was bringing his new found girlfriend into his bed later so he could "give her one."

On receipt of this rather daunting news Fred wished he had opted to share a hotel room with anyone else but Jack. He didn't begrudge anyone getting their end away but when you were forced to listen to it while you laid there unmolested was taking the piss.

Fred need not have worried; as part of a group of boozy "Brummies" they all intended to sink a fair few pints of beer between them each day so, while Jack performed to his usual standards, ensuring the woman's holiday experience was far better than she could ever have dreamed of, Fred snored away happily, blotto from the amount of alcohol he had consumed.

For the group of lads the week went by in an orderly fashion, dominated in the main by the consumption of beer and chilling out. Two lads had been lucky and found "steady" girlfriends, one of these relationships, built from the holiday romance, became permanent, the engagement was cemented with the purchase of a ring from a Jersey jeweller. The happy couple had already created a guest list to include the holiday bunch; the newly appointed Best Man, also chosen from the group, offered a few sample speech lines for approval, reciting these with jest, one for example; 'Sally had just been issued with new glasses by the opticians when she first saw Mike and thought he was good looking.'

He attracted only heckling and laughter in reaction which was obviously all part of the plan.

Constant fun and frivolity ensured the week bobbed along at a steady pace, however the general wedding conversation now thrown in made Jack feel uneasy, bored even. Needing a break from the happy family aura he wandered off alone one morning to check out Jersey's beautiful St Ouen's Bay. If you were in need of some space there was plenty to be had at St Ouen's Bay, which boasted a five mile beach. And Jack had, just lately, begun to feel in need of some space.

Wandering aimlessly along the impressive beach, kicking the odd shell from his sandy path, his thoughts flitted between his family and life back home. *Where the hell was his life going? Did he care? He earned good money, £300 quid a week. He must find himself another place that he could call his own. He shouldn't have given Josie the house. Working in the Philippines would help. He could buy another home from the Local Council; the Government had for once come up with a good idea there. Pity he didn't have the dogs with him, they would have loved this beach.*

His thoughts were broken by the sight of a shapely young woman walking toward him. She appeared quite pretty, her face surrounded by long curly hair, the loose strands of which she frequently pushed behind her ear while the sea breeze repeatedly insisted blowing them back. As she walked toward him they smiled at one another uttering 'Hi' in unison, which made them both laugh. Jack asked if she thought the beach impressive and was she walking anywhere in particular.

She replied, 'Yes and No' which encouraged more laughter between them.

Jack enquired, 'Do you mind if I walk with you for part of the way?'

'No, I don't mind at all, I could also try to make conversation using some longer sentences!'

'Don't do that!' said Jack, 'I'll get confused.'

Laughing quietly into his face she offered, 'I'm Sarah, nice to meet you.'

'Hi Sarah, call me Jack.'

Conversation between them was easy and uncomplicated encouraging the pair to spend the rest of the day together; however, spoken communication was suspended temporarily while they consummated their meeting within just a few hours amongst the sand dunes of St Ouen's Bay.

Jack spent the last two days of his holiday alternating his attention between Sarah, and his workmates. The holiday party had doubled in size due to the remainder of the lads eventually finding themselves a girlfriend. The atmosphere was lively, with never a dull moment.

A mass outing to Gerald Durrell's' Zoo was hilarious entertainment for the inmates let alone the visitors. The antics that young males can achieve with an ice cream cornet in the quest to amuse a female are impressive. I refer to human young males, not the animal kind. The whole entourage were suitably impressed with the male Gorilla, Jambo; unaware they were in the presence of a future celebrity. Jambo would, in a few years time, astonish the world with an act of compassion, never before expected by, or demonstrated to, humans, expressing concern while at the same time gently touching the little boy who would fall, by accident, into his enclosure. This most revealing form of empathy had previously not been thought possible from what was largely considered to be quite an aggressive primate. Could they really be gentle giants?

On the last evening of the holiday the whole group met up in a pub that had become a favourite. Relaxed and happy among friends, Jack was feeling good. Unfortunately, the aura didn't last long.

Shit! While nonchalantly scanning the bar of its occupants his gaze stopped short by the main entrance. The pub was fairly crowded but through the maze of heads he recognised the woman he had sexually entertained in his hotel room while Fred had snored, asleep and oblivious.

Fuck! She had seen him.

She smiled, then, raising her hand in recognition, she began to gently push her way through a sea of various hair styles in order to make her way toward him. He turned to check the position of Sarah, his beach girl.

Good, she had momentarily moved away and was now talking to her friends. The woman reached him faster than he had anticipated, he wondered, *what was her name again? Bugger he hadn't bothered to even try to remember.*

Smiling at him she asked if he had enjoyed his holiday.

'Great! Yes great' he nodded, as if a puppeteer had strings attached to his head and jaw.

'And you?'

'Yes, I've had a brilliant time, my holiday turned out better than I expected, pity I haven't met up with you again since, still, I expect you and your friends have painted the town red!'

Jack laughed weakly in response to the sly look with which she delivered the words. From the corner of his eye he noticed Sarah's imminent return to him; she also had a friend in tow. What should he do now? To introduce them would be polite but might be awkward for the woman. If only he could remember her name. *I must make more of an effort to remember names.* It surely would be obvious to her he had met someone else during the week. But what should he say. *Oh, eh, Sarah, this is the woman I shagged a couple of nights before you, sorry I didn't get her name!*

It was okay. No introduction was necessary from Jack. Sarah performed it for him. Putting her arm snugly round his waist as she stood alongside, her pretty face breaking into a big smile, she directly addressed the woman with no name, 'Oh, Hi Mum, I see you've met Jack!'

Chapter 9

Sat on the plane, en route to the Midlands, in rather pensive mood, Jack wondered why he kept finding mother and daughter duos lately. Spending a few minutes to ponder the unexpected events of his holiday's final evening he mulled over the resulting conversation.

Sarah's mother had graciously said nothing, just smiled back at her daughter, 'Yes, we have met darling, have a nice evening and ill catch up with you later', then moved away, returning to her friends on the other side of the bar.

And so, the final evening passed by without any unpleasant scenes.

At the time Jack's own guilt assumed both the mother and daughter would get the picture; the daughter, he felt probably did not; the mother however, he was sure, probably did. The two women flowed out of his mind; relaxing back into the seat his thoughts turned to his future.

Jack still had a few weeks at home before he flew out to the Philippines; they were promising to keep him busy. Apart from turning up for work each day in the usual way, he also had two evening security type jobs lined up. An old school friend, Kit, had telephoned Jack's home one evening and left a message with his Mother while Jack was on holiday.

Possessed of a good memory, his Mother had carefully recited the message to him the very day of his return; 'Kit said to tell you, did you fancy a spot of, it sounded like, "crowd control" in the City's Dance Hall for a couple of nights? He said he's the Manager of this new Band and they are playing there next week or something. He said they are gathering quite a following and he needs to arrange some sort of guards for them. He told me their name but I've never heard of them! They'll not be anything as good as Perry Como I bet! Ah he's lovely. Now there's a man who can sing!'

Grinning as he recalled his Mum's rather dismissive description of the unknown Band and their hopes for success, they would obviously be shit scared if they didn't sound anything like Perry Como, he found he was actually looking forward to a spot of "bouncing" at the well known, Bingley Hall. Up and coming bands performed there often. He had seen Slade play there once in the early nineteen seventies.

His memory flew him back in time, but without the aid of a snowman....he was standing amongst the crowd, circa 1973; attired in his Ben Sherman shirt, jeans, red braces and Doc Martens, he was almost a complete skinhead. If you are thinking I say "almost" because he had not shaved off those curly sandy locks at the time you would be gravely mistaken.

Stomping up and down to the loud, noisy music while simultaneously laughing, as they tried to keep time, Jack had attended the concert with, and now stood alongside, his best mate Cookie. Cookie was of mixed race origin (of course this description was not widely used at the time) and had a wonderful permanent suntan to confirm his ancestry had not wholly originated from the UK. Along with a pair of "cherry reds" as footwear and red braces holding up his black "skinner" jeans, he looked no different from Jack when you absorbed the whole of his appearance.

Cookie also had a very beautiful, dark skinned, sister that Jack was dating at the time. He was pleased to remember she had later been successful in London as a model. Unfortunately his Mother had displayed signs of xenophobic behaviour when he had brought Donna home for the first time in order to introduce and show the leggy beauty off to his parents. His Father's 'Hello Dear' did not help to quash his Mother's look of astonishment. She nearly fainted, her look was aghast. Jack's thoughts now annoyed him; *his Mother could be a stupid cow at times.*

Shutting the embarrassing home grown racism away he turned his thought to remember the posters promoting the show had announced the band would tour as far as Plymouth. *Where the fuck was Plymouth?* Somewhere down south below Bristol he supposed.

His mind wandered back to the new band and his old school friend. Kit had always liked music, Jack hoped things would go well for him as their manager. Most of his schoolmates were aware of Jack's boxing skills, Kit, remembering how handy he could be with his fists, if ever there was a spot of bother, had not seen this as the only requirement for the job however. Kit knew Jack's large boxer build was an ideal security guard shape and so, had contacted him to ask if he fancied the idea of deterring the odd (I mean odd in the sense of an individual person, not to single out people behaving in an odd manner) over excited fan from clamouring on the stage while the band performed.

Jack had quizzed Kit, 'Are they that good that people want to get at them on stage?!'

'Come and see for yourself Jack, you'll even get paid for it!'

It seemed he might have a laugh if nothing else so he agreed to turn up at the Hall on the following Thursday around 6.30pm.

Chapter 10

Crowd control was a complete success. Jack was impressed, the Band were pretty good. Kit asked if he would be up for a few more gigs in the future. It was plain for all to see that the Band did indeed have a future and was heading for the "Big Time" and without the aid of the said named TV programme. Jack explained his future four on, two week off schedule but it didn't worry Kit, quite the reverse.

'Nothing can be planned with this caper Jack, if you can fit in with them, as and when, then even better.'

So, Jack had every reason to wear a smile on his face during his last couple of weeks before flying East. However, one person was very put out by what they considered was his wanton desertion of duty. Reality had eventually hit her hard.

Geanie would be the second woman to be scorned as part of Jack's life. When he had steadily explained that yes, he was now divorced but no, he was not going to marry her, Geanie finally realised she had failed. The handsome man she craved as a mate for life had let her down stinking. For breaking her dreams into shattered, scattered pieces he would pay. Oh yes, she would make him pay. Unaware of the pain she would cause him in the future he patiently sat beside her making arrangements to pay regular maintenance for his daughter. She screamed and cried at him.

'You said we would get married!'

'Geanie, I never said I would marry you. You said we would, not me. It would never work anyway'

'Why on earth not? Don't you want to be with your daughter and me?'

'Geanie, you're forgetting, I have a son as well, what about him? It's not that I don't want to be with you and my daughter but I can't be with my son either because, well, I just don't get on with his mother anymore. We wouldn't get on together either'

'Jack, you're not giving us a chance!'

Ignoring her protestations he instead offered her a list detailing the monthly payments he would provide in the future for their daughter. It was pointless to argue. She realised he could not now be swayed. Unable to think of anything else to alter his decision an awkward silence prevailed while her thoughts took over. *I don't want bloody maintenance. I want him!* Her anger increased because he just sat there being nice! *Fucking nice! Why could he not see? He only needed her. They could be a neat family all together with their own home. Bastard! She would make him pay. Yes Jack, you will pay for this.*

Jack was surprised that Geanie had been so savage. At no time in the past had he ever said he would marry her. One should never assume... He was equally surprised when Josie gave a fairly civil response to the news of his impending shift eastward. He just did not realise the intricacies of a woman's mind.

Josie had assumed, incorrectly, that Jack would marry Geanie when their divorce became final. When the local gossip, referred to as the "jungle drums", had informed Josie that Jack was not going to marry the mother of his daughter a strange feeling of relief washed over her; cool like a soft mountain spring, it felt that good. She considered she had almost won something. And her prize was? Satisfaction.

Josie had been devastated when Jack informed her, with some regret, it has to be said, that Geanie had given birth to a daughter, which was his; and only three months after she had provided him with a beautiful son. How ***could*** he do it to her when she loved him so much? She was well aware that he had always been popular with the girls at school; she smiled at the memory, her so called friends had been so jealous. All had wanted to date him but she had been the only one interested in accompanying him fishing, sat on the riverbank for hours; eventually it had all become rather boring for her, whatever did men see in fishing? When they had married (okay they had to because she was pregnant but she was his only girlfriend at the time and they had already planned to get engaged to each other) she thought it would be forever. In his defence, she knew the little tart had, almost certainly, acted in her most seductive manner toward him, *why the hell had he been so tempted?* Geanie had not been the most attractive girl in their school either. Josie would have taken Jack back into her arms even now but something told her it would only be temporary, he would never settle. There would always be some woman after him somewhere, watching, and waiting.

Her new man was nowhere near as handsome as Jack but he was kind and happy to spend time with her. Jack, on the other hand never seemed able to rest. *Yes, that must be it,* Josie's thought pattern explored deeper philosophical lines; *Jack was possessed of a restless spirit. Would he ever find peace?* Surprised by the unusual conclusion she had created, Josie realised that she now virtually, felt sorry for him.

Alone in her bedroom Josie stood with her head held high, an aura crammed with superiority surrounding her, in front of her dressing table. The bold theatrical portrait she displayed into the mirror slowly withdrew to exchange its place with a malicious smile which spread all over her face in confirmation of her victorious triumph over her rival, the "other" mother, Geanie. She addressed the mirror in a superior tone of voice and without the prequel "Mirror, Mirror on the wall"...... to state 'And it serve you right you silly bitch!'

If Geanie was the abandoned bride then Jack's Mother was the frustrated bridesmaid.

'What about your children? What about their mothers? When will you come back? What do you want to go out there for? Running away from responsibility, that's what you're doing my lad!'

Slightly exasperated, trying to explain to his Mother that a four week on, two at home work pattern could hardly be classed as desertion, Jack looked to his father for support but the glances they exchanged indicated that it was a waste of time trying. Didn't some foreign King try to turn the tide without success?

At least there was one place where he would find the atmosphere agreeable; Angie could always be relied upon for a spot of solace when required. She was pleased when he said 'Yeh thanks Angie, I'd love for you to write and keep me up to date with the local gossip while I'm away' and he might even attempt to send a reply back. Even if he couldn't find the time to write he would be back to sleep with her. He most certainly would.

*

Glad to escape from the circus of sexual thrills that his life had somehow evolved into, Jack relaxed back into his seat, settling himself in for the long flight to the Philippines. At their last meeting, the day before he flew out, his Manager had updated him with details of the situation at the eastern site. He also felt it might be prudent to provide Jack with some personal advice that, when received, suggested his Manager also subscribed to the jungle drums information network because he appeared well informed of Jack's reputation with the opposite sex.

'Don't mess about with any of the local women Jack; one of our lads came back last year with some sort of VD but the Docs aren't sure what. It's completely fucked the lad up. He's never been the same since.'

For once, this worrying tale was allowed a storage slot for future reference in Jack's brain because during the two years he spent working his four week on, two off pattern, Jack kept away from the local women. And it wasn't easy. They were virtually forced on you, as he was about to find out, within the first few hours of his arrival.

Chapter 11

Jack's Manager, as part of his formal pre-site prep talk, had to impart not only the personal, carnal warning but also disclosed a crucial piece of corporate information. He asked Jack to be careful when dealing with the local Philippine pimp come drug dealer. Jack's face took on a hitherto rarely seen, serious look. 'What the hell are we doing business with him for?'

'He rules the supply of the local labour, I know how it looks but that's the way it is, he could close down the site for us, so don't fuck it up Jack. I know you're handy with your fists.'

Christ! Jack thought. *He must subscribe to the jungle drums weekly gossip. This bloke knew it all!*

The flight had been long but grateful for a complete change of scenery and domestic situation, for at least four weeks anyway, Jack attempted to settle while unpacking his luggage in the hotel room which would be his home for the duration. Another employee, Mike, had been sent out with him, having been allocated the room next to Jack, he was situated just along the corridor.

Mike was returning to the Philippine site from UK leave so the company had sent them out together deliberately. His employers possessed a superior ability; this particular element of their success was clearly demonstrated by their recognition throughout the industry as a prestigious construction company; they realised their workforce was an asset to be valued and nurtured. Wise in the use of this wisdom, they had arranged for Jack to arrive at the strange new site knowing at least one person and therefore quell any possible feelings of isolation, helping him to settle into his new job in a more efficient manner. The company's preparatory, Human Resources, planning paid off handsomely; both men struck up an immediate friendship which also helped the long flight to pass pleasantly.

At one stage during the journey, while dozing quietly, Jack's eyes flickered open to exchange glances with a rather shapely Air Hostess as she made her way through her passengers checking their comfort. She gave Jack a look of appreciation but just before he let the smile appear on his face, complete with an indication of interest, his Manager's warning suddenly leapt out from its memory storage shelf persuading him to look away and sever all amorous thoughts mid flow. He was sure she was interested and, with respect, his Manager, he was sure, did not mean to infer such a multi-lingual educated woman as part of his warning, however, Jack decided to give the famed, Mile High Club, a miss; for now anyway. He could always apply for membership at a later date.

With their usual efficiently, the company had arranged for a taxi to transfer both men from the Airport to their Hotel on arrival. After checking in and being escorted to his room, having packed a sparse supply of clothes, Jack had just opened his suitcases and hung a pair of jeans and some trousers in the wardrobe, when he turned to the sound of a knock at his door. Slightly annoyed, as he had planned to relax in his generous personal bath before meeting Mike in the Hotel bar for a few beers later, he impatiently crossed the room. *It could be a message from his new Site Manager,* he thought.

When he opened his door to scan the corridor outside, his eyes took a few seconds to adjust as they struggled to make sense of the little show displayed directly before him. Offered as a form of friendship, the presentation of the unwelcome live gift had the unwitting effect of expanding Jack's anger level, like a firecracker, from passive green into red for danger.

Stood in the corridor just a few paces away from him was a petit local man of seedy appearance; wearing jeans and a white, short sleeved T-shirt that enhanced his olive skin, the whole ensemble was complemented by a glowing, all over greasy shine, there was also a suggestion of sweaty pores. The entire package was completed by thin, unwashed, black hair that swept untidily across his forehead. Uneven, unclean, yellow stained teeth were shaped into a huge grin now beaming straight toward Jack. A picture of something from The Muppet Show popped into Jack's head. At approximately five feet, two inches in height there was not much of an excuse for the red means danger flag to be issued, laughter mode would have been sufficient. Unfortunately, for the seedy little creature, it was the scene to his right hand side that had raised Jack's anger level by such a fast pace.

Stood to attention in a bedraggled line, ranging in height and age, was a row of young girls. Their ages were, from what Jack could assume, maybe only eight to twenty years old. Fear and misery flowed through their pinched faces. Jack found it difficult to control his anger but before he could say, 'No thanks' the slimy little man grinned even wider and said, with an attempt at persuasion, 'You like one?'

'No! Go away.'

Mr Slime, slightly astonished, was persistent, 'You no like?'

'Fuck off' said Jack and sharply shut the door in his face.

Walking back across his room to the bath he repeatedly muttered to himself, 'Fucking little bastard!' he wished he had hit the slime ball.

Jack had enjoyed many women to date, no mistake; however they were all consenting adults, not slaves or children. Trying to shut the upsetting sight out of his mind and lower his anger, he started to run that long awaited bath.

Leaning over as the hot water streamed out of the tap, creating a mini waterfall flowing into the bath below, Jack breathed in the exotic aroma of the luxury foam soap spreading its sweet scent through the production of multiple air filled bubbles. Relaxing back into the hot, aromatic water he focused on the enjoying thought of those long, cool beers patiently waiting for him in the Hotel bar. He could easily have lain in the warm water till his skin crinkled but his thirst began to protest.

Exiting the bath he wrapped a crisp white towel round the lower part of his wet body and let the soapy water escape down the plughole after fulfilling its purpose within the luxury bath. As he rubbed a second towel around his upper half, destroying a few determined mini soap bubbles in the process, he heard a knock at the door. *Mike is probably ready. I'll let him know I'm just getting dressed.* He quickly shrugged into a pair of jeans and opened the door.

His placid expectation of a friendly face the other side was, for a second time, wiped away by the same dirty cloth. Mr Slime had returned, but this time there were no unfortunate girls in tow. Speechless at the new sight set before him, all Jack could think of was, *the fucker's brought boys!*

If the seedy little git was a red flag then Jack was the bull and an absolutely raging bull at that. Unaware of the bomb about to explode immediately in front of him the little bastard spread his teeth into a confident yellow grin. *The English man didn't want girls, he preferred boys.* He thought it but he didn't get a chance to actually say it. Jack's fist smashed straight into his smiling grimy teeth. The assorted row of boys jumped in shock. The yellow teeth behaved in a similar fashion. The boys' weary faces appeared hollow as their dark eyes grew large with amazement. A couple of the older lads stifled back laughter. They should have stood still to recover from the shock and await their Master's command. However, it appeared to the little row of janissaries that their Master was not going to be issuing any commands for a while and they took the chance as an excuse to run off.

Jack did not stop at one punch. The intensity of his anger meant more than one punch would be produced. He knew he was the bigger of the unofficial pairing and always fought by the rules but the sight of the little boy at the end of the row, perhaps six years old, fuelled his fire, so in his opinion, the little bastard needed sorting out.

The noise brought forth other hotel guests as spectators. The husband of one couple who had left their room to watch the unsanctioned punishment said in encouragement, 'Well done mate, little bastard!'

Mike, however, appearing from his room just along the corridor, started to run toward Jack in panic.

'Christ! Jack, No, no! Stop! For fuck's sake Jack, stop!'

It was difficult for Jack to slow the tirade of blows let alone stop but stop he did, puzzled by the look of grave concern he perceived on Mike's face.

'Jack, don't hit him, I know it's difficult but didn't they tell you about him before you flew out?'

'What?'

'Jack he controls our labour force, he could shut the site down!'

Mike urgently went on to inform Jack that he had been knocking seven bells of shit out of the local drug dealer he had been specifically asked to deal with respectfully.......

Chapter 12

Work had indeed stopped at the site, even before Jack had set a foot upon it. A well respected J.M McDougall employee, permanently based at the Asian site and fully qualified in the noble art of diplomacy, was sent immediately to placate the slimy pimp come drug dealer. The Asian Office thought there would be no end of disruption on site but perhaps the beating he received encouraged the little horror to negotiate without the need for any backlash. Work was allowed to start up again within a couple of days but Jack was given a very wide berth by Mr Slime during the rest of his contract on Philippine soil.

*

Over the next few months, each time Jack returned home, he was aware that changes had taken place. One of the most positive of these related to Josie who had settled well with her new man; he was kind to both her and her son and quite affable toward Jack. Quite possibly, this helped restore her affiliation with Jack, it was clearly apparent to him that their relationship had improved immeasurably. At the end of the day they both realised they had their son's future happiness to consider, neither parent wished him unhappy. Josie was well aware that Jack loved their son she was also astute enough to know he could always be relied upon to provide maintenance, if not faithfulness, to her. To deny her son his father was pointless and cruel, and so, the father and son relationship would continue unopposed, throughout the years to come, enabling the nurture of love and respect.

Jack did his very best to avoid Jenny and her mother. *Let sleeping dogs lay*, he thought. Angie was still a regular girlfriend, ensuring he was kept informed of any home scandal he might miss by writing to him religiously, while he was away, as promised, she even moved into the enviable position of number one girlfriend for a few months but Jack, during his two week visits home, had recently come across a rather vivacious young female going by the name of Linda.

The Dog & Duck Public House had landed itself a very capable manageress through The Brewery, in their insight of appointing Linda to the post. Times were changing in the UK with more women being assigned to managerial roles; The Pill had certainly aided the allocation of more quality jobs for women en-mass if not providing indemnity to Jack in particular. Jack found himself frequenting this pub more often than his other favourite local, where Angie reigned, on each return to the UK, purely to avoid

Geanie, who on a couple of occasions had been waiting for him outside the entrance to the Public Bar when he had sauntered unawares around the corner en-route. Unlike his relationship with Josie, which was improving, his dealings with Geanie were becoming very difficult indeed.

Twice in the past she had sprung at him just before he entered his local, angrily shouting 'Where's my maintenance money?'

'What are you on about? You are paid regularly by my bank'

'Well I haven't had any money so don't think you are seeing my daughter if you can't be bothered'

'Don't be stupid! Why would the bank stop paying you and she's my daughter as well, not just yours'

'You'll see her on my say so Jack' and off she would storm leaving Jack angry and stressed.

One weekend Geanie made the pretext that he could not see his daughter due to her being ill. The next Saturday that excuse was replaced with another; this time Geanie and the little girl were going away visiting friends. Jack returned to the Philippines having not seen his daughter at all that particular leave period. This pattern continued until there came a time when Jack had not seen his daughter, or, because it works both ways, the little girl had not seen her father, for twelve weeks in total due to an assortment of various reasons offered by Geanie. Jack knew she had lied about the maintenance money and the jungle drums confirmed his daughter had not been ill. Geanie did her absolute best to continually punish Jack using the ultimate method available, their daughter, and there was nothing he could do about it either. Unlike his son, who was allowed to love and be loved, his daughter was encouraged to hate.

It is possible that Geanie was responsible for completely ruining Angie's chances of a future with Jack (Angie had so nearly succeeded); he would not have met Linda had he stayed a regular at his local where Angie worked. Although she had been successful, albeit temporarily, in becoming his sole girlfriend, her attraction started to wane due to the hostile single picket that chose her moment, at random but with success, to accost Jack's person on virtually every attempt he made to either enter or leave the Red Dragon.

There was simply no contest, two pretty women, and two nice pubs, however, one pub occasionally took on the appearance (with imagination) of Pitcairn Island to Fletcher Christian, who chose to crash his vessel on the rocks in order to gain dry land. Jack preferred to sail in good weather only, ensuring he might moor up alongside with all his essential equipment intact. With a local fair weather pattern ensuring constant safe passage into The Dog & Duck, Linda won hands down.

Angie, at first disappointed her relationship with Jack had not blossomed as she would have wished, appeared upset when Jack suddenly declared, 'I'm sorry Angie, you're a smashing girl but I can't offer anything more serious at the moment', was not forlorn for long. Her Mary Quant bob and sultry figure ensured her plight had not gone unnoticed, one or two other young men had secretly envied Jack the cute female attached to his arm and were quick to declare their interest when they heard he had given Angie up. His loss was their gain as far as they were concerned. Angie had the difficult task of choosing one man over the other; there was certainly no need to cry over Jack.

As his two year base in the Philippines passed, an unusual situation developed. Jack became faithful to Linda. A witty girl, 'Are you cleaning that glass in an attempt to pretend you are going to put it ready for use on the rack or sneak another pint when I'm not looking Jack?'

'Just one more my sweet, I'm thirsty'; she kept his attention.

During his regular two week breaks at home he started to help Linda run the Dog & Duck, eventually moving in to share the one bedroom flat, situated above the pub, with her. Not only humorous, Linda had also been provided with an enquiring brain, which aided her success in the brewery trade; her day to day business of running the pub averted Jack well away from boredom. And he only had to cope with the odd tart comment from his Mother when he informed her he would be moving in with Linda,

'How long will this one last I wonder'

'Mum, pack it in please. Dad fancy a spot of rabbiting this weekend?'

And so, his life slowly manoeuvred into a more settled pattern.

Even Jack himself observed how easily he had matured into a more sedate pace of living. Surprised at the subtle change that had taken place in his life; while changing a barrel of beer one afternoon Jack's thoughts were jolted back a few years in time, when he had found himself enjoying quickie sex with a barmaid over the beer barrels in the back yard of another local pub.

They had been flirting over the bar when she coyly asked if he would mind helping her change the barrel "out back." Far from slow on the uptake, Jack made his way straight to the yard, only to find said doxy bent seductively forward showing stocking tops in a lame attempt to select the next barrel. Hearing his footsteps, she turned to smile saucily at Jack whilst still leaning forward, both hands on the barrels, stocking tops waving blatantly in invitation for him to come and stand directly behind her. Jack happily did as he was bid and with the added delightful surprise of finding her knickers taking a short break, took her from behind over the beer barrels. She was quite a few years older than him as well. *Yes, we both enjoyed changing that barrel but did I remember to shut the door back into the pub from the yard at the time,* he wondered? He doubted whether any of the customers back in the bar heard her cries of pleasure. *It was long ago, who cared? She was quite a cheeky piece*; the usual lazy grin lit up his face at the memory as he wandered back into the bar shouting, 'Linda, I've changed the Bitter barrel' and carried on cleaning the beer glasses.

Most of Jack's friends, including Tom and Jim, came over to visit him at the pub, nearly every weekend he was home in the UK, accusing him of only helping behind the bar in order to get at the beer faster.

'Christ how do you do it Jack, women always in tow and now beer on tap!'
'Hey! There's no women in tow any more mate, anyway, there's nothing stopping you doing the same thing you sad git!'

With the nineteen seventies fun, musical records such as "Oops upside your head" and the new wave verses punk music invading the duke box list, the atmosphere was always lively and happy punters meant lots of beer sold so, the Brewery were happy too. Saving his eastern earnings well Jack contemplated buying a house again. Also keeping him busy, in an entirely different area, was the occasional security work for the band.

They were now very well known indeed, having developed quite a following, possibly because unlike some of the bands of that era, they could actually play their instruments and read and write music. The fact that some "Heart Throbs" of the day lacked any musical skills (a humming bird possessed more) would not become public knowledge for quite a few years to come, but at the time who cared?!

Jack was amazed when he had to rescue the Lead Singer from being mobbed by hysterical girls at a couple of gigs. At first it was simply a laugh but the fans became more determined as the Band's fame increased, this unexpected development required the recruitment of a few more security chaps at each gig.

One day, Kit asked Jack if he would mind body-guarding the Lead Singer exclusively from then on; apparently their front man had explained he felt safer that way. *Cripes! What was up with some women!* Jack could not stop wondering, *their behaviour was crazy!* He was convinced they wouldn't rip the clothes off a bloke they fancied in the street! He was aware that a lot of women looked at him but he was bloody glad they didn't try to get his gear off as he made his way up the town! These thoughts, however, sent his memory swooping back to explore the memories of one or two Saturday nights in particular when he had returned temporarily from the Philippines.

Jack and a few of his friends would normally enjoy a night on the Town at least once, each time he returned home from abroad. He laughed remembering one occasion which had turned out really funny. Attempting to stay upright while messing around on the dance floor, trying to keep in time with the music and their preferred hapless female partners, intoxicated with good spirits as well as booze, Jack had turned about only to recoil in surprise at the sight of Smelly Simons, dancing with a real live girl, right behind them.

Jack, who had by now drunk enough to say just about anything, was instantly struck dumb. Mystified, he wondered how the hell he had omitted to detect Peter's presence amongst the stale sweat and beer fumes swirling and wafting rampant among each body gyrating on the dance floor, especially in the area immediately beside his. Notwithstanding his slow, intoxicated reaction, it became apparent that Peter was surrounded by a strong but most pleasant aroma, possibly freesia or violet. Jack felt an inebriated urge to offer some sort of comment.

As he staggered puppet like, amongst the make-up decorated jiggling, giggling bodies, still trying to gyrate in time with both his girl partner and the harmonious flow of the music, Jack put a thumbs up to Peter.

'You smell...sgood..!, he shouted over Cyndi Lauper, excitedly informing anyone who could hear through the sweat, sexy moving and singing on the dance floor that, "*Girls just want to have fun*", gorra ssoap's...ssorted then?'

'Yeh, sort of, I took your advice Jack'

'Wha'davice? I din give you any a 'vice'

'Yeh, you did, Air Fresheners. I've got half a dozen air fresheners in my pockets.'

Chapter 13

Poor Peter, life was so unfair to some; however, air fresheners had to be a better option than moth balls stored in your pockets. Jack let the memory pass, drifting on to another occasion when an old rugby team mate of his, Tom, had suggested they go into the City one evening; 'Jack, have you heard of that new night club "Fizz"'

'What a name!'

'Yeh, I know but it recently opened for business and its reputation is good.'

He smiled remembering how they both had been delighted due to receiving plenty of attention from two very good looking Air Hostesses whom they had met as part of the evening's festivities. Part laughing as they danced, while mouthing and gesticulating to the words "*take on me*", along with A-ha, there was something about the two women Jack could not place. You could almost say he had trouble putting his finger on it. However, he was not the type to over analyse and so, instantly dismissing any more curious thought he turned his attention to enjoyment and chatting up his quarry.

The jovial pair succeeded, without much difficulty, in securing an after disco trip back to the girls' flat. In spite of this triumph, immediately on their ascending the stairway and crossing the threshold of their home, the success of which encouraged Tom to mutter in celebration, 'Open sesame!' under his breath, Jack, once again, felt uneasy.

After only a few minutes of their entering what they had hoped was basically a 'shag pad' it became apparent that neither Jack nor Tom would be performing any shagging or placing their eager fingers on anything particular that evening. Although the two women had given the impression they were really keen for sex when they had invited the pair back to their flat and, with the expectation of a possible shag each when they got there, both Tom and Jack left the Club in good spirits. But it now became clear to both men that they were probably not required to physically participate in any sexual games.

Wondering in which direction the early hours of the morning were now going to take them and whether they should make a move home, Tom shot a puzzled glance toward Jack. Noticing their confusion, the two women made an attempt to break the ice which had promptly sliced its icy spikes through the previous sexy atmosphere, with an encouraging 'We want to show you both an alternative way to have some fun!'

It was said in earnest; almost pleading by the woman with fabulous chestnut coloured hair who Jack surprisingly remembered was called Gina, probably due to her likeness to the beautiful Italian film star who also shared the same Christian name. The other air cabin beauty, adorned with flaxen hair and a very striking pair of green eyes, now poured drinks for them all, encouraging the lads to 'Please sit back and enjoy the special show we want to perform for you!'

As a preliminary, they explained teasingly, to the now fairly excited, if still slightly bewildered, men, that they would enjoy the fun much more if they removed all their clothes. Even better fun if they allowed the girls to do it for them. *Who am I to complain!*, thought Jack, perplexed, still struggling to place his fingers with clarity. Slightly inebriated, they giggled at their laborious attempts to help the women, which required a fair bit of manipulation, to remove their large male limbs from their shirts and jeans. After more drunken laughter, the two women completed the removal of Jack and Tom's clothes, albeit in a rather rough fashion, reminding the hapless pair to sit back and relax. At this point you could say the light bulb was switched on; Jack instantly became both excited and very disappointed at the same time.

His finger, now slotting perfectly, rather like the little Dutch boy, into the Dyke, brought forth the realisation that had eluded him earlier in the evening. Slightly disappointed that a quick shag to round off their evening was now definitely well out of the question, Jack turned to Tom, 'Shit mate, I've just realised! These beauties are lesbians. We may as well pack up and go home'

'Aw Jack what a bugger! I thought something was wrong. Aw, come on girls, this is not fair!'

Using their timing well the two women returned to the living room, wearing Chanel and a few scanty pieces of silky underwear, just as Tom made his protest, and without more ado commenced their show and tease...

All was not lost; the early morning hours gave up a new experience to both men. They had both been very excited by, and had enjoyed watching, the all female show and even if they didn't sample any form of sexual intercourse at the end, the flaxen haired woman performed a very satisfying blow job on Jack. Tom told him it was handed out (think about it) as a consolation prize and 'trust you to be the bugger to win it.'

He was rather surprised to think that he had quite enjoyed watching their display, physically describing how one woman can bring another to orgasm as well as any man. At one stage during the performance, Tom felt totally frustrated, part laughing, part exasperated he turned to Jack saying. 'Aw fuck! How are we supposed to keep our hands off them! What a tease!'

At one point sexual redundancy flew past Jack's mind and it troubled him slightly. It didn't last long.

As they wandered, without haste, back to their own homes, the jaded pair laughed together over the whole episode, 'Now that's what I'd call a bizarre alternative evening out!' stated Tom.

*

A few months later, during one of his regular trips home, Jack bumped into the two Air Hostesses again, at the same club, Fizz. Just to prove that you should never throw in the towel too early...., Jack spent a fair bit of the evening entertaining the duo simply because they were not only stunning but intelligent and fun to be with. Sometimes you had to breathe a bit and just chill out.

He was thoroughly enjoying himself, wallowing in the exclusive company of two beautiful women, even though there was quite a large probability he would not get his end away to round off his evening. However, the proof of the pudding is in the eating...

As the evening flowed on into the early hours of the next morning and the gregarious trio had danced and drunk their fill; always the gentleman, Jack insisted on escorting both ladies home safely.

'Come on girls, time to get you both home to bed. He burst out laughing, Shit! With each other I mean. Shit! I didn't mean it like that, not taking the piss or anything. Oh ignore me!'

The two beauties just laughed back 'No problem, don't worry!' but both glanced toward each other only to raise their eyebrows in a joint smile as they did so, this look had been unnoticed by Jack. So, when the taxi they hailed in the street outside the club eventually pulled up outside their flat Jack was surprised, but unconcerned, to be invited into their home for a nightcap. He could probably cope with another show if that was their game.

However, the early hours of the new day turned out to be very pleasant for him indeed, and not such a tease as he had expected, not only was he was allowed to play with both women in bed, all to himself, he was utterly delighted to be informed that the flaxen haired, green eyed beauty was bisexual .....

Chapter 14

Linda's Mother had once lived down south. One morning she informed her daughter that she was going to move back there for her retirement.

'Well love, since your father died there's nothing to keep me here in the Midlands and I've kept in touch with my friends down there, so I think I'd like to go back.'

Linda didn't like the idea of her mother moving all that way on her own.

'But Mum how will you manage on your own?'

She knew some of her mother's friends, they were nice people but they were all advancing in years and who would look after her mother if she was ill? Happily, she realised the beauty of running a pub is that you can run one anywhere. She could easily manage a pub down south and at the same time be close to her Mother, but what about Jack? Would he come with her?

Also, should she tell him the pregnancy test kit, she had bought yesterday, had tested positive? The little blue line had appeared to her joy. She was surprised how happy she felt inside, even though she had no idea of the reaction the news would bring when she placed it directly into Jack's lap, so to speak; would he be happy too? Linda thought it best to tackle him head on and hopefully, he would want to stay with her and be pleased she was going to have a baby.

His two years in the Philippines were nearly finished and the company had already suggested a similar work routine, only this time at a site of theirs in Jersey with one or two ad hoc projects in London thrown in for variation. *It didn't really matter where Jack lived,* she thought; *a base was all he required. All the same, I'm asking him to leave his family in order to help me be closer to mine. Ah well, if I don't ask now I'll never know and perhaps now is the time to find out what his real feelings are and whether we have a future together.*

Linda had been blessed with fairly rational thought so, without worry, she explained her predicament and was not only surprised but over the moon when Jack replied 'Good idea, why don't we get married at the same time?'

'What! Do you mean it?'

'Of course, I love you!'

Jack had settled well with Linda. He thought he might actually love her, so he said so.

'But Jack, what about your children'

'Josie could always bring him to visit me or I could go back home for a visit.' 'It won't be so easy with Geanie but we'll see.' He mused, if he stayed overnight with his parents he could see both of his children at the same time.

Linda so wanted to inform him she was pregnant, it would have been the icing on the cake right now but suddenly, that very morning, without warning her period had appeared. Ah well, not to worry she would have fun trying again.

Jack was delighted when Josie happily agreed to the plan that he suggested, she also wished him well for the future, contented as she now was with her new man. He wouldn't see his son so often but he would still see him and the lad would not forget his father.

Geanie, however, was not so accommodating. Her bitterness flowed like the lava of Pompeii, destroying where it lay. She had always been as difficult as possible whenever Jack wished to see his daughter. He had deliberately stopped paying her maintenance at one stage, in an attempt to blackmail her into producing the little girl. The twisted seed of hate was spreading through Geanie's slender body, destroying any thoughts of her daughter's right to a relationship with her father. *Oh no! No way was her little girl becoming a 'Daddy's girl.'* For once, she had power over him, ultimately becoming his Judge and Jury; so when Jack asked if she would keep in touch all she said was, 'I'll think about it.'

While his thoughts were with his children he suddenly stopped to wonder why Linda had not become pregnant yet. They were doing nothing to stop a baby developing in their lives. Jack wondered if sperm were stubborn little shits, only swimming well when you didn't want them to. He dropped the thought from his head as he switched on another. *What would his Mother think of it all..? How would he tell her?* He had a fair idea that his impending move down south, when announced, would once again cause friction with his mother. If the thought of him going abroad to work had emitted spiteful, selfish comments from her lips, the news that a woman was taking him away from the Midlands, possibly for good, might not produce the positive thought and wishes he would prefer.

He was right. On his arrival at his parent's home, the very next evening, he knocked as he opened the front door calling, 'Hi Mum, Dad, how are you today alright?'

'Yes Jack, why?'

His mother appeared from the kitchen situated at the back of the house at the end of the hall.

'Oh, nothing I'm just glad your okay and anyway I need to talk to you'

'About what my son.'

Led into a false sense of security by the easy, introductory sentences as he followed her into the sitting room, where his father sat in his armchair reading the daily newspaper, his sudden, 'Well, I'm going to move down south to live with Linda', brought forth an eruption of smouldering, slanderous words and statements.

Not only were words thrown but they were also accompanied by the glass ash tray, snatched from its usual place of residence on the coffee table only to be hurled at Jack's head once again.

His father ducked further behind his paper. He obviously thought it had hidden defensive properties against glass. You knew it was the final straw when women threw things at you.

'The little whore, got her claws well into you hasn't she? What on earth do you want to live down south for? She's just after your money! Or have you got this one pregnant as well?!'

Her last statement increased Jack's anger level speedily toward overload. He wished she would temporarily turn into a bloke so he could hit her. Jack was too much a man to resort to such base behaviour toward women. But why say such things? *Linda was lovely and worked hard; he wished she was pregnant, why the hell was his mother such a bitch at times?*

He accusingly looked to his father for support but knew he was on his own even as he did so. Jack's father, Don, (his mother referred to him by his full Christian name, Donald, in anger or when his support was required) had never been able to stand up to his wife. Jack felt sorry for his father now.

'DONALD! Say something to your son! Make him see sense.'

His face looked sad, downcast, totally lacking in the drive to stand up to her, feeling too weak to intervene and back his son. Jack decided long ago that '*no woman will ever dominate me like that!*'

What he didn't realise was that his mother loved and would worry about, him. The only way she felt she could show her love and fear was to shout abuse and throw the odd, heavy, glass ash tray at him.

She had tried her best, ever since he had become a teenager, but never could succeed in controlling him like his father; it worried her when she thought about it. *If he would only have listened to her in the past he would never have got involved with those two bitches. Both women deliberately got pregnant just to catch him. Now this one was going to take him away from her altogether. And Jersey! If he was working in Jersey during the week she would hardly see him at all.*

His mother then made a decision that would ruin her own world, and her son's, albeit temporarily. *Right!,* she thought, *for taking my son away, I will never, ever, see or speak to that woman.*

'I obviously can't save you from making this ridiculous decision but I don't have to see her! So I won't, EVER.'

Jack sighed, downcast he mumbled, 'Dad, Mum, I'll see you later' and left the house. A small grey cloud trailed behind him.

*

During the years Jack and Linda were together, his mother never saw Linda, refusing even to go to their wedding, held in the local Registry Office, however, this was no detriment to their day, they both had many friends who helped to bring joy and delight to the occasion. Jack proudly smiled down into the excited, sparkling blue eyes of his second wife. Linda was a beautiful bride; her brown curly hair was decorated with a corsage made of freesia and gypsophila flower and she carried a small posy constructed of the same. If you had suggested to Jack's mother that only she herself was responsible for the loss of her son, she would have thought you mad.

Jack was very upset by his mother's comments. He was angry and confused. He was sure he loved Linda. Why was his mother so awful to her? *Well if the silly old cow wanted to be like that, so be it.* Jack had wandered away from his old home feeling quite sick. He also felt like he had lost something but what? He set a course for his old local, remembering the laughs he had had socialising and playing darts with his many friends.

For one split second a concern shot like a comet across his mind, *would*

Geanie be standing outside waiting for him? He shook his head at the thought of her. *She was one nasty cow! Pity, they had had such fun together before she had become pregnant.* His thoughts still on Geanie, he didn't notice a large man exit the pub, then, after spotting Jack making his way in, deliberately head straight toward him. Brought swiftly back from his thought, Jack looked toward the big man, now shouting directly at him. 'Hey! You! I've been looking for you!'

Gazing steadily at the man, now only a few paces away from him, Jack's brain discerned the tone of voice, unquestionably, as male not female. At first hearing the accent sounded angry but the bodily stature bearing down upon him was definitely not a woman's, so he could rule out Geanie at least.

Coming to a halt, directly in front of Jack, was his old rugby team mate, Julie's husband. *Christ! Here's more trouble!*, thought Jack.

'Look mate...I told you.....'

Jack only had a second to prepare for the punch he was expecting but the man extended his right hand towards him slowly, not compressed, but open flat in greeting, which confused Jack who, within the last few seconds had been preparing for the speed associated by a clenched fist flying toward him. He looked directly into the man's eyes.

'What's the problem?' but all Jack could detect in return was a sort of grateful expression, not anger.

Then, without warning, the big man landed a real planter on Jack, but not with his fist, with his words. Taking hold of Jack's right hand in his, he looked around in case anyone could hear what he was about to say then, out it came.

'I want to thank you for saving my marriage!'

Jack froze on the spot, totally dumbfounded. Julie's husband had scored a knockdown with just one sentence but with his next two, he would win the match, the invisible referee completely counting Jack out, Seven.., Eight.., as he now spun in a vortex of confused thought, unable to think straight, Nine... The man leant forward to whisper the words;

'I tried doing what you said so I wouldn't get excited so quick. Well it worked and our sex life is now brilliant! Thanks Jack.'....Ten and OUT!

The big man strode away, upright, oozing confidence, leaving Jack with a rather jaded expression on his face, slightly, and only slightly mind, similar to his father's appearance only a short while ago. Collecting his thoughts Jack started to smile, then pushed open the door and entered his old local for a last pint.

Down South in our thirties

Chapter 15

They both settled well "down south". Running the gauntlet of what lay below Bristol, in order to reach Torbay, was not as bad as Jack had been led to believe. He encountered no, white smocked, straw covered, verbally challenged country folk, and boldly gave in to the Landlord, who had, with persuasion, offered him to try a sample glass of Cider at a beautiful country pub while making a stopover on their journey. As noted before, Jack never minced his words but luckily for him, the Landlord took no offence when after just two slurps of the golden liquid (and a dry version at that) he reacted thus, 'Yuck! Shit!'

The Landlord simply grinned rewarding this, in his opinion, philistine reaction, with a 'You obviously don't have the taste buds to appreciate it Sir!'

Linda giggled, 'At least it's not compulsory to drink Cider in these parts darling. There are quite a few real ales lurking in Devon and Somerset!'

Jack retorted that to drink such muck regularly would destroy any senses he had been born with, secretly deciding that as long as he avoided drinking the stuff, like bypassing some poor bugger with the plague; he wouldn't end his days covered in cow shit mumbling inaudible dialect.

Jack remained busy travelling to Jersey and London on the usual, four on, two off, working pattern while still performing the odd security duty for the Lead Singer. As part of the preparations for their move south, both Jack and Linda had debated the work involved to run a pub of their own. After allotting the enterprise fair consideration Linda decided not to take on the unenviable task of running her own pub; Jack was inundated with work and due to Kit's advance notice of a few more ad hoc bodyguard duties, planned while the Band completed a European tour, was very well paid. Happily they discussed their future, deciding that Linda should take a part time job instead, just to keep her busy during the times Jack was away from home.

'You could always fly out to stay with me in Jersey now and again. We could spend the weekend there together then you could fly back when you wanted. What do you think? Would you like that?'

She was even more overjoyed when Jack suggested they could start a family. 'Oh darling do you mean it? I mean you've already got two of your own!'

'But I don't have one with you! I recon I must be slowing down, I'm surprised you're not pregnant already!'

'Oh Jack! I'm so excited! To tell truth I did a couple of pregnancy tests a few months ago and they said I was pregnant but they must have been faulty because my period arrived anyhow, even if a little late. They say you can't trust them.'

Linda's body levitated, overflowing with happy thoughts, *now I can start a family! I can't wait for us to have a baby! It will be wonderful and Mum will love it! I know she'll want to help out, when and if, I go back to work.*

At last, Jack felt content with his situation, *Linda looks prettier every day*, he mused; he had also not failed to notice the sunny glow that had settled around her face in the past few weeks. Just thinking about her sent strange feelings around his body, which surprised him as he'd not come across this sensation during his earlier wanderings; he spent a few seconds in search of a suitable reason but didn't waste time in deep thought. Grinning toward his bride he suggested 'Shall we go to bed and get started?'

Linda giggled as she put her arms around him, cuddling into his huge frame. She felt safe.

Lying back on the bed in her husband's arms, Linda's body bubbled over with joy and satisfaction. She wondered *I could be pregnant already!* Unfortunately, while she lay in their bed enjoying the warmth of the after sex relaxation, she decided to nurture a worrying thought which kept returning, unwanted. *On two occasions in the past since she had been sleeping with Jack her period had been late. Both times she bought a pregnancy testing kit. Both times they said Positive. Surely they both could not be faulty? Forget it, you silly girl. It's probably nothing.* She shivered with excitement.

'Are you okay sweetheart?'

'I'm fine sexy man'

Jack grinned at her thinking, *she is beautiful!* 'Want to go out for dinner tonight?'

She giggled, 'Yes please'

'What are you laughing for? You look like you're up to something'

'I'm just happy'

'Good! I want you to be happy!'

'Yes but I'm also happy because I could be pregnant right now!'

'Well, shall we try it again just to be sure?'

'Can you hang on till after we've eaten my handsome man? Anyway I want to show you off in the town tonight. All the women will be jealous of me with such a handsome man on my arm'

'Rubbish! I'm the one that's showing YOU off! I love you'

'I love you too Jack'

People did indeed stare at the happy couple but with kindness and rye smiles, Linda was not of model stature but her radiant face, lit softly by the restaurant's discrete lighting, plus the personal effort made by the little candle flickering in the middle of their table, gazing at her very handsome animated husband as they interacted intimately with each other across their table, created an aura of "feel good" around them. What's the saying? The world loves lovers?

For a while things went well between them but after a year or so Jack noticed Linda had become slightly distant and appeared to have gone off sex. It had been good between them and for once he was being faithful to one woman only, he felt he should congratulate himself on this unusual situation. So, was there now a problem? He wondered if she had become fed up with him or found another man while he had been working away, *why else would she become so distant?*

On his arrival home one Friday evening, Jack boldly broached the subject, in a matter of fact sort of manner, and asked her direct, 'Linda, is there a problem? You seem to have gone off sex. Have I upset you? Have you got fed up with me? I'll go if you're not happy.'

Linda smiled at him in reply, as if he was a child asking a silly question 'Of course not my sexy man!' She carried on to assure him there was no one else she wanted, only Jack, she also told him he was kind and thoughtful when he stated he would not stop her if she wished to leave him for another man.

No way would Jack make a woman stay with him if she didn't want to. Why insist one person should stay with another, therefore condemning them to slavishly endure untold misery during, what is really, a short time on Earth, when wisdom, if possessed, clearly shows that a happy soul radiates positive vibes to others around them. Jack wouldn't have entertained the positive vibes stuff. If it didn't work for him he just thought, *fuck it! Let's try somewhere else.* But Jack was deeply happy with Linda and had no intention, this time, of walking away just yet; however, this frank exchange of understanding between them still did not alleviate the problem. And there was a problem, but Linda could not bear to tell the handsome, virile man she adored as her husband the extent of the difficulties she now found herself subject to.

In reply to his blunt enquiry which popped into his head like a light bulb being switched on, 'I thought you wanted a baby?', she did offer up part of the problem; she had suffered three miscarriages in the early days of pregnancy, one had happened during the time he had been working away.

'Linda! I'm so sorry! But why the hell did you not tell me? Surely you realise I do have a right to know? I'm supposed to help you!'

She placated him by explaining that after the first she was not too worried as these things happen. It's what nature is capable of. But after the second she had started to worry and just recently she had miscarried for a third time, she found herself unable to say anything at all for fear of upsetting him and causing worry.

Jack now felt slightly concerned. He was very fond of Linda. And yes, he did love her. Being a big man he felt he should defend her in some way, but how? How could you defend someone from nature? A doctor, yes, it was time for the intervention of a doctor.

They discussed the issue. Jack was full of compassion and, feeling slightly higher in spirit by their mutual agreement to involve a doctor, left Linda to sort it all out. He assured her things would be okay. He felt it should be and so it had to be. Unfortunately, Linda did not tell him the other part of the problem.

She had already seen a doctor and what he had said to her had not been okay. Instead of sharing this information with Jack, in the vein of "a problem shared is a problem halved" Linda kept it hidden, locked away reminiscent of a shameful secret. Approximating grapes shut into a vat, the dilemma began to ferment but, aided by a lethal mix of fear and sadness the result of this mutated process of maturity, was far from the nectar associated with joy and happiness.

Negative thoughts are strong, depression aiding the fruit discomposure, manufacturing misery through rot. Linda, unaware of the detriment of holding these ill thoughts within her body, became sullen and distant.

Any man may have started an affair after time, perhaps feeling guilt at the stolen moments of pleasure denied within their marital relationship. For Jack there was no guilt. And there was no delay in finding a mistress. Women had not stopped wanting him just because he had moved south. While busy travelling with work and keeping just one female satisfied, Jack had not bothered to respond to the regular advances made toward him but now, with sex not on offer as regular as he would have liked and Linda becoming ever cooler toward him, for reasons he could not fathom, he began to engage in the occasional one night stand.

Chapter 16

As the Lead Singer's bodyguard, Jack often spent the night sat in a large comfy arm chair placed directly outside his hotel room door (the Band usually booked out the whole of one hotel floor). And don't think for one minute he was attempting to ruin the front man's sex life. He was there to protect him from unwanted attention whilst asleep. It was not necessarily the risk of female fans planning a way to break into his privacy; the Press were also a damn nuisance and ready for any juicy story to embellish out of proportion from its simple origins.

While on duty one night, as part of the Bands' European Tour, Jack found himself in a difficult position. Sleep, in a first attempt to exert its will over Jack, pursued in its mission to transport him into the land of nod. Winning the second round with ease, Mr Sleep had managed to tempt Jack by lulling him into the preliminary stages of relaxation. Fighting back, Jack awoke with a start to realise he had dozed off; aided in all probability by the luxurious leather, Belgian Hotel armchair he had taken possession of, placing it directly outside the Lead Singer's room door.

The Band was appearing on a bill alongside the impressive Depeche Mode, among others, in Belgium and, as usual, Kit had reserved the whole of one floor for the band members' use. His senses now on full alert, Jack fixed his sleepy gaze toward the figure that had just exited the elevator on his floor. However, Jack's initial reaction of alarm relaxed when it transpired the possible threat to his sleeping charge had now manifested itself into a stylish and quite stunning English chambermaid.

Entering the corridor from the lift, her presence and purpose was valid; she had made her way from the hotel's kitchen in response to a room service, food request from another band member. Impressed by the vision of loveliness making her way tentatively toward him, victuals arranged on the tray she carried, Jack immediately sat up and paid attention. Security was the last thing on his mind as he studied the approaching beauty; he deduced, partly due to her waitress uniform, there would be no attempted invasion of the Lead Singer's privacy here. He laughed inwardly, thinking how his charge would probably protest, 'you bastard Jack!' when he informed him the next morning how he had stopped such a gorgeous creature from throwing herself at him.

Realising Jack's purpose, and before he could ask, the vision explained that she was by no means a fan in disguise.

'Oh, please don't wrestle me to the ground! I'm delivering food not offering sex!'

'I'd be delighted if you were offering sex to me' retorted Jack, meaning every word, 'but no way will I wrestle you for it unless that's what you fancy!'

They both stifled laughter then started to chat quietly, aware of the sleeping guests surrounding them. Angela described how she wanted to escape the UK after completing a Law Degree at University. Unsure whether to further her studies and take up Law as a career, she had decided to travel a bit and learn another language, initially making her way to France but ending up in Belgium where they preferred to speak English rather than French! The chat provided a welcome break for Jack in his quest to stay awake during the long, tedious, slumber hours but the chambermaid could not linger.

'Gosh, I better deliver this order before a complaint is sent to the hotel's kitchen! But before she left to complete the remainder of her nocturnal work pattern, they had arranged to meet later that morning, when the world had awoken to a brand new day and the two of them were both off duty, ready for sleep, their night shifts ended. The main reason for this meeting was purely that Jack had kindly offered to obtain for her, a free ticket for the next concert later that day. It truly was intended as a brief meeting to pass over what was quite simply, a gift from one person to another but when they were reunited a few hours later at Jack's hotel room door, the chambermaid was in no rush to collect her ticket and graciously accepted Jack's offer to 'come in for a coffee.'

Angela barely noted how quiet the hotel floor appeared even though it was now daytime hours, silence reined mainly due to the fact its musically talented inhabitants had left for the day, rehearsing; she was admiring the handsome face and body stood directly in front of her. She hoped he didn't guess how attractive she found him as she walked into his room. On the contrary, Jack was thinking how stunning she was. *Oh to be able to sleep with him*, she wished but spoke instead, 'Gosh it's as quiet now as it was in the early hours of this morning! Thanks so much for the ticket but I better not detain you if you are trying to sleep?'

'Yes, I do need to lie down but I don't actually need to sleep, just rest.'

Jack wondered if she might offer him free passage to roam all over her shapely looking body if he enquired politely. Before his speech section could form this suggestion, her thoughts gave her courage, *Go for it girl*,

'Want some company while you rest?'

Jack grinned with delight, 'That would be very nice indeed.'

And there we have it; Angela immediately pulled her top over her head to reveal her breasts, free to roam without a bra.

'One piece less for me to take off', said Jack grinning.

The conversation that had started with simple but sincere, verbal thanks to a kind gesture; swiftly lead into a deep physical union of their bodies. It was sheer pleasure for both of them. Jack had been living without sex for a few months now and was finding the whole experience difficult and stressful. Not least due to the erection that plagued him every morning on waking. It wasn't the sort of item you told to go away and leave you alone either.

Angela was a beautiful girl. They both made a stunning pair. Pity the joint picture they produced was only seen by the hotel's bedroom. Lying together breathless and elated, they didn't arrange to meet again as the Band were returning to Britain the next day; anyhow Jack felt, rather bizarrely one might add, that one night stands were not quite the same as a full blown affair, keen as he was to stay faithful to one woman. He really wished he might return home to find the happy radiant bride he had married had returned and that her quiet, sullen twin had crumbled away. Anyhow, Angela was a stunning girl, he was sure she would not be interested in a relationship with a married man when she could attract whomever she wanted. They both had the freedom to move on having enjoyed each other just the once.

Later that evening, while The Band wowed a crowd of approximately 30,000 people with their performance, Jack roused and refreshed himself from a sound slumber. Among the enraptured fans, their loyalty and awe confirmed by their knowledge and enthusiasm to join in every chorus with their idol stood the chambermaid. But the elated smile on her face was not simply due to her unexpected attendance at a concert where The Band, now famous the world over, were performing; as she too sang along with the crowd, her body still tingled from the memory of her rapturous sexual session with the Lead Singer's bodyguard. Always in tune with reality, Angela realised that the Lead Singer was well out of her grasp and anyway, at the end of the day he was just another man, albeit a famous one. As for his bodyguard however, she felt that with him she had experienced the best sex ever. She had scored on a level not too dissimilar from the Lead Singer if you wanted to look at it that way. She grinned to herself as she thought, *if there was a chart for sex sessions instead of records, I've just been part of a carnal duet that's gone straight in at Number One!* Nevertheless, one minor detail had begun to nag at her, she was annoyed with herself. *Why hadn't she been bold enough to ask for his phone number in the UK? She'd been fast enough to get into bed with him. He was a handsome man, probably had his pick of women, No, let him go, he wouldn't want to see her again.*

A couple of months later, Angela discovered she was pregnant.

Chapter 17

As the one night stands increased, Jack's second attempt at marriage slowly flowed away to join in with the great ocean that is divorce; it was a shame as there had been good times that were unable to be built upon due to Linda's reluctance to reveal the extent of the problem and Jack's tendency to just move on if the situation became too difficult for him to bother with.

In spite of this situation his children, in their summer holidays, had made the journey south to stay, individually, with their father for short periods. Josie kept to her word and delivered their son for a visit whenever possible during school holidays. She would take him to his father, making the trip south and Jack would handle the return journey to take him back up north, using the time to spend a day or two with his parents while he was in his home town. His mother still refused to see Linda and so Jack made the journey on his own, once, he had been annoyed with the situation always marring his trips but, as the tension between he and Linda increased, Jack was glad for any chance to escape.

Josie had long since moved on with her life, remarried and given birth to another baby with her second husband. She was keen for their son to spend time with his father and encouraged contact between father and son. Conversation between them was good at 'handover times' which provided a stable background for the lad, however on one occasion Jack was moved to tears, when, as he drove away from Josie's house, he stopped the car to look back and wave only to see his son, now nine years old, crying his heart out. He had been bashed once or twice in the boxing ring but the sight of his son crying at his leaving tore his heart in two. *What a fucking mess I've gotten into,* Jack admonished himself. By the time he had returned home to Torbay he considered asking Josie if the lad could stay with him permanently but his work pattern was hardly helpful and he was sure she would never agree. He was always away from home and he could hardly expect Linda to look after him. Anyway he wasn't sure he wanted to stay with Linda himself. *No, the lad may cry but he was well looked after by his Mother. He could depend on her for that.*

On the other front, Geanie, resigned now to the fact that she would never marry Jack, had relented slightly and on occasion allowed their daughter to visit her father. She had also found a new man but in her mind he would never be Jack. And so, her dissatisfaction would stay with her throughout the remainder of her life. She refused to make the trip south, insisting Jack collect and return his daughter himself. Occasionally, if it could be arranged, he would collect his daughter and son at the same time and drive them both home with him to stay. Jack was keen they would know each other, however, synchronising school holiday visits was nearly always scuppered by Geanie, there was no way she was going to be accommodating for Jack's benefit. Driven by the desire to wound, she gave no thought to her daughter's feelings and future happiness, only hers. On every possible occasion she would emit spite. The last time he had delivered his daughter home Geanie spat a malicious question at him, 'Not had any more children with wife number two yet then? Just as well. You'll be driving all round the country to collect them eventually!'

Jack wondered how she felt she might profit from her actions. *Did it make her feel better? Why couldn't she let go of the past? Did her new man realise how angry she was? Ah well, it was her problem.* As long as he could see his daughter he didn't care.

Linda was always kind and attentive to his children when they visited, always careful to hide the deep sadness within her. Paignton Zoo was a popular, annual holiday destination. Both of Jack's children enjoyed the day, their attention captivated while observing the variety of animals. Each year there would be a new addition or enclosure and they were nearly always lucky with the weather, enjoying ice creams in the sun in the afternoon, sat in a picnic area. Jack wished he could spend more time with them both; watching them run and play with no care in the world, made him aware of how big a chunk of their lives he was absent from, he mused, *life was far from easy.*

If Jack felt life was difficult for him at times, Linda's opinion of it was pure torture, annually catapulted as she was into a family environment within which she felt the alien. It was tough for her to entertain Jack's children without experiencing the desire to have one of their own. Every time they arranged themselves, as a family, around the table for a meal, Linda wished with all her heart that her own child could be sat alongside. She often wondered, *what bad thing have I done to be cursed so?* Many a time she had left the dinner table, feigning a headache, only to cry silently and alone in the bedroom upstairs.

*

Construction was big business in the late nineteen eighty's and Jack had plenty of work due to the building boom. House prices were rocketing like the space shuttle, skyward. After a few years since moving south with Linda, Jack decided to expand his knowledge of building and took a job as a Site Inspector for another building company. In the main this involved travelling around Cornwall, inspecting various construction sites. He still occasionally worked as a live-in bodyguard to the Lead Singer or joined them on tour if his work pattern allowed.

For the next two years Jack spent his working week staying in Bed & Breakfast near each specific site as required, returning home for the weekends. During this time Linda suffered two more miscarriages, each one pushing a greater wedge between them both, increasing the downward spiral their marriage was already locked into. On Jack's normal Friday evening return home, Linda was often withdrawn and tetchy, creating more frustration between them, decreasing their desire to talk and spend time together and more importantly, make love together. The situation was unchanged when Jack finished early one week, arriving home on a Thursday, enabling him to eat his dinner off a cushion balanced on his lap while sitting in his armchair, a vision not dissimilar to his father, apart from the TV programme he was watching, Top of the Pops. A video of Depeche Mode's latest hit came on screen; Jack reminisced over his meeting with the group's members and hearing their music, which he enjoyed, while touring with The Band in Belgium. "Enjoy the Silence", Jack realised, was the name of the song. He started to laugh, as he watched their Lead Singer walk up a hill, dressed as a king while carrying a deckchair.

'Christ he seemed a sensible bloke when I met him', he stated while laughing out loud to no one in particular 'What they put in these videos!'

Temporarily transfixed by the music he stopped eating, forkful of food mid air, poised to enter his mouth, distracted, he started to hum along to the video, 'Dum dum dum de dum, dada la, la, dada, la, dada.....he turned to his little girl...'Hey Linda, do you remember I told you I met them in Belgium? They are good aren't they?'

Linda just smiled at him in reply from across the room. She was laid back on the large sofa watching, in silence. Jack shot her a frustrated glance, *Enjoy the silence! What a bloody joke! If Linda couldn't be bothered to speak to him what was the point of him being there? Bugger it; he could always go down the pub later...and take his own deckchair with him.*

About a year had passed since his new job commenced, Jack had taken to the work with ease due to the building knowledge he had accumulated since leaving school. J.M.McDougall had trained him well. During a visit to one of his employers' Cornish sites, Jack came across a very nice blonde piece, who, for some reason her family and friends could not fathom, was living with (what they could only describe as) a complete twat. Jack guessed the relationship had started off well but now, because she had money tied up in their building project could not afford to leave the idiot and lose everything. A parting of the ways would prove complicated and expensive, requiring solicitors. Either way, Jack was about to improve her sex life; this would leave her less concerned over her partner (who worked nights) and their failing joint monetary investment. Jack told Linda he was required to work over the next weekend and quite a few more on an ad hoc basis. He did, but only on the blond piece, whose name was Cindy.

On one of these clandestine weekends they were ensconced in a very lush hotel room in Tintagel, birthplace (or so 'tis rumoured) of King Arthur, for a dirty weekend. Why do we describe sex as dirty? I'll try again...They went to Tintagel for a naughty weekend....sounds childish? Whatever, they went off to enjoy sex for the weekend and due to the historic / romantic surroundings plus Cindy's high level of imagination, she felt like Guinevere and I suppose you could say Jack appeared to be a modern day Lancelot. The two men obviously had something in common as both were guilty of shagging other bloke's wives.

'The rugged North Cornish coast; wild and windswept at times', Cindy, compared sex and her relationship with Jack to a description she had just read in an eye catching glossy brochure dramatically describing the surroundings of the famous cliff top hotel, where they were staying, overlooking King Arthur's suggested birthplace. She closed her eyes, transporting herself into a previous world, circa 1050AD, her long blonde hair, braided, and reaching beyond her waist. She was wearing a long flowing green coloured dress that crossed over at the front and fastened at the back, it was easy to untie.... awaiting the bidding of her lover. Her man entered the room, oh; how she wanted him.....he looked just like a Viking... Jack had returned from making a phone call.

'You okay Cindy? You look a bit; oh I get it......come here baby...'

If Jack could have shared her day dream he'd have thought her nutty as a fruitcake.

The affair lasted nearly a year with the usual inevitable expectations becoming expected by Cindy. While the relationship lasted it was confirmed that her boyfriend was indeed an idiot but due to the money she had invested toward his project she felt it would be difficult for her to break up without quite some financial loss. One weekend however, not long after the Camelot caper, she broached to Jack the subject of their eventual legal union, she could divorce herself from the building project with her awful boyfriend, forgoing her investment as there was only one man she wanted now. Jack was completely surprised; he had not realised, or in keeping with past performance, bothered, where her thoughts were going, they apparently, were definitely not along the same lines as his, which were the usual, fun without commitment.

Letting her dreams down in what he hoped was a gentle manner he explained fairly straight that he had no thoughts in that direction 'Cindy, I'm sorry, I had no idea this meant so much to you. As you know it's not going well for me at home but to leave my wife for you won't make everything right'

'I thought you had come to love me Jack'

'Eh!?' confused he wondered, *When the fuck did I say that? I'm sure I didn't say that!*

He realised with gloom that he had been in this situation before. Jack's memories flew back to the Midlands and one or two historical, or should he say hysterical, conversations he had held with Geanie in the past. Just when he thought he might have a problem an unusual escape route, which would help exonerate him from the situation, albeit temporarily, came in the form of the music scene.

The Band was recording at a studio in New York and by all accounts they were having a ball. To show their gratitude for his help in the past would Jack like to come over and join in the fun for a few days? Yes please, Jack would love some fun, anything to escape the repeat situation of women and life that he found himself once again spiralling toward with no specific plan of campaign for avoidance.

Chapter 18

Relaxing back into the flight, destination JFK airport, Jack smiled at the Air Hostess moving toward him, appreciating her curves; his mind flew to another pleasant thought, no aggravation for a few days, bliss. Kit had arranged the flight and transfers stating on the telephone, 'It'll be good to see you again mate.'

Jack started to unwind and his spirits lifted, they were first class just like his passage on board Concorde. His recent problems flowed away with the tide; deliberately he shut away the fact that the tide has a troublesome habit of flowing back still accompanied, on some occasions, by the debris that should have stayed out at sea.

Within ten minutes of Jack's arrival, the Hotel had a preliminary viewing of the forthcoming 'laddo' behaviour that would be the norm for the next few days. In reply to the Lead Singer's greeting of, 'I feel safe now your here mate!' Jack retorted with a small display shouting, 'I'll show everyone why you need a bodyguard my friend!'

The remainder of his initial verbal greeting, to this now very famous man, was to shake his hand then make a grab for his black, combat style trousers, pulling them down, fairly easily, around his ankles. Of course it was hilarious; all persons gathered in the immediate vicinity literally collapsed in group mirth, however, the joke had its own punch line. The Lead Singer was not wearing any underpants, widely referred to in most of the western world as "going commando", thereby exposing his tackle to all and sundry. The extra laughter generated by the all male presence grew higher, like the notes of a song, as if on an imaginary 'clapometer' and not altogether different from the rugby bathrooms that Jack had long since ceased to join in, having given up playing that particular game due to lack of time. Luckily, or unluckily, depending on which side of the fence you sit, there were no members of the press around to photograph and broadcast worldwide the image of such a famous todger.

During the next few days, recording of The Band's new material was somehow achieved to a very high standard, encouraged it would seem by the aura of playground type antics surrounding the musicians and their staff, resulting in yet another, quality album for the fans. Jack merged into the proceedings well and heard some wonderful musicians and backing singers; one or two of whom would become famous in their own right in the years that followed. And Jack had been there to enjoy the moment when their stories had just begun. If only his own chronicle could flow like a song without discord.

Not only were the Band engaged in the studio, recording, while in New York, they were also booked to play Madison Square Garden. Jack, however, was due to leave for the UK the day before the concert took place but accompanied the others to watch rehearsal and part of the setup for the venue the morning he was due to leave. It had been an enjoyable and uneventful 'all lads together' trip for Jack, with surprisingly, no women around to tempt him. Only one episode darkened the trip.

Jack nearly always had to say 'Fuck off' to someone; it was a regular phrase in his vocabulary. In this particular case, two skinny, leather clad drug pushers were on the receiving end of his verbal warning the minute he first noticed them, hanging around near the Band members, literally loitering with intent on the pretext of collecting autographs. Well experienced as he was by now in the art of spotting trouble, his radar detected this particular form of human straight away. The simple two word request, more politely put as 'bugger off' appears well known the world over in English, it needs no translation really, however, in this particular case it didn't appear to be understood when Jack verbally threw it at the two men after signing them away and out of sight of his friends behind some stage equipment.

He knew they spoke some form of English as they were American. Whether they both understood or not, they gave good indication they were not going to comply, throwing Jack rather an aggressive, threatening look which translated literally as "No, what are you going to do about it tosser". Jack tried the phrase a second time, along with a hand gesture advising the direction in which to travel, only to receive much the same response in reply so without further ado he smacked one of them, planting a punch straight into the guy's face. Slightly shocked but none too happy, they felt there would be no benefit in retaliation, there were too many people around for a start and there was always someone else to pester, so they promptly slunk off to peddle their wares elsewhere leaving Jack, after bestowing his goodbyes and good wishes to the gang for the concert the next day, to take a yellow cab straight to JFK airport and head home to uncertainty.

He had a smile on his face while waiting for his hold-all to rejoin him at Heathrow baggage collection after landing. He had obtained the phone number of an Air Hostess on the way home. They grinned to each other in temporary farewell, as she strode past, elegantly dragging her blue, wheeled, over night case behind her, on the far side of the room. Jack's eyes followed her very long legs, appreciating their pace as she glided past the collection area heading straight through Immigration, accompanied by other members of the crew.

After such an enjoyable, relaxing few days, surrounded by laughter and positive vibes, Jack was not prepared to return to Linda and the silent negative world that had come to dominate his life. He broached the subject of their future together the instant he returned home from Heathrow only to receive a single, empty, 'Okay' in reply to his greeting and enquiry of 'Hi! You okay? Sorry to leave you but it was good to see all the gang again. Would you like to go out for dinner tonight?

Jack wished he had been party to a full blown affair then he would have understood this miserable situation but it had now reached the point of no return for him, he had had enough, he stated, 'Linda, I can't stick this any longer. I can't live like this. You obviously don't love me any more so I don't think there is any point in us staying together. I know you longed for a baby but I just don't know what else I can do. I wish I could help you but I can't and I won't stand all this not speaking. I've had enough.'

Linda immediately burst into tears, prompting her to confess the rest of the information she had held secret for so long. But she would still never disclose to Jack the real reason for withholding all within. Even after her explanation of the various problems she had been faced with; their relationship was now so strained that they could barely talk to each other.

'Linda, we can make another go of it if you wish. I don't care if you can't have a baby.'

'But I'll always feel useless Jack, like a bloody spare part attached to you.'

Jack studied her sad face; he didn't have a clue what she was on about. He gave up. It was obviously far too late to go back and start again. They then both agreed there was no point in Jack coming home at the weekends at all now really.

After making a cup of tea then settling down on the sofa, as if resigned to her fate, Linda eventually described how she had met with her Doctor after having some tests, only for him to inform her that she would never be able to have children due to a problem with her uterus. She explained that, at the time, he had said for her to continue to try but he had to advise it could, not only lead to complications during pregnancy but also, possibly, cause detriment to her health. This problem had now escalated to the stage where the only option left to her was a hysterectomy. Jack was devastated for her. His sadness encouraged his anger.

'Linda, why the hell didn't you tell me this before?

Women are tricky, sometimes even their own enemy. Linda lied 'I didn't want to upset or worry you.'

She just could not say that she loved him so much but felt useless in not providing him with a child. As only she imagined, a virile man stuck with a sterile woman. Yes, Jack already had two children but he was not so insensitive to realise Linda would have liked one of their own. But the fact that she could not provide one was of no bother to Jack. No bother at all.

Jack's mind searched back to the Midlands remembering some of the women in his past. One at least had had a hysterectomy. He smiled remembering her warm experienced touch. *She was HOT stuff!*

He didn't feel this piece of information, offered up just at that moment, would be an appropriate way to encourage Linda. He knew it bothered her but he also read her frustration incorrectly. All he could see in front of him was a woman who was never going to be happy because she could not have what she wanted. It was also something he could not provide for her no matter how hard he tried so what was the point of trying?

He supported her as best he could through the operation but the intimacy between them, kept buried for so long, had now dissolved away altogether, like precious ingredients lost into the earth. Jack continued in the only way he understood that could help him to escape difficulty, work and women. Not necessarily in that order.

He never knew whether Linda eventually found out about Guinevere or whether she had just called an end to the now empty relationship but on returning home one Sunday, after spending a few days visiting his parents in the Midlands (fitting in a bit of pigeon shooting with an old friend at the same time) he found a selection of filled black rubbish bags on the driveway of his home. They contained the bulk of his clothes. Linda had thrown him out.

Always an organised woman, she had telephoned a friend of Jack's, who lived in Torbay, to arrange a temporary home for him on his return and enforced eviction.

After about a week had passed, Jack went back to collect the rest of his possessions. Linda opened the door to him but said nothing, Jack said nothing in reply. As he walked through his home collecting up his belongings he noticed their wedding photo was missing from its usual place in the window of their bedroom. He recalled she had been such a pretty bride and those lovely flowers in her hair...

He wasted no time in moving out, personal items were quick and easy to collect. Once again, he left the home and contents to his wife. He felt sad that the relationship had ended in such a way. He felt for her. He wondered, *why the hell did people beget children so easily when they didn't want them and those who would provide the most loving of homes could not?*

Whoever was planning the manic, unpredictable events that influenced his life was about to have a real laugh, sending him into a fast lane where the throttle could not be eased off. He was on the brink of living life in a very expensive world where the women desired him just the same as the girls in the Midlands only these Birds of Prey wore exotic perfumes, designer clothes and basically had more money......

Chapter 19

As his life with Linda came to an end so did his job. The company he worked for had enjoyed and profited from the boom of the early nineteen eighties but now all was coming to an end so Jack, ever the entrepreneur, started his own building company. He felt optimistic for his new business, had obtained a new (rented) home, plus a new life. He would go, as always, where life would lead him.

A very pleasant and rather grand job, restoring a listed house, came to him through a friend, who was an architect. The owner was a very, very wealthy man whose passion was wine and he had a huge cellar full of the stuff to prove it. Knowledgeable and affable, he loved describing and imbibing his various wine collections with anyone he liked and trusted. After a reasonable amount of time had elapsed and his building skills had been proven, Mr Wine began to trust Jack; one evening he invited him to his home in order to, 'taste my new addition to the cellar.'

These 'tasting sessions' became a regular occurrence with both men unaware that Jack had become a sort of 'wine tasting apprentice.' And so, Mr Wine explained the qualities of some of his favourites to Jack, allowing him to view and study his most prized bottles. He handled each of his rarer bottles with an air of secrecy, much like Jack felt he himself would handle a woman, with a caressing but firm hand.

'Never lose your grip when studying them! He warned Jack. You may drop a priceless bottle'

Jack grinned inwardly at hidden thoughts; *he had never yet found a woman he thought priceless.* Mr Wine introduced Jack to another world, far away from the boozy beers he had, until now, enjoyed and which were part of his upbringing in the Midlands.

He teased Jack's pallet, never before had his pallet been teased...., with beauties such as:

Top quality, Grand Reserva Rioja's,
Montrachett (a white)
Amarone from Italy,
A Pinot Noir from America grown in American vineyards called The Cigar,
Whites from New Zealand, such as Cloudy Bay and

Australian wines from the Hunter Valley.

Over the next few months Mr Wine's home was restored to the high standards for which Jack's company would soon become renowned, while Jack himself was slowly transforming, literally redesigned from the original handsome beer swilling lad, frequenting local pubs, into a well dressed, sexy man who could appreciate fine wines and pen ultimately, entertain at a dinner table.

His business gathered momentum and was now well established mainly due to his good reputation based on quality work. Success had not been awarded to him lightly either. He smiled remembering his earlier life in the Midlands working for J.M McDougall; *yes he had served his apprenticeship well.*

Due to these excellent references and a recommendation from Mr Wine to a friend, Jack suddenly landed a gem of a job consulting for some building projects in Antigua and Jamaica. This entailed visiting the islands on quite a few occasions over the space of a few months. His duration on each could be anything between a week and ten days at a time. A dream job! He knew he must keep well out of trouble at these times, concentrating on the job in hand which was high profile. His employers enjoyed an exemplary reputation. *No fisticuffs or wording such as, fuck off, tolerated here*, thought Jack, smiling at the memory of his first experience abroad in the Philippines. Evidently there were no exploited children or seedy persons, sporting mangled yellow teeth, forced upon you either. Everyone he met, everywhere he stayed, appeared wealthy and / or happy.

On one occasion, while visiting Antigua, the weather was blissful but one evening, for some unknown reason, Jack could not sleep. He rose early (the hotel guests were not known for breakfasting before ten o'clock in the morning) and set off for a swim in the Hotel's luxurious heated indoor pool. The sumptuous area was deserted at eight o'clock enabling Jack to relax after his restless night. He thought that while he had the chance he would make use of the Jacuzzi as well.

After a refreshing and lazy swim, enjoying his exclusive use of the whole pool, he reluctantly exited the water regally, strutting his fit body across the expensive marble flooring to what may as well been his own private Jacuzzi. Alone in such rich and opulent surroundings he felt like a King, his mind wandered into pleasant thoughts, *if I made enough money perhaps I can build my own swimming pool and Jacuzzi and maybe have my own queen to share it with.* His mind played on into a daydream, for a split second he felt sad; *shame he was alone in such beautiful surroundings*. He had slept with a couple of women since his split with Linda, one, the air hostess he had exchanged phone numbers with on his return flight, after his visit to New York, from JFK but neither possessed the spark that might tempt him to embark on a more regular relationship.

As he pondered whether he felt peaceful and serene at that particular moment because of the glorious surroundings or *was it due to the fact he was single?* His pensive thought was rudely interrupted. No rest for the wicked? It could only happen to Jack. As a make believe sort of King Henry VIII, he was about to meet his many 'Wives.'

He settled his back into the Jacuzzi helping the water swirl around his muscles, his daydream flowing vibrant, fuelled by the mesmerising sound of bubbles, transporting a satisfied smile to his face. But the sudden sound of lively female chatter brought Jack out of his peaceful world with a snap! The bright and bubbly human picture that unfolded before him, as it made its way into the Jacuzzi room sent his senses reeling. Jack sat bold upright amongst the fizzing effervescence. *Fuck! Was he dreaming?*

Twelve stunningly beautiful bikini clad women were filing into the Jacuzzi room and were heading straight toward him. The sight of such a handsome man all alone and, let's face it, looking every inch a virile King in his own private domain, led to an explosion of various saucy, teasing comments playfully emitted from the girls in turn. 'Oh, he's mine girls, give us some space!'

'No-way! He's mine! Wait your turn sweetie'

A third beauty brazenly suggested, 'Come on girls lets share him!'

With a giggling 'Yes, let's all take a turn', shouted from somewhere amongst the mêlée in reply, their collective laughter filled the air to mix with the gurgling bubbles as they entered the Jacuzzi, gracefully picking their way down the few narrow steps into the tub, to sit, six girls either side of him.

It's raining Legs! thought Jack, grinning as a Cheshire cat at the situation he now found himself in; surrounded by a bevy of beautiful Valkyrie type women (all were around six feet in height) but unable to touch them! *What a bugger!*

The girls were fun and friendly, chatting to Jack amicably, teasing the two gay male models to come and look at a real man, then playfully banishing them from the room altogether. The two males both feigned disgust with Jack and the girls but joined in the good spirit and chatter of the moment. For one hopeful minute Jack thought he might have to perform twelve times. He had to consider it; after all, the situation was bizarre enough!

However, the Powers that controlled his life had not allowed for such an orgy in Jack's lifetime.

While the fun ensued (a photograph of our boy and the girls, six either side of him in the Jacuzzi, was taken) Jack didn't fail to notice the shy wardrobe mistress, standing quietly in the background talking to the photographer, a very famous man, well known in the world of photography.

After enjoying around half an hour in the company of his make believe harem Jack, his mind, ninety five per cent on his work contract, bade farewell to Odin's maids. Nevertheless, as he made his way out of the marble palace the remaining five per cent stopped to exchange brief conversation with the wardrobe mistress.

Jack arrived at work that particular morning with a smile on his face; it matched the one now being worn by the wardrobe mistress. He had secured a dinner date for that very evening and she was definitely mortal.

Later that day, she became Jack's Queen, consummating their union in the fantasy kingdom, if only for a short period. She may not have been a famous model, her body sensuously displayed within an infamous motoring calendar that men the world over would dream about and lust over, but it had been displayed privately for Jack and he had made her feel like a supermodel in her own right. You could say she had become Miss Month Thirteen (lucky for some?).

Where Months One to Twelve would mainly be hung on a wall in various garage locations, their suggestive shapes ogled and prodded by many oil splattered men, greasy fingerprints an indication of their guilt, Miss Thirteen received a romantic candlelit dinner, complemented, later in the evening, by an exquisite menu of nocturnal physical pleasures; all provided by the most handsome man she had ever come across. In the world she worked that was truly saying something.

Patiently dressing some of the most beautiful women in the world, every day as part of her job, she often felt drab in comparison but right now she cared not a fig if her picture was not part of the famous motoring calendar, this man made her feel every inch a Bond girl! Joy!

Chapter 20

Back home in Torbay, Jack, along with various other projects, had been asked to price a patio extension on a bungalow. He had known the owners, Tom and Sally, for some time as they were customers of one of the local pubs Jack visited. He stopped by at their bungalow, having left one of his building sites early for the day, in order to take some measurements and confirm the ground would be suitable, on the way home. Sally opened the door to him with the usual British greeting of 'Thanks for coming. Would you like a cup of tea while you're here Jack?'

Jack replied that he would indeed be grateful for a cup of tea and followed Sally through to the kitchen. She was a petit woman, her slender shape accentuated by her neat, brand label, denim jeans and her black 'skinny rib' button through t-shirt. Jack left her to prepare the drink and carried on out through the back door, so he could take a look at the ground to make sure it would be suitable for a patio, while the kettle boiled.

He noted the basic quantities of sand and other materials that would be required for the job by roughly measuring the area. He thought their idea, to create a patio, was good as it would cover the grass to give a hard standing area directly in front of a pair of sliding doors which were a feature of the master bedroom. At present they opened direct onto the grass.

Jack discussed the project with Sally over the cup of tea, 'Do you know what design of patio slab you want'

'You better check with Tom, I don't think it matters. We just want to be able to walk out on to a dry area rather than grass and we can also sit there to have breakfast, you know the kind of thing? It's okay in the summer but you can imagine how the grass turns to mud in wet weather! I understand you have been enjoying the Caribbean sunshine just lately, lucky you. You also have quite a tan to prove it Jack.'

'Yes, perks of the job. I must admit I did pretty well with that contract!'

She was pleased when he said there should be no problem and the job would be straightforward. He would telephone later to let them know how soon he could fit the work into his schedule. Preparing to leave, he thanked her for the tea but as he turned to make his way out, Sally suddenly exclaimed 'Oh! There's something else I wanted to ask you, hang on a minute'

Jack waited politely for her to return to the kitchen before he left. But as Sally walked back into the kitchen Jack felt something was different in her. She also had a wry smile on her face. As his brain struggled to find a reason for her strange smile and behaviour he suddenly noticed the buttons on her t-shirt had been undone to show more of her cleavage. In a split second Jack was convinced all indications were pointing toward another little job he might be able to perform, she was damn bold if his inkling was correct. His thoughts were confirmed completely as she walked right up to him, chest bursting out of the buttons, thrust right under his nose, only to purr at him sexily, 'I've always fancied you Jack, would you like to play with my measurements right now?'

Mildly surprised, but always willing for action, Jack grinned 'But of course! I'll get my ruler out.'

Her face now alight with excitement, she turned and signed for him to follow her into the master bedroom.

The action that immediately took place between them on the bed can only be described as quick hot sex. However, just as the heat increased the temperature of this volatile steamy session, they heard the front door shut. Tom had returned home from work. Trying not to laugh, Jack leapt into his jeans (let's face it, he had an unofficial honours degree in getting your kit off and back on faster than a woman can arrange herself into a new pair of 10 denier tights), and gently made his way outside through the sliding doors into the garden. Lucky for the guilty pair, that Tom had entered their home then headed straight through to the kitchen, exiting via the back door to arrive direct into the garden and greet Jack, with a 'Hi Jack, knew you were here as I saw your van outside'

Jack was now feigning the recording of measurements for the intended patio. Oblivious to the hot, spontaneous, sexual session his wife had enjoyed with Jack only moments earlier, Tom was also unaware of the wide grin she threw Jack from the master bedroom patio windows.

With a sigh Sally turned to make her way to the kitchen, her orgasm had been terminated prematurely by Tom's unexpected return to their home; selecting a bottle of wine from the fridge she poured herself a glass of white liquid, *how soon would Jack make a start on their patio*, she wondered.

Chapter 21

The Band, with their distinctive style of new wave music, were now famous the world over. Quite a few of their top ten hits had already etched their words into the minds of music followers across the globe, never to be forgotten.

Kit telephoned out of the blue to ask if Jack would fancy becoming a live-in bodyguard for the Lead Singer and his family while they were based in London for a short while. 'Can you fit it in around your work pattern Jack?'

'Kit, I'd like to mate but I'm really busy at the moment. I've got a hell of a lot of work on.'

'Go on Jack, do us a favour. He trusts you and would be really pleased if you could help him out. It would almost be like a crazy sort of holiday.'

'Yes, yes, I get the picture mate. Okay, I'll do it but only you would class it as a holiday!'

'Cheers Jack, I'll tell him the good news. I'll phone you with the address later in the week. You can arrive anytime after the 10th; your room will be ready for you.'

Jack, who had not yet found a regular girlfriend, despite his handsome looks, agreed in principal to help his friend, however, as he made arrangements with a trusted Foreman to run the business in his absence, he realised it really would be a chance to break away and enjoy a complete break from building every day. His fantastic Caribbean contract was nearing completion, he had been surrounded by luxury every evening but he spent most of his day on a building site and sometimes, for reasons he couldn't understand why, he kept wondering how Linda was. *No, she wouldn't want him back, best to keep busy.*

He was glad Kit had contacted him and as they say "a change is as good as a rest". Come to think of it, Jack had recently heard tale of a new type of working holiday where you could help restore old Roman or Historic sites as a holiday, living in hostel type accommodation, just for the pleasure of a couple of weeks residing in the private, surrounding countryside. He, on the other hand, would be staying in an exclusive house in Holland Park, all expenses paid and all he had to do was walk around London a bit and swot the occasional human fly that might attempt to buzz into his famous employer's personal space. Jack grinned at the thought, *now that's what you really did call a holiday!* His spirits lifted and he now found himself eager to reach the City.

His building company now enjoyed a high turnover; he had also been wise, employing some very reliable men who could be trusted to run the work while he was in London. However, Jack was meeting new contacts all the time due to the wide geographical spread of the building work he was involved in, he had already been offered building contracts in London as well as Jersey; he could visit one or two while he was there. He now considered the working vacation ideal, so, after the promised phone call from Kit, he made his way to the capital by train, very much looking forward to a temporary change of scenery.

He had left Sally and Tom's patio to his Foreman to arrange. He felt it would be in his best interests to avoid Sally. Some women had a sort of 'look' to them, trouble normally. He had come to ascertain the onset of possible trouble over the years. Was it maturity that now suggested he avoid such situations?

After his first week, of residing as part of the Lead Singer's family, had passed without incident and therefore could be labelled a success, Kit telephoned to ask Jack if he would mind escorting another celebrity on a shopping trip, just for the day. 'It's okay with the family and they thought you might like a change Jack, especially when I told them who it was!'

Jack readily agreed to escort the mystery shopper; it would certainly be a complete variation from taking the children shopping or to school. Although easily classed as an absent parent, Jack was a natural Dad. During his first week he had mainly escorted the children around the select city surroundings that were part of their home, as he walked and chatted with them, his memory recalled his weekend and holiday outings, with his own offspring. He smiled at a fond memory; there was absolutely no requirement to tie pushchairs together with builder's string for a trip into the town here. *I might have one of those particular pieces of string lurking somewhere in the back pocket of an old pair of jeans.*

His thoughts stopped to linger in the past; he wondered how his daughter was. He had not heard from Geanie in some time now and it was up to him to contact her otherwise he would be informed of nothing. Slightly annoyed at this particular thought he made a conscious effort to return to thoughts in the present moment.

Always a 'down to earth' type of man, he was in no way fazed when informed the secret consumer he would accompany was Diana Ross. Jack was delighted and, after a jovial, informal introduction set off via limousine with his charge for the day. She was witty and engaging, Jack found her easy to converse with; all in all, he thought her a lovely woman. *What a job! What a life!* Jack felt he had arrived at the pinnacle; he was so enjoying the whole experience. He was also free.

Escorting any famous, beautiful woman you would think would be the penultimate for any bodyguard, however, being present when a 'famous moment' takes place is a unique event in time and our boy just happened to be in the vicinity on one such occurrence.

As part of his two week bodyguard duty in London, Jack was required to escort the Lead Singer to the film premiere of 'Four Weddings and a Funeral.' The vast crowd of well wishers and celebrity 'spotters', erupted with a mass cheer as the Lead Singer exited the limousine under Jack's guard. Unperturbed as usual, Jack turned away from the vehicle, performed a quick scan of the direction in which to escort his charge safely up the main stairway, instantly raising one of his huge hands to block the lens of a camera thrust aggressively into their path as they attempted to make passage. Forcing his way, with determination, through the gauntlet of photographers wildly taking pictures, in order to deliver his wares safely inside the Odeon cinema, with mild surprise he noticed the cameras suddenly go crazy, flash bulbs exploding into the night air like lightning. Their aim was directed toward the handsome couple, now right in front of Jack; their progress had been arrested by the mêlée.

'What the fuck is that all for?'

Jack totally confounded, looked to the Lead Singer, 'No bloody idea, mate! Come on, I'll get you round'

He knew his own charge was famous but then realised after a few seconds that it was the woman of the celebrity pair who was drawing most of the attention from the press. Jack immediately became conscious that, not only was the man one of the 'stars' of the film but his partner, famous in her own right, wore a stunning black dress held together with oversized gold safety pins. People the world over would eventually refer to this inventive piece of couture as 'that dress.' Jack exchanged a few more words and a laugh with his charge when they realised that Liz Hurley had been striding up the stairway right in front of them along with her escort, Hugh Grant.

'Christ mate, if you want the paparazzi to take more notice of you, you're gonna have to wear a more revealing dinner suit and a shirt held together with safety pins to these sorts of do's'

'Fuck off Jack, No way!' was his wry reply.

The Versace dress would be admired and spoken of for a long time to come but a few days later Kit produced a press photograph of Liz and Hugh making their way into the cinema foyer, the background of which clearly caught Jack striding up the stairs with the Lead Singer in their wake.

'You're famous now Jack, you may even make the tabloid front pages', Kit grinned, but all he received in reply was a quiet smile.

Jack sighed inwardly; *all I want is peace and bloody quiet, no way do I want to be in the limelight,* unaware his own actions and looks (which in all fairness were not his fault) would rocket him far into the spotlight, locally if not globally, in the not too distant future.

In an 'ad hoc' sort of way, Jack travelled a fair selection of the world with the Band. While on tour in Italy, they spent some free time shopping. The whole entourage entered the Valentino shop. Kit, Jack and the band members partook of some boyish fun trying on leather coats. Jack's choice of a black, three quarter length style hung superbly from his shoulders accentuating his athletic shape, it simply looked stunning. One bright spark suggested he resembled a young Mafia boss; the comment raised the shop assistant's eyebrows but her face, smiling quietly at Jack, confirmed she had appreciated the joke and also the fit of the coat. The Lead Singer then insisted, 'Jack, It's obviously been made just for you. I'm buying you that coat as a "Thank you" mate'

'No, you don't have to do that!' protested Jack, feeling slightly embarrassed. 'You will offend me if you don't take it. You've been a great help on many an occasion so please take it mate.'

And so, the coat was duly purchased.

Their successful journey through the music industry to date meant the Band could now attract audiences far greater in size than their Belgium gig however, a 'Save the Rainforest' concert held in Rio would be the penultimate, with Jack included as part of the security arrangements, stood immediately in front of the stage with nearly five hundred thousand people breathing, excited, enthralled, directly in front of him, as part of the historic event.

The magnitude of the experience didn't really hit him until he gave the whole episode some thought quite a few months later. *I was stood in front of all those people! What if they had all charged for the stage in one go? The power of the crowd! What a feeling! What memories! The women in Rio! Fabulous!* Jack's broadest smile appears every time he thinks of the party capital. He occasionally ponders on how it all started, along with his Mother's suggestion that they would do well to sound like Perry Como; the group of lads who originally played Bingley Hall, Birmingham had really hit the big time.

'Rave' had taken over now; heaven knows what Mr Como would think of that, but what about Jack? His life was about to take another turn and this time he would be the star attraction. He would also be involved with a form of charity; basically this meant he would not charge for the services he provided...

Chapter 22

Meanwhile, Jack, in ponder of the enormity of the Rio concert, was completely unaware of a result from one of his favourite memories; the festival style gig, attended by Depeche Mode, among others, held many years ago now, in Belgium.

Nine months on from her rapturous sexual liaison with Jack in his hotel room, Angela had given birth to a baby boy.

He had the same sandy brown hair and big brown eyes as his father; unfortunately the local Registrar of Births would not allow him to use the same surname. They prefer the father to be present when the surname is recorded into the register and are not known for taking the mother's word for it.

A lot of women, who don't expect to get pregnant, do. It's an unsafe assumption. It's also probably safe to say that some of these women don't obtain the surnames of their partner because of this assumption. Angela had made an unsafe assumption. This had given her a few major challenges to deal with all on her own:

1. Should she keep the baby?
2. Where would she live and how would she work?
3. Should she tell the father? She would like to.

Challenge numbers 1 and 2 were decisions she could make by herself, but number 3 was slightly trickier due to the fact she didn't have a surname with which to commence a search. Even after their rapturous love making session had ended, both parties had not bothered to swop phone numbers, mainly due to the additional assumptions, that had been assumed incorrectly, in existence at the time.

At one point, soon after discovering she was pregnant, Angela considered contacting The Band's Admin department in an attempt to trace the handsome bodyguard and inform him of the impending birth. After spending quite some time in the construction of a suitable letter, she instantly tore it up. *What the hell would they think of her?! How could she be so stupid!* Sighing she decided, *anyway, he would probably laugh and pretend it was nothing to do with him.* This just goes to show how a one night stand can entwine all sorts of feelings but not necessarily trust. This was sad, because Jack would have wanted to be involved.

After giving the weighty subject some thought Angela eventually dismissed number 3 as a no hoper but went for 1 and 2. With the passing of time she would build a solid future for herself and her son, pity Jack could not be part of it, once again.

In the years that followed, the little boy grew into a handsome man, just like his Dad. Every time The Band's songs are played on radio or CD and now, iPod, Angela looks toward the picture of her happy, full grown son and smiles contentedly.

Chapter 23

Moving toward his forties, you could safely declare Jack had achieved a fair bit with his life, especially where his building company was concerned anyway. It had become a resounding success, with contracts held not only in London but also in Jersey. He seemed to have an affinity with Jersey. He never thought he would return to the island as a successful independent builder after that first boozy lad's holiday back in his twenties! He also remembered sex in the sand with the girl at St Ouen's Bay all those years ago and grinned, he started to hum *...we're gonna have sex on the beach......* a jokey tune flowed into his mind stimulated by his thoughts.

Whenever possible, Jack still allocated time to the Band. Occasionally the Lead Singer would contact him direct and ask if he fancied a few games of chess. A keen player, he considered Jack a worthy adversary. However, the venues for these thought provoking tests of brain and strategy were far from staid, Jack would be transported to wherever the Lead Singer happened to be, which was nearly always abroad, for an all expenses paid, "be part of the family and play chess with me", session.

Where a woman would not be disappointed at the loss of his company (there was still no permanent mate in his life) he would often accommodate and pay his friend a visit for a few days. One such request entailed a visit to Corsica lasting a fortnight. Jack, on cloud nine, boarded the plane; grateful he had been instructed, from a boy, by his Grandfather in the game of chess....

Mr Wine was still a valued client, a shrewd businessman, he controlled other assets apart from vineyards; however, his most prized biological asset would manifest itself in the form of a very attractive, well educated daughter, Valerie, who aided her father in the day to day management of his business. She was about ten years older than Jack. Sent, with a message relating to a new building contract for him, in person, Jack, immediately taking a fancy to such an elegant, classy dressed woman, boldly asked her out to dinner and was pleased to hear her reply 'I'd be delighted Jack.'

The first dinner date went swimmingly, not only did they make a handsome pair worth staring at, they mutually enjoyed more in common than just good looks, mainly because they had both travelled extensively, also preferring such expeditions to be accompanied by a champagne lifestyle. By the end of their first course a relationship between them was assured. Conversation flowed with a sparkle complementing the expensive bottle of bubbly Jack had ordered as an aperitif. 'My Father is very fond of you Jack, he trusts you implicitly'

'I admire him. He is an astute businessman. Not only is he my best customer, helping me to build my business and my career, that Caribbean contract he put my way certainly helped build my business and knowledge but I also respect him. He has also, I think, invested a lot of his time in producing you to a high standard!'

'I can see you are full of charm! It wouldn't surprise me to hear you have left quite a few broken hearts behind on your travels?'

Jack shifted uncomfortably on his seat, 'Err, you could say I've left a fair bit behind. Some things don't want to follow.'

He was not sure what he meant by that statement but it helped avoid an awkward moment, well, for the time being at least.

She studied him quizzically, appreciating the masculine line of his face as he sipped his champagne, *what a handsome man! To be seen with him on my arm would be wonderful.*

Jack's own thoughts suddenly came over all prim and proper, obviously an emotion held in reserve for the odd emergency (was this moment an emergency?), he thought Valerie a beauty and he craved, more than anything, to sleep with her as soon as possible but somehow tonight felt too soon. Which felt strange? And he wasn't sure why things should feel 'strange' either. His thoughts offered, *probably because she appeared a completely different 'kettle of fish' (as his Mother might say) than he had previously entertained to date.* Her conversation was intelligent and fun but not as he was used to, there was no obvious flirting, perhaps posh birds didn't flirt, *No, don't even go there mate. Let's take this one step at a time, maybe you'll get it right for once.*

And these thoughts, surely, were all two people needed as a base for a lasting relationship. Oh, and yes, our original 'brummie boy' could now afford champagne whenever he wanted, impressively possessing the ability to distinguish between quite a few varieties and the odd vintage, courtesy of the Mr Wine school 'Introduction to Quality Booze for Brummies' course.

However polite, and slightly formal, their dates appeared to Jack, one easily led to another and so, after only a few weeks, and, primarily as a result of their preferred complementary lifestyles plus his engaging personality, Jack thought it might be worth having another go at a monogamous solid relationship. Psychologically he didn't stop to wonder why he persistently felt the need to be in a 'normal' relationship. After attracting and bedding so many women to date, you would think he would be happy to stay single. His head told him that things were once again going his way and what a beautiful woman to go any way with!

Jack had worked hard since leaving school to enjoy the lifestyle he had ultimately attained, which was commendable and now with Valerie as his other half, notwithstanding her beauty, enquiring brain but also vast wealth, he really could live the high life. He patted himself on the back, *I've worked really hard over the years, and I've now finally made it. Bliss!* So, his heart congratulated him, he was obviously sailing with grace, straight into the sunset. Meanwhile, his head was screaming a warning but couldn't get a look in.

Chapter 24

Within a few months they had set up home together in a rather spacious luxury flat while Jack modernised the house they had chosen to buy together. Sometimes we make light of those niggling inner messages we receive don't we? Running along with the scent, keen to find the pot of gold at the end, Jack gave no thought how he would support this lifestyle in the long term and bugger preparing for old age!, that was for when you reached old age. Scooped hook, line and sinker into an exciting new world he knew nothing about, swept along with Valerie's expensive, every-day lifestyle, Jack was ecstatic. Don't forget, money meant nothing to him. He fancied Valerie and that was it, but his head would not give up; annoyed to have lost out to Jack's heart, winning literally every round of his life so far, it launched a campaign of attack.

Jack began to suffer from annoying questions invading his head at the most bizarre times of day, the most prominent of these only served to encourage his curiosity. Shortly after their unofficial honeymoon stage ended, Jack began to wonder why Valerie was so very difficult to turn on in bed. This appeared a novelty at the beginning, just for a while. He thought she might be, of all things, shy, and would relax, given time. Let's face it, he was a master at turning women on, so, within a short space of time, confusion set in, especially when he discovered she was not so keen to melt into his arms for even a cuddle, basically, he found her bloody hard work. By the time he had turned her somewhere close to 'on', he had turned off completely. Frustration then settled in, as Jack could find no logical reason that might affect her ability to enjoy sexual fun and games with him and as they were now over a year into their relationship he had become rather worried. It was evident that Valerie was quite happy in herself giving the impression she was naturally oblivious to all sexual desire.

They say there is always a first time, for Jack it was the first time he had come across a woman totally uninterested in enjoying sex with him. And he didn't feel he should question her either, it sounded juvenile to offer up something like 'Why don't you want sex with me? Do you not like sex? Is there a problem? Are you ill but won't tell me?'

Thing is, time has a habit of passing so fast that before you know it, year one rolls into year two and so on, till one day you wonder what you saw in your chosen one in the first place and where had the time gone meanwhile? *I'm sleeping with a fridge! Bugger! I could have been shagging someone else all this time!*

Jack threw these accusations at himself in the years that followed along with the most baffling of all; *why the fuck did she want to live with me knowing the type of man I am and the sexual drive I have? I'm not arrogant but I'm far from ugly! Why start a relationship with me if she didn't want to love me?*

However, he was keen to try harder this time around, third time lucky? So Jack deliberately made conscious efforts to try other tactics and so, on the odd occasion when they were out together, especially when conversing, and at ease, amongst her friends he would, at an opportune moment, take a chance and suggest something along the lines of, 'You are looking gorgeous tonight, can I show you how much I appreciate your fabulous body, later?' only to receive an imaginary slap in the face with, 'Jack, don't be absurd! She would laugh, 'We have another engagement tomorrow evening, and I'll be shattered'

'We could just cuddle up together then?'

'Tut, oh Jack, not now, people are watching us' and that was it.

And so, it came to pass that Jack, unequivocally, had been looking at his future life through rose tinted spectacles. Instead of taking action to abort the whole situation, Jack, once again, buried his head in the sand, ignoring the immense problem now looming ahead due to the distractions of running his own business and once again, obtain/provide sex from/to, other sources. He did sit bolt upright and take notice while having a shower one morning however...

Chapter 25

They had been together for eighteen months or so when Valerie's best friend arrived for a short visit to their 'house which Jack built.' The split level house boasted commanding views over Torbay. After completing the repairs and moving into their first home together, they had immediately discovered a 'must have' plot of land, situated close to the town but in a private, quiet area. Money was no problem for either of them so in due course the land was purchased allowing Jack, after attaining the correct planning permissions etc., to build his own home. This was a personal achievement for him, the realisation of a dream he had nurtured from his elementary days as an independent builder.

Anyway, we return to Rosalie, who had become, due to her efforts at camaraderie during their time together in their exclusive Swiss school, Valerie's best friend. She had flown from her home in Italy, at invitation, to inspect the brand new unofficial marital residence, along with her husband, Carlos. They had planned to stay for a week only as their return journey would be via Paris where Rosalie, with no disrespect for her friend, could not wait to let herself run, distributing money wildly in return for the latest fabric, or otherwise, creations, among the Parisian fashion houses she so adored. Torbay's presumptuous Fleet Walk, along with the tempting slogan, 'open till 9.00pm on festive Thursdays' promoting the Town's seafront shopping, didn't quite cut the same sort of cloth Rosalie was used to adorning herself with. Even 'an audience with' the fabulous Joan Collins, who would appear at the famous Pavillion Theatre, could not offer temptation in the form of 'if it's good enough for her....' Rosalie possessed the tenacity to abstain patiently until she visited Paris to shop. That was how she envisaged sumptuous shopping.

In keeping with regular habits, Valerie had risen early in order to let her dog run free as part of its early morning exercise, leaving Jack alone in their bed to once again ponder why she never seemed to want sex, it was certainly an easier way to keep fit and lose weight, rather more so than donning welly boots and trudging around with a dog in the rain (Torbay may be classed as the English Riviera but that does not deter the water from falling frequently from the sky..). He also thought it best he forget any ideas of suggesting sex for breakfast (again), when she returned, he could not be bothered, he knew he would receive the same irritable smile and 'Not now Jack I've things to do'; just get up out of bed and take a shower before attacking what had become another samey workday.

Just recently he had come to realise that his life was actually very boring, only his work gave him any form of enjoyment. Even the two very expensive holidays they had taken abroad in the last year were not tempting Miss Excitement into his life. Some of the places they had visited on these holidays were fantastic, the views often breathtaking. However, the holiday scenery had become the only aura creating any stimulation for Jack in recent months. The situation had started to play roughshod in and around the daily thoughts sweeping in and out of his mind; *yes come to think of it, he had not had sex for six weeks and three days.......*

Feeling slightly concerned, mainly by wondering what he should do to alleviate the problem, he abruptly aborted this thought then shoved back the duvet cover and headed straight for the walk-in shower.

The hot water forcefully sprayed over his head washing away any troubling thought of, *how should he tackle this dilemma?* Water felt refreshing and invigorating. Actually now the bloody watery stuff was not really helping at all, it encouraged Jack to want sex. *Was it a water thing*, he wondered? *It was definitely not easy living with a fine looking woman that you could not really touch. She was almost a piece of fine china, too precious to use so kept for display purposes only. It was quite a tease.*

Jack's mind produced a mini fantasy, portraying him breaking the glass surrounding this most treasured possession in order to fondle her all over, unfortunately he set off the alarm and two security guards rushed in only to drag him away before he had any chance to leave sticky fingerprints anywhere.

He felt despair from the knowledge that the closest he might get to enjoy a session of sex, in the immediate future, was probably striding across the local beach, wearing muddy willies, at that very moment, *did he just think willies instead of wellies?* He mumbled into the cascading water, shaking his head to avert the soapy liquid entering his mouth as he did so, 'Somebody help me please!'

Jack was now very alarmed, muddling the spoken word was a common occurrence among folk virtually every day and the invention of short fantasy sketches in your head, well, we all day dream, however, mumbling into waterfalls was surely an unnatural condition to observe in a virile man. You may have realised by now that Jack did not pray and was not at all religious, however, someone somewhere must have felt he was a little hard done by and thought it time he was cheered up a bit or, slightly scary, his mumbling may have actually been heard.

This little mercy appeared as a very bright, ray of sunshine while the water was spraying, mid flow, over his head in the shower.

Chapter 26

Due to the force of the water and the movement of his hands developing bubbles with the shampoo over his hair, he didn't hear the glass shower door open and shut gently but his heart jumped as he felt a gentle hand slide down and over his soapy back, massaging the lather onto and over his bum.

Wow! His facial muscles spread to set free a huge sexy grin encouraged by the smooth touch as it spread slinky bubbles over each individual tight buttock squeezing each one in turn. 'Oh Yes! Yes! Game on baby' He groaned.

For approximately two split seconds Jack felt overjoyed that after all this time Valerie had suddenly developed a yearning for sex, and, in the shower of all places. Hell! Any sort of sex with her was fine by him, but then his heart jumped as if shocked by electricity. Turning around to open his eyes through the warm torrent and plant a kiss on his woman in gratitude for the bestowal of such sensuous touch he immediately recoiled backward in horror, hitting his shoulder against the cold, wet tiles. Laughing at him through the warm and steamy waterfall was Rosalie.......

Did Jack ask her to come to her senses and leave? In true John Wayne form, "The hell he did!" Wow! What a wake up for Jack! The woman who had attended finishing school with Valerie was about to terminate the stressful sexual situation, Jack had recently found himself a party to, with a flourishing finale; admitting unashamedly to Jack, 'I want you and Now!'

Willing, with every piece of gusto, gusting Jack's way, to participate in any sexual game she might suggest, he made a start by putting his right hand behind her left knee; she had already raised her left leg up and around his thigh. Holding tight to his slippery shoulders she used his right hand as a lever, and for balance, to lift her right leg up so he could hoist her up and across his lower body. With much fun and laughter, as they arranged their lower body equipment to line up with one another amongst the torrent of water, Rosalie eventually connected to her desired object, suds, bubbles, water and all ... and Jack got sex. The smile lay on his face for the rest of the day and for once in a long time; his day went very well indeed.

Unfortunately /fortunately, depending on your opinion of the morals in this situation, things became better /worse for Jack.

Although two more discrete, sex filled, sessions were accomplished during that particular stay, Rosalie, in the future, developed the need to fly from her home in Italy to visit her best friend more frequently, 'We should make the effort to keep in touch more often Darling' she suggested, but with each visit she secretly demanded more of Jack's sexual attention.

On two occasions both Jack and Valerie travelled out to stay with Rosalie in her home, however her husband was away working over both dates, 'Oh what a shame Carlos has business to attend to again', said Valerie, 'We are not planning these trips very well.'

'Oh it is annoying but can't be helped', Rosalie offered with a wave of her hand, 'Some important business deals, you know how it is, never mind, it's YOU I love to see!'

However, in a fairly short space of time Jack became slightly concerned as Rosalie was demanding his attention at every opportunity, in fact, so demanding had she become that Jack would, in future, make any excuse not to be at his home when he knew Rosalie would be paying a visit. She had also taken to visiting her best friend without the need for her husband to accompany her at all. 'Nice for just the two of us to spend time together!' she would say to them both....individually.

Racey Rosalie seemed to kick start the next chapter in Jack's life. Whether he suddenly became invisibly 'marked' as a sex object who could say but after a relatively steady period dealing with Rosalie only, the demand for Jack's talent spread like a persistent and rather annoying pest, a bit like Ivy really.....

Pheromones, they say its pheromones that attract people to each other. Jack must have been born with an overdose of them. Or do randy people just attract each other anyway? Let's face it Jack would always be on the lookout for sex due to its not being available at home. Mind you, if it had been available at home he probably would still have wandered but perhaps not so much? Then again, apparently, if you are a sexy person and have a good sex life you make a lot of pheromones. It's absolutely unfair; you can't win, really....

Jersey in our forties

Chapter 27

A black BMW awaited Jack's arrival at Jersey airport. Immediately on clearing customs he was transported in this most stylish form of vehicle, built of renowned German technology, across the island, only to make an exit, via St Helier harbour, aboard a fast cruiser, destination Majorca, within an hour of his arrival.

'Jack, help yourself to a drink please, we can eat later once we have got under way', the bikini clad driver of the BMW (now left behind in the Marina car park) called as she turned back to look at him; her face animated with excitement, happiness and, lust.

Jack nodded in reply but stood, as if in a daze, while he studied the luxurious nautical surrounding he now found himself a part of. *Where had he landed? This was surely no regular part of the Earth he knew!* He almost plodded, dumbfounded, with his holdall, down the staircase which lead into the accommodation and galley. Letting his bag drop to the floor, his gaze alighted on a beautifully crafted wine rack. Tenderly handling the, evidently, very expensive bottles he nearly laughed out loud, his confidence growing along with his penis size. Amongst the very select collection of wines, stored within the galley of the cruiser, were quite a few of the famous named beverages that Mr Wine had already introduced Jack's pallet to, ultimately helping to develop his 'vino' education.

Delighted to also notice two bottles of vintage champagne cooling inside the galley fridge, Jack's eyes eventually alighted on a bottle of Montrachet. One of his favourites, Jack took hold of the bottle, as Mr Wine had instructed, with a firm but caressing touch. Jack grinned at the thought. Oh, he would be very gentle and caressing. The beautiful woman, now at the helm of the cruiser was quite unique and he was going to do his best to tease her into total sexual ecstasy, he would enjoy every minute of pleasing her throughout the coming week. He became excited at the thought which instructed his penis to harden. Bugger the wine; he had to taste her too.

The galley produced, after a frantic, random inspection, an expensive designer wine cork and two very nice crystal wine glasses. Jack headed back up the narrow staircase to emerge on deck with the nectar and accompanying drinking vessels he had collected from below.

'Nice choice Jack! Do you like fine wines?'

Jack replied 'I do indeed enjoy fine wines but I also enjoy the company of a fine woman.'

He quietly, and with feeling, told her she was very much a fine woman. She didn't believe him but then again she did, *what a handsome man! And all mine for the next week*. She also became very wet the minute Jack, bestowed these complimentary words upon her.

She had been treated indifferently during her marriage and had simply been ignored by her husband of late; she suspected he had a mistress in America. He was in the USA, supposedly on business, at that very moment; well, albeit taking into account the time difference anyway. Now was the time for her to enjoy herself and boy was she going to indulge! Jack was ready to reciprocate her every wish and she knew it.

When they had exchanged telephone numbers at a mutual friend's birthday bash on Jersey, she was not sure if he really intended to meet up with her in the future; she was over the moon when he had agreed to her suggestion of him accompanying her while she sailed her cruiser to Majorca. It was the ideal smokescreen. She could even inform her husband of the truth over the telephone.

'I won't be home for a week or so Darling, I'm keen to take the boat over to Majorca while the weather is good. I've already taken care of the berthing arrangements in Palma so I can fly back once it's installed there for the season. I'll call you so you know I've arrived safely and also each time I make port during the journey. Are the business negotiations going well? Oh good! That's marvellous Darling, okay take care, and I'll call you the day after tomorrow.'

Driven to distraction by loneliness she had already turned to the services of an Escort Agency, however the date had not produced the sexual attraction, albeit attention, she craved; her feelings had been confused. Although her selected man had been very attractive, and certainly attentive, no spark of intimacy had lent itself to the evening, the whole situation had appeared false and she had not been able to relax enough to sleep with him. The money she invested, in the hope it would bring her some measure of excitement, had only brought frustration and a huge knock to her confidence. Jack, far superior to any escort, was going to entertain her for free. She mused; *he could easily become a male escort.*

As Jack made his way back toward her at the helm, she turned to look at him, a seductive and sultry smile upon her lips. The designer bikini she wore encouraged the sun to visit every possible part of her firm, tanned body. The lads back home in the Midlands would have described it as minute pieces of material kept together with string.

Jack wanted to touch her right there and then but the liquid prize he had discovered was also tempting him, it wouldn't hurt to make her wait just a little while longer, to tease her would add to her enjoyment, almost akin to the practice of allowing a bottle wine time to 'breathe.'

After smiling softly into her lovely expectant face he kissed her gently then turned to place the Montrachet onto a small fixed table along with the glasses. *Come on Jack don't drop the bottle, concentrate!* Their glances to each other were teasing, promising untold delights in as short a time as possible. Jack took his time to open and pour the wine. She studied him carefully, her excitement increasing, absorbing the detail of his strong forearms as he opened the bottle gently but with a confidence that suggested much practice. He gave the impression he had opened thousands of bottles but this one, she felt was especially for her. He poured the lovely, pale liquid delicately into the two glasses, and then offered her one.

'To us both, may we enjoy an interesting week together!' she smiled, almost shyly.

He sipped the wine. It was beautiful. Aperitif over, he put his glass back on the table, firmly put his left arm around her shapely waist and with his right hand took hold of her glass, placing the delicate crystal vessel carefully beside his. Just the feel of his arm circling around her waist took her breath away. When Jack took hold of you, you knew it! He was firm but gentle, all very sexy. There was no rush to reach Majorca.

'I think we had better cut the engine for a while or we shall hit the rocks!' she smiled.

With the journey, en route to St Malo, momentarily halted, Jack moved to stand behind her then gently ran his hands over her supple, tanned, stomach. Murmuring a soft 'Oh... Jack', she looked up toward the sky in ecstasy of his touch; pulling her gently back into him by placing one hand on her stomach he sensuously kissed the back of her neck as his other hand ran down her body and into the front of her bikini bottoms.

*

Lust and longing replenished with a fairly quick session, they started up the cruiser's engines, resetting the course for St Malo where she intended to anchor for the evening.

Not only was Jack skilful at sex he also had a penchant for cookery. Nothing over the top mind you, he would not worry the TV chefs of the future but he could manage more than egg and bacon. The lovely woman could not believe her luck; her body was still warm and tingling from the sex she had received when they had stopped the cruiser earlier. His lovemaking had been fantastic, gentle, and meaningful. Replaying the session in her mind only made her yearn for a repeat performance. Now, while she showered, he was cooking her supper. It felt very intimate to have a man cook only for you and, she knew what was planned for dessert. Her body quivered in anticipation as she dressed. Applying her favourite No5 French perfume, for the first time in her life, she felt like a million dollars; which was almost sad because she had married a man worth well over a million dollars, many millions of dollars in fact. Unfortunately, love was not included as part of this presumed, brilliant society marriage. The Beatles gave warning with their message, 'money can't buy me love' but suddenly now, she was showered with Jack's brand of amore, she didn't even have to pay for it, Jack gave everything for free.

She washed down fillet steak and the accompanying stilton cheese sauce with a second glass of Petrus wine. Jack had eaten fillet steak a plenty but never drunk such a beautiful soft red wine as an accompaniment before. Jack thought, *like the woman, the wine was out of this world.* It was also very expensive, like the woman.

Sat aft of the 40ft, triple engine cruiser, enjoying the fine spring evening with a glass of champagne in relaxation, Jack studied the beautiful fortresses protecting the historic St Malo harbour. Feeling happy and contented his thoughts travelled back to the Midlands bringing forth favourable memories of the beer swilling youth he had once been. He smiled remembering how he would probably have verbally assaulted anyone who might have offered him a glass of wine in those days. He had once rated the liquid on a level similar to Cider, well, perhaps not as bad as that foul stuff. And his thoughts now, *Wine? Beautiful!*

His hostess was also beautiful. His facial expression morphed from pleasant memory into contented grin as his thoughts returned to the present. She really was a lovely woman but, as any thoroughbred livestock investor would admit (well they probably wouldn't admit it) prime bloodstock was expensive in upkeep. In fact, so besotted with our northern boy was the lovely woman; while he reminisced over beer and the women he had attempted to love in the past, she had thoughts of offering to maintain Jack at any base in the world he wished. You might, right now (if you are a bloke reading this) say lucky bastard! I can assure you he gave the offer some serious thought when she mentioned her plan to him later in their relationship but in the end Jack decided not to accept. Her offer encouraged him to deliberate maintaining the lovely creature himself and don't think it was purely a man thing, that Jack felt it was his responsibility to maintain her. He just somehow could not commit to any woman permanently, yet he felt the urge to. Confused he shut away his thoughts but then Valerie popped into his head. His head, in an effort to make him concentrate and ignore his heart, was working overtime throwing as many Valerie thoughts as possible into his stubborn brain. *And what about Valerie? He felt mean! Mean! Had she not been mean? She could have told him she didn't like sex.* Okay, we are all different, she was allowed not to like sex but if we should all be allowed to live our lives in a happy state then Jack needed sex where Valerie didn't. *Who was in the right? Was anyone in the right? Who cared!* Jack struggled to dismiss his glum thoughts, he really liked this woman. She was fun, lonely and willing to please. He also wanted to please her. Turning women on had always been the biggest turn on for him. His thoughts turned to the first time they had met, at a Birthday party held by one of his clients on Jersey.

He had been invited partly as a 'thank you', in recognition of his quality building work and partly because both client and builder had become friends. The invitation had helped Jack to, not only win more building work but also more women. He had given his telephone number to two women at that party. They had both approached him, and with a similar chat up line, 'I wonder if you might be interested in a little project I need some help with?', the word "help" was accompanied by fluttering eyelashes. *What were they like?!*

Jack could not believe how desperate some women were, vying for his attention, and attention was what they wanted, NOT babies. No way did they want their life styles interfered with by parenthood. He was still slightly puzzled by their clamouring for his company, they could easily hire a classy escort with discretion but he was not going to analyse the situation too far.

Leaning toward her, Jack took her hand in his, softly kissing the base of her neck as he did so. 'What a lovely perfume you are wearing. What is it?'

'Do you like it Jack? It's only No 5. I have other far more expensive perfumes. Does it suit me?'

'It's lovely, I like it very much, but then, anything would suit you; you are beautiful'

'Well then, I shall have to wear it just for you, every time we are together!'

Moving gently to kiss her lips, he then offered, 'Sweetheart, are you ready for my dessert?'

Chapter 28

Oh dear, as I said previously, the relationship with Valerie had not gone well from the start. Good looking though Jack was, you don't need me to remind you that looks are not everything.... Now there are some relationships around that survive all sorts of traumas but to expect Jack to live his life solely with you but not indulge in sexual activity with him would be very naive. Valerie didn't realise or would have given it much thought anyway but basically Jack was a 'trophy' with which she could impress her friends. Jack's Mother had said as much, in private, a short while after first meeting her.

His mother, in time, admitted she had made a disastrous decision ignoring Linda. Contrite, his mother was grateful she could visit her son and his new partner, however posh she seemed, enjoying the opportunity to stay at their Torbay home. His parents had now taken advantage of their gift of hospitality three or four times in the past two years. Time marched like a relentless army in search of a worthy foe but Jack had kept in touch with his parents, old anger and frustrations temporarily kept at bay.

One day, whilst his parents were saying at his home, his mother quietly took her troublesome offspring aside. 'Son, are you happy?'

Jack replied in a flippant manner without thinking about his answer much, 'Yes Mum, I'm fine. Why do you ask that?'

His mother could read behind the text uttered nonchalantly. She scrutinized the look in his eyes in the hope of identifying a few seconds of his thoughts that might be serious and take heed of her warning. Talking in a quiet, steady tone she stated gently that 'My son, I find Valerie very pleasant but I just don't feel she is the "One" for you', verbally running on to inform him that 'I know ten years age difference should mean nothing but Jack, my lad, I can't get it out of my head that you're just a form of trophy to her.'

Of course, his mother was absolutely correct. Some mothers have the inbuilt, sometimes annoying, ability to predict the future, tapping into just a simple 'feeling.' Before you rush out to collect your mother, breaking your journey only to buy a pack of Tarot cards en route, I should warn you, sometimes these "feelings" can be unreliable, clouded with personal bias and emotion. In this case however, Jack's mum had knocked the nail on the head without the aid of a hammer.

Annoying as it was for her to admit her son was a 'trophy', 'after all the chaos you caused me in earlier years with your wanton disregard for responsibility and your lack of morals.....' , (his mother went on a bit which started to annoy him slightly) *Here we go again!* Jack thought, she only wished her son happiness in his (as she saw it) crazy, out of control, life.

Valerie was fond of Jack, very fond indeed, but he really was only another of her possessions and in the quite selfish world he was now moving, other women were talking about him, wanted him, wanted sex with him. Unlike the girls he had run amok with back in the Midlands, the majority of these women were married. They had no intention of leaving their wealthy husbands for a life with Jack but they were keen to experience his brand of sex. They could not shout from the rooftops they had slept with him but incredibly they would vie with each other for his attention, the bird 'of the moment' preening herself over her rivals.

Birds indigenous to the wild (the natural feathered variety) were high on Jack's list of respected creatures. The sight of a buzzard, its array of intricate feathers enabling it to circle with agility in the sky, awaiting just one neglect in security arrangements by an innocent mouse or the detection of carrion, thereby spotting dinner and a ready meal, Jack found amazing and part of the wonder of country life. And of course a feather lightly touched over a human body as part of sexual play can be quite a turn on (apparently) or off, depending on personal preference. However, the attachment of bird feathers to material items such as clothing etc. can be received with admiration or repulse, by an audience, in a similar fashion. Jack, never slow to come forward and issue an opinion where his passion lay, found himself in a situation where he was confronted by one particular feathered, artificial item.

Chapter 29

Another summer had arrived, however Jack, now bored at the prospect of attending a wedding on the isle of Jersey with Valerie, was largely unaware of the entertainment that awaited him at this convivial celebration or indeed what surprises would be lurking for him at one or two more of the island's weddings in the future. For the moment we will concentrate on the first of these celebrations where Valerie insisted he accompany her and reminded him, very much like one might tempt a reluctant child with a treat for good behaviour, that he might meet potential new clients.

'Jack, you must come with me! Georgina has made a huge effort arranging her only daughter's wedding. You knew you were invited! The invitation has been in the office for months. You will enjoy the food and wines if nothing else!'

Jack had to concur with this statement and as superb catering and fine wines were guaranteed as part of the day's age old ritual of joining a man and woman in matrimony, Jack had to accede, and so, retired to his dressing room where he put some serious thought into which attire might be suitable for the occasion and made a start packing his suitcase for the weekend stay.

'Jack! Don't forget to pack those new trousers I bought for you. They look wonderful!'

'Yes Mum', he muttered under his breath. *Shit! This had to stop but how?*

*

The taxi smoothly drew to a halt outside the church gates enabling Valerie to exit the vehicle within a few feet of the entrance. After arranging the return journey, from the church to the hotel where the reception was planned, Jack paid the driver, who couldn't help but notice Jack's aura of boredom prompting a cheeky retort 'Enjoy your day mate!'

Raising his eyebrows with an 'I doubt it!' Jack turned and made his way around the back of the cab and into the church grounds where Valerie now stood waiting for him to join her.

They both noticed the usual clique of guests assembled. Most knew each other. Surveying the gravestones, wondering how peculiar society could be at its simplicity in mixing both joy and death, Jack's gaze halted on a group of wedding guests standing close to burial plots chatting happily; Jack's day suddenly brightened, as if by a flash of light. Standing on the path just outside the entrance to the little church, he was extremely pleased to spot the beautiful BMW driver in conversation with another wedding guest. Both were about to enter the church. Slightly piqued, it goaded him to think he could not greet her as a lover should, he almost sulked, forced to watch her, untouchable to him. With difficulty he tried to ignore her, now standing elegantly in conversation with two other guests. The sunshine made her shapely outline appear in silhouette as she stood with grace, in close proximity to a cherry tree, its blossoms delicate, floating gracefully, enhanced her femininity, making her appear vulnerable. Jack thought she was looking very sexy, but so alone, with almost a suggestion of sadness. She was the epitome of elegance, wearing a long delicate summer dress with a matching pastel coloured wide brimmed hat. Jack was unaware she had been invited and wondered if her husband might be lurking somewhere. He hoped not, and then he could use the opportunity to surprise her, especially if she was unaware of his presence.

His thoughts flew back to the trip on her cruiser and the lovely bottle of Montrachett, his grin widened as he mentally mapped her lovely body remembering her ecstasy at his touch..... 'Are you with us Jack?!'

Sharply brought back from his pleasant daydream only to find Valerie staring at him, an enquiring smile on her face; he reckoned the smile would have vacated with a fair amount of speed if she had known his thoughts.

Replying with the aid of a short grin, a hint of suggestion in his tone, 'Of course my Darling! Where do you want me?'

He continued to scan the church grounds in case he might identify one or two affable men friends in the hope they might entertain him with lively conversation throughout the day's events. Within a few minutes his wish was granted as he caught sight of two men he knew fairly well due to their financial involvement in one of his own island building projects.

One of the men was very well built, possibly the next size up in suit measurement from Jack, with a generous nature to match not only his size but also his fortune. Jack, from past experience, had found him most agreeable and started to make his way toward him in greeting. But as Jack moved forward the big man's wife came into his range of view. She had been standing to her husband's right side, out of sight. Jack, instantly and without composure, allowed a very loud audible gasp to escape which registered easily with the guests surrounding him due to the fact that they too had noticed the large man's wife and had also found her an object for hilarity. However, the assembled guests managed to register their acknowledgement of her arrival in a far quieter manner than Jack, who without one shred of decorum leant his body back slightly to let out a huge string of 'Hah, Hah, Hah's!' in wild laughter.

Valerie, her face colouring brightly at the very loud outburst made by her handsome escort, quickly scolded Jack to, 'For heaven's sake shut up!' as quietly as possible, from the side of her mouth, due to their being surrounded by other guests (who in all fairness to Jack were also trying to stifle their own individual mirth).

The good humoured, affable man had resignedly accompanied his wife to the occasion whilst she wore a most ridiculous huge round hat, the edges of which being adorned with long black feathers, gave the impression that a huge bird nest had alighted on her head in an upside down position. Jack could not stop himself uttering, to those within his volume range, a self made joke suggesting the hapless husband was an Eagle with his own nest to rest in as and when required. Apart from a few quiet sniggers uttered by the guests in range of his outburst, no one appeared to be offended by Jack's frank opinion of the much feathered haute couture hat, apparently purchased in Harrods, and both he and Valerie made their way toward the day's festivities.

The nest, however, was never far from view due to its very similar comparison with an upturned Scottish eyrie, maintaining Jack's laughter level to near overflow throughout the day. He made a mental note wishing he could thank the woman for her contribution, which without doubt, had brightened the whole event for him in particular.

As the evening festivities unfolded and having socialised well throughout the day, imbibing a fair quantity of good quality wine on the way, Jack eventually found himself sitting beside the affable large man. Both immediately started up lively, amiable conversation. Jack's etiquette score, which due to his impeccable behaviour throughout the days' events, loud laughing at silly hat misdemeanour already forgotten, had hit an all time high, unfortunately, they were only ten minutes or so into their conversation when both Valerie and the Eyrie shuffled into view, wiggling in unison on the dance floor not far from the table where the two men sat in cahoots together, each enjoying a large glass of brandy and an even larger cigar.

The black nest feathers were magnificent, gently flapping up and down in a rhythmic pattern. Jack tried very hard to concentrate on the immediate task of conducting a sensible conversation, without accompanying laugher, as he did not wish to insult his kind companion. Rescue came to most of the spectators trying, with difficulty, to hide their glee and entertainment from the big man, in the form of a gust of wind (most guests were aware that, silly hat withstanding, he was a very wealthy man and they did not want to offend for that reason in the main). Television nature programmes have shown an eagle nest withstanding powerful tempestuous storms whilst wavering precariously on the edges of a spindly, extremely tall, tree branch. The haute couture hat was never intended for such inclement weather so when the French windows leading from the disco area to the sweeping lawns outside were opened, allowing the summer breeze to rush in, the feathers, mid wiggle, as nature intended, rose to the thermals, lifting the imitation eyrie from its position atop her head only to deposit it ungraciously upside down on the dance floor next to Valerie's, still shuffling, feet.

The big man surprised many guests within hearing distance as he proclaimed in a statement for all to hear, 'Thank goodness for that! Perhaps now the crows will nest in it!'

Jack let out a huge roar of laughter that did not end too quickly. The big man smiled at him through his brandy glass and asked, 'Have you been laughing at my wife's choice of hat Jack?'

Never one to lie, Jack admitted 'I've never seen anything so ridiculous in quite a while, Sorry!'

In response to his truthful reply the big man admitted in return, 'don't be sorry, what the fuck possessed her to waste money on that load of crap I don't know!'

The most productive part of the day's festivities manifested itself in the form of the BMW who had invited our boy to sail her boat back from Majorca to Jersey before autumn appeared. The secretive pair had been able to speak for a few minutes without attracting any enquiring eyes from the other guests. Their passion locked away while they stood so close together, just talking. Well aware of the warm reception he always enjoyed with this woman, her appetite for fellatio was enormous; he was keen to participate in the return journey.

'What I would give to be able to take you upstairs and make love to you right now!' Jack whispered with a sigh.

'I would give the same. I miss you. I wish you would take up my offer, it still stands, always will Jack. I've not met anyone quite like you before!'

'Are you saying you're in love with me or just commenting on my ability to keep you in sex? You smell beautiful and you've got No 5 on again. Am I right?'

He moved closer, she giggled nervously, 'Yes, but Jack, move back, people will notice'

'I don't give a fuck!'

'Don't be ridiculous, you will cause a scandal. You know I want you but we must wait. Unless of course, you want to give up Valerie, I can match her wealth you know?'

'Money is the last thing on my mind, only you. I'll look forward to sailing the boat back with you. Until then, okay?'

'Okay, miss you...'

Without further ado they arranged a date not too far in the future; Jack knew an easy excuse could be found in the form of viewing new work somewhere, in fact anywhere. They parted with difficulty, Jack wishing he could retire for the night to an upstairs hotel room with this beautiful woman. Alas, he must return like a reprimanded hound to his cold mistress.....

*

Within a couple of months, the usual, 'I've a new project to quote for on Jersey but the owner lives in the Balearics' excuse accepted by Valerie; Jack flew out from Exeter to Majorca.

The flight time of just two hours, could not pass fast enough for him. He felt like a boy on a first date, inwardly he reprimanded himself, *Idiot!* Eager to meet his favourite, he knew she would be waiting to collect him at Palma Airport ready to transfer him once again from air via a rented car onto the boat. His impatience transferred into daydream, *one short train journey and I would have completed every form of Earth travel. You couldn't really count the space shuttle as a regular form of public transport, yet.* It had occurred to Jack that he actually missed this particular woman's company and would be glad to see her again, albeit he still managed to put any thought of a permanent arrangement out of his head and live in the moment once again, but don't let this tempt you into thinking him Buddhist.

Jack was a 'live life to the full' master, taking every day and situation in his stride, as you should by now, be very aware. However, let me draw your attention back to the fact that this woman had made him think, seriously, of accepting a kept man life style. The offer still stood, having not been withdrawn.

Always eager to indulge in sexual activity with Jack, she demanded his attention the minute he alighted into the car putting her hand straight between his legs while she kissed him, coming up for air with a, 'I've missed you my sexy man! Just wait till I get you back on the boat!'

Jack's reply was to run his hands all over her curvy bits, one can only assume to ensure they were all correct and present, offering, 'I'll see what I can do to accommodate you darling!'

As for the 40ft cruiser, his home for the next week, the customary bottle of wine and crystal glasses had earlier that day been placed ready for their joint arrival, below deck. Of all the women he had known this one seemed to become more randy each time she met up with him. During the short drive to Palma, gleefully teasing, she informed him 'I have a particular fantasy I will enjoy performing on you during our journey back!'

'I look forward to it you sexy minx!'

It appeared to Jack she may have spent the time they had been apart planning this one. Well, if it made her happy, that was fine by him!

Jack loved shellfish. His present lifestyle enabled him to experience some of the finest sea foods. Our lovely BMW driver/woman, along with Jack, just happened to have a penchant for oysters and, after completing quite a few exercises from the Joy of Sex during the previous evening, they had bought some fresh from the local fish market the morning they set sail.

Lazily, the cruiser made its way back to Jersey, skirting the south west coast of Majorca. The morning was still and sunny, the Mediterranean Sea glistening with the reflection of the sun. She anchored the cruiser off a small deserted cove close to Valldemossa. Jack's immediate thought guessed she probably intended for both of them to indulge in a bit of nude swimming. *She was beautiful and always so randy*! *He had kept her busy a fair bit the previous night but she was always ready for more*! His thoughts broke into a smile, finding they had travelled along the correct lines, as almost immediately upon dropping anchor she stepped out of her bikini, disregarding its designer label, to drop the expensive minute pieces of material straight onto the deck as she made her way toward the back of the boat.

'Come on Jack, don't be shy, surely you're not shy?' Holding a pose in front of him for just a few seconds, she turned, then, with a graceful arc, dove into the crystal water. Jack had appreciated the little show of her curves with a grin, *she could be a fantastic burlesque performer, and she certainly knew how to tease. It's all for you, you idiot, stop gawping and go get her!* Laughing, Jack followed her into the water with an ungainly jump, his thoughts ecstatic *what a life! Fantastic!*

After messing about childishly for a while in the warm water, their tiredness dictated they end their refreshing swim and relax their bodies dry. Climbing back up the small chrome ladder onto the cruiser's sun deck, they spread out over a sun lounger each, to bask regally in the warm sunshine. Back on board, Jack was completely unaware of the unusual sexual experience awaiting him but the secret smile he glimpsed on her lips betrayed some mischief afoot, 'What are you up to Minx?'

With a slight raise of her eyebrows and a naughty, schoolgirl type smile lighting her face, she gave no reply, rose silently from the lounger with a sexy stretch, and walked toward the galley.

Returning with the oysters, purchased in the market that very morning, which were now arranged on a plate along with a few thick slices of lemon, she settled the dish on her sun lounger then made another trip back to the galley, returning with a bottle of Rully Premier Cru AOC.

'Would you kindly open this beauty for me darling?' she asked Jack.

He sat up, and, corkscrew in hand, opened the bottle with ease. 'Nice choice sweetheart but what are you up to? You're smiling as if you are up to something'

Part filling one of the crystal glasses, she passed it to him regally but the schoolgirl grin would not behave, dancing all over her face. They toasted each other but Jack wondered why her minx like grin persisted. *Come to think of it she had been smiling quietly ever since she had purchased the oysters that morning. She was obviously happy, let her be.*

Jack stretched back out on his sun lounger, enjoying an all over tanning session while the salty water simultaneously dried on his skin. Suddenly, with a giggle, his hostess put her glass down, then knelt on the deck beside him and took hold of his penis. *Wow!* Jack thought, *fantastic, here we go again!*

After teasing Jack with her hands and tongue it was not long until he was at the peak of explosion. Slightly puzzled, worried even, to realise he was at the stage where he was very much under her control, he managed to gasp 'What are you doing? Why have you put them there?

Giggling, because she had just positioned the plate of oysters onto his flat well muscled stomach, she reassured and encouraged him with 'I want some of your special sauce on my oysters darling!'

Laughing in astonishment, he joyfully complied with her request, relaxing in ecstasy, sprinkling all he could produce over the dish of unsuspecting shellfish. Still slightly confused, he continued to laugh with amazement as she delicately tipped the first oyster into her mouth along with the unique sauce, supplementing the flavour with a sip of the beautiful dry white ruiy, ensuring a smooth journey as she swallowed. Jack was almost speechless. He could only laugh to himself, *what was she like!*

Managing to recover he suggested tartly 'If that's what you wanted why did you bother to buy lemons?'

They burst into laughter together. The smile has never really left his face. I sometimes catch the bugger smiling quietly and ask him if he's thinking of oysters.

Chapter 30

Jack returned home after that particular week feeling fairly tired but happy. Rather reminiscent of a dog that has wandered off after a bitch in season, only to return home triumphant to a kind owner that does not beat it. However, not too far into the future he would return to his kennel completely knackered due to the soaring demand for his sexual prowess; with a carefree air of nonchalance, Jack would walk the whole experience full of fun with no expectations of debacle. Eventually, quite dumbfounded, he would come to realise that unwittingly, over the space of a few months, he had collated a sort of Isle of Jersey 'harem.'

He first became aware of this unusual situation when Valerie informed him, after opening the post one morning, 'Oh Jack we've both been invited to another wedding on Jersey, in the spring.'

Unaware of his mumbled derogatory 'Not again!' she ran on to verbally list, for his general information, quite a few names of acquaintances that had also been invited. Unwittingly, three of the women she mentioned Jack had recently slept with; as part of the Jersey elite, their presence was automatically requested. It was almost a routine.

Time passes quickly, and as Jack had need to visit the island on business trips at least thrice before the actual wedding day, Valerie suggested 'You already spend so much time there, we might be better off actually moving to the island permanently!'

Slightly alarmed he dismissed the comment as one that should not cause too much concern and certainly it was not worth losing any sleep over. 'I expect the work will end eventually' was his hopeful deterrent.

*

With the wedding imminent and their suitcases packed with suitable clothing once again, for a few days stay, they both left Exeter Airport, the short flight depositing them once again, on the biggest of the Channel Islands, in no time at all.

The ceremony was performed in the same local church, by the same Vicar and in the usual fashion, where the previous wedding they had attended had been held and thankfully, no headgear similar to an eyrie was worn. Jack, always a keen participant at any reception, was one of the first to escape the church and slide elegantly into the awaiting taxi.

By the time they arrived at the hotel reception venue there was plenty of Veuve Clicquot La Grande Dame flowing (Jack, as part of his sommelier education, had been lucky enough to have imbibed many bottles of this special cuvee de prestige) and could identify this particular nectar if presented with a choice. Valerie, always aware of the envious looks other women gave her when she entered any public building with Jack, strode importantly, notwithstanding her Louis Vuitton suit, up the grand entrance into the hotel.

Arriving at the edge of the splendid ballroom balustrades; she stood to one side, accompanied by her trophy while she surveyed the already very busy dance floor, scanning the guests for faces known to her. With no regard for Valerie's direction, *would she dance or drink first?* Jack chose drink, plotting a course straight for the Bar, his heart jumped, surprised to spot the lovely BMW in conversation, elegantly holding a glass of the delightful afore mentioned champagne, *I didn't see her in the church?*, with two other married, neglected, wealthy women along with Julie, a divorced woman, well into her fifties, of whom Jack had also become particularly fond in the past few months. A harem always has its favourites...

The wedding was special for the couple attempting to spend the rest of their lives together but the day would also be memorable, in fact, unforgettable, for Julie, who had been lucky enough to be seated next to Jack during the wedding breakfast. A close family friend, she had influence. Fortune had placed her in the family home while the seating plan was deliberated over and drawn up, the Bride had laughed, declaring,

'Aunty Julie, I understand quite a few women secretly admire Jack. I don't want my seating plan to cause any jealousy!'

'Really! Ellen! I don't see how, I'm far too old for him!'

'Well, with Valerie on his other side he should be safe from you, she teased, and Valerie must count herself lucky to live with such a handsome man!'

Julie smiled inwardly, from what Jack had told her, while she lay snuggled into his strong arms, his naked body wrapped protectively around hers, Valerie didn't realise just how lucky she was. Her neglect of her handsome beau was Julie's gain. She was delighted she could provide such a virile man a little love and comfort.

Excited by the thought of his intimate and sensual touch, she remembered the last time they had made love together, he had shown her one or two things she had never before experienced resulting in such an orgasm; her face needed no lift! Her friend had paid a top Plastic Surgeon quite a price to look ten years younger, she wondered, *perhaps I should have given her Jack's phone number!* Her body shook to the thrill that shot across the upper part of her body as she thought of him, Julie came back to reality leaving the Bride slightly concerned, 'Are you okay Aunt Julie? You seem a bit distant.'

'I just felt a bit chilly darling'

'Oh, are you cold? I'll fetch a shawl'

'I'm fine darling, full of fun!'

The resulting final, table arrangement caused quite some jealousy in one or two corners I can tell you. And so, during the sumptuous dinner/wedding breakfast, Julie was able to imbibe freely of her desire, touching thighs with Jack under the table.

She was a down to earth sort of woman who had married an older man of vast wealth but since the death of her beloved husband from cancer three years earlier, found her life, at the time, devoid of love. Young at heart, she declared all suitable men of similar age, suggested by friends as a potential mate, boring old farts. Not the type to consider escort agencies, she had tackled loneliness by busying her day with pleasant but tame, social lunching and charities until she had had the good fortune to be introduced to Jack at a mutual friend's Birthday party a year ago. Her life, once dominated by continuous days of "Ladies that Lunch" was now interspaced with sporadic hot sexual encounters which she coquettishly referred to as, *Fuck with Jack*.

Never one to miss an opportunity for sexual activity with a favourite Jack, delighted with his table position on Julie's left side and without delay, took the chance whenever possible, to put his right hand under the tablecloth and caress her left thigh. They had managed a fair conversation, with each other and the remainder of their table guests, throughout the meal but as the wedding speeches commenced, Julie deliberately moved her leg closer to Jack, allowing his hand more leg area, a tease for him to explore further while muttering 'What do you think of that Jack!?'

Little did she realise the lengths he would stretch to as he replied quietly 'I'll show you, little tart!'

His masculine reply brought forth a wild rush of excitement all around her body leaving her face radiant. Her youthful looks did not go unnoticed by two of the other guests at their table prompting one to offer

'Julie you really are looking well these days! Have you found another man! You deserve to be happy!'

'Why thank you! But I just enjoy life and I keep busy!'

Jack glanced sideways, catching Julie's attention then murmured, for her ears only, 'Would you like to expand and provide me with a little more detail of how you enjoy yourself and keep busy? By the way, that perfume you are wearing is nice. What is it?'

Julie suppressed a giggle, managing to turn it into a pleasant smile in the hope their amorous conversation would not be detected and replied, 'You know very well the reason why I smile so much these days and I'm surprised you haven't recognised my perfume, I always wear it, it's No 5'

Confused, Jack nearly blurted out how he knew another woman, who wore just the same perfume, but its fragrance smelt totally different on her body. Julie detected the quizzical look on his face, 'Do you not like it Jack. I'll wear something else in future'

'Oh no, no it's lovely, it's just that, well, actually my Mother wears it but it smells totally different on her.'

'Oh, that's simple to explain Jack. Perfume can smell different on different women, a lot of people don't realise that fact.'

'Well, I never knew that. Now where were we? Oh yes ...little tart.'

The table was deep and the lush tablecloth covered any sight of Jack's wandering right hand from the other seated guests. Julie jumped inwardly with what she hoped was an undetectable small gasp, her steady breathing pattern had been momentarily interrupted by the fingers on Jack's hand working their way under the hem of her dress to reach the very top of her left inside leg then push gently under the edge of her pants and move on to touch her clitoris. The slightest movement of his finger dictated Julie breathe in small gasps. Well aware of the surrounding diners, the risk of being caught and the sensational feeling, Julie had difficulty concentrating and was grateful the surrounding guests were captivated in full by the Best Man's witty speech. Quietly, almost pleading, she murmured to Jack, 'Oh my god..!'

Jack's face gave nothing away. A quiet smile innocently covered his face while he drank his brandy holding the delicate cut crystal glass with his left hand while the middle finger of his right hand was gently moving on a precise spot under the table.

Oh, what naughtiness! She could have shifted but she just did not want to. Oh the price of being caught! The serene expression hovering over Jack's face did not match the increasing excitement within Julie's body. She had been unable to meet up with him for some weeks till now, however, now was not the appropriate time for Fuck with Jack. She knew she only had to move away slightly and the feeling would stop. She just could not let it stop. *Oh my god! How am I going to keep quiet*, she bit her lip in an effort to stop the sensation escape her mouth in small verbal moans. A couple of times she shifted on her seat, tortured by ecstasy but this only served to increase the feeling and *Oh No! I'm going to come!* No way could she stop now. Incredibly, not one person had noticed the under table action, engrossed as they were in their desserts, coffees and the speeches. With no thought for the other table guests, some still sipping their sorbet, Julie let out an audible gasp, 'Oh! Ah!'

The inhabitants of Julie's table, number 8, plus all of 6 and a few on 7 and 9, turned to see what was amiss but Julie, far from stupid, had found a smart way to cover her illicit enjoyment. Shutting her eyes with a second small 'Oh!' she dropped her head to one side, immediately sliding sideways off her chair and onto the floor, feigning collapse...

Concerned she had suffered a "funny turn", half a dozen guests from nearby tables rushed to her aid, helping her return to her seat beside Jack, who had carried a look of slight bemusement on his face throughout. One guest bitchily suggested to a friend, 'I expect it's her age, you feel the heat a bit when you get past fifty I'm told.'

'Julie, are you alright?' Valerie and a few other guests asked in unison.

Julie explained that she was indeed alright. 'Please not to worry, Oh how silly of me! I just came over all hot and must have fainted, how embarrassing!' She was so sorry to cause a fuss. 'I'll just freshen up in the powder room.'

Accompanied by a concerned friend, she made her escape; only to giggle like a schoolgirl once the privacy of the rest room had been attained.

Later in the day Jack took her aside to ask quietly 'Are you going to faint every time I make you come in the future?!'

Oh! He was so handsome, she thought, as she grinned back up at him. She could not wait to enjoy his lovely body when they were alone again and told him so. Jack, always willing to please, like a moth to the flame, said he would try to arrange something soon. If he was careful he could make more than just one woman happy on his next visit.

Chapter 31

Unbeknown to Jack, another woman, who had just moved to the island with her husband, had been secretly watching him during the day's celebrations. She had been quite envious of the female guests placed either side of Jack at the dinner table. She thought him gorgeous and something also told her he might be persuaded to entertain her on occasion, without her husband's knowledge, if she was careful in her approach. *But, how could she ask him?* Do you fancy a shag sweetie? Was not a phrase that would ever have entered her head or one she would verbally utter, although it might as well have been? Handsome though Jack was she could not explain exactly why she had to have him. She just did. *How would she meet up with him without her husband's knowledge? How would she introduce herself? That older woman must know him; I saw her smile saucily up at him earlier.*

Jealousy offloaded a bag of spiteful thoughts into her mind. *Surely he would like to spend some time with me; I'm much younger than that older woman. Okay she was sort of married but her spouse had become boring of late so she deserved some attention!*

Had Julie read the younger woman's thoughts she would have supplied a tart retort, confident in the knowledge that she herself was single at least.

It was no good. She could not take her eyes off Jack. He was gorgeous and she just had to have him! Desperation and mild jealousy delivered her a quick, not too well thought out, but cheap, plan. She would follow him to the toilet and think of something to say when she caught his attention outside the function room. Simple!

*

Jack was very much enjoying himself. The wedding was pleasurable; the quality of the catering was superb, as usual. The Bride's family had been very generous. Jack, still inwardly grinning at his amusing and amazing, secret act with Julie under the table, continued to enjoy a sensation of quiet mirth probably due to the peculiar fact that he now found himself part of an assemblage that included four women, all of whom he had slept with.

Three of the women, Julie, the BMW and Lily (who had terminated their affair some months previously, due to her constant worry her husband might find out) were gaily conversing with Jack and Valerie, Valerie being the fourth. The BMW and Lily were attended by their husbands. The group were engaged in pleasant, fairly normal discussion albeit for Lily and Julie respectively directing shy glances toward Jack when they considered their airwaves, full of sexual understanding, to be clear from detection.

Jack offered no indication of comprehension on his part, slightly distracted due to the annoying actuality of the BMW abnormally escorted to the event by her supercilious, hedge funder, husband, 'I like to keep my finger on the pulse' he boasted in reply to Valerie's polite enquiry of,

'How do you find the financial markets at the moment Jason?'

Jack kept his opinion in his head, *you've no idea how to use your fingers to increase your wife's pulse, twat.*

Boredom began to creep around the vicinity, Jack searched for an excuse to abscond. Moving his eyes to glance briefly at the BMW standing, attentive and elegant, no indication of the passion she could produce, in a fuchsia pink Chanel coatdress and matching wide brimmed hat, setting off her brunette hair and deep blue eyes, beside what Jack felt mimicked a letter day Napoleon, he excused himself from the conversation and made his escape. What a joke the man was! Jack stifled a loud laugh by coughing.

'Are you okay darling?' enquired Valerie.

'Fine dear, tickle in the throat; I'll just go get some water.'

Another distraction arrived for Jack in the form of a humorous thought, *If the pompous little prat was Napoleon, was his wife Josephine? 'Not tonight Josephine!'* Jack roared inwardly, he could easily imagine him say it. Still coughing from his delightful inward joke he set off for the rest room.

Julie, revelling in a sense of elation, felt secretly superior to the other members within the little circle due to her earlier surprise 'under the table' treat, plus she had no husband to entertain as a result of her being a widow and a wealthy one at that. Still, she didn't want to cause a fuss with Valerie. She pondered whether Jack might be persuaded to leave Valerie and come and live with her. The thought of living with him was exciting. She so enjoyed cooking breakfast for him when he stayed with her, 'Would you like some breakfast Jack?' she would call, as he prepared to shower.

'Only if it's no trouble sexy' he would reply.

'Oh it's no trouble Jack. No trouble at all.'

Every time he prepared to leave she became conscious how lonely her life was without a man. The two or three days he could offer intermittently were barely enough. However, Julie was unaware of the proposition the BMW had already put to Jack, equally she would have been quite perplexed to know that it had been considered with serious thought, if not success, when submitted for Jack's consideration.

Jack, relieved to dodge out, made his way to the plush men's toilet eager to escape the constant female attention, asinine characters from the last century and find a place to enjoy a quality cigar. The hotel oozed sumptuous furnishings throughout its nooks and crannies, the toilets being no exception. Red and gold embossed paper gave an aura of wealth and relaxation.

Further along the corridor he spotted a friend, Jerry, now making his way back from the rest rooms toward Jack, his personal mission having already been accomplished. Jack, raising his hand, smiled at him in recognition only to allow his thoughts to immediately wander away in admiration of the excellent effort made by the interior designer who happened to be a friend of his. He wondered whether she actually got stuck in with a brush and a bucket of wallpaper paste or employed others to do so. He grinned inwardly and made a mental note to tease her by asking that very question when he next saw her. She was a comely wench and Jack's thoughts wandered franticly from a vision of her splattered with wallpaper paste while wearing lose white decorators overalls. She was wearing nothing underneath them. These slightly different but exciting thoughts of his friend's success with the wallpaper and paste were sharply interrupted by a short, spoken sentence emitted tartly and in a slightly bored fashion.

With his arrival at the lavish latrines imminent, Jack, surprised to see Jerry, was about to ask how he could have missed him as part of the wedding guests or was he in the hotel on business?, when Jerry, now drawn level with Jack, instead of performing the usual greeting, looked straight past Jack and stated (in bored fashion) to persons unknown behind, 'For goodness sake Tilly, there's no need to follow the man! If you want Jack to shag you just give him your phone number!'

Astounded by his friend's abstract greeting, simply lost for words, Jack's prepared salutation of "Hi Jerry, how nice to see you" momentarily put on hold, he immediately spun round, keen to discover to whom Jerry had directed his blunt address. Incredulous! Only a couple of paces behind him stood a petit blonde woman now wearing, apart from a very fetching pastel blue two piece, a very red contrasting flush across the 'caught in the act' surprised look on her pretty face.

Jerry had known Jack for quite some years, originally through their attendance at meetings to discuss building works and legislation in particular to the island. They had become friends after discovering they both had one or two interests and a similar outlook on life in common. Jerry was also well aware that Jack provided special services, such as discrete shagging, to one or two of the local inhabitants. A very good friend, he had covered for Jack on a quite few occasions in the past when Valerie had rung from England, or abroad, to speak to Jack, providing an excuse for him if he was unavailable due to being engaged in sexual activity with one of his harem.

'Sorry Valerie, I gave Jack your message yesterday but he's been tied up with planning complications and there's no telephone line on site.'

Grinning, Jerry thought he had never before come across a woman named 'Planning Complications', and the thought of being tied up with her brought forth images of playful bondage. Jerry mischievously referred to Jack's collection of female fans as "Dollybirds".

'Yet another dollybird enquiring after you Jack', he would say, sounding almost sad for him.

An easy going type of guy, Jerry thought the female interest Jack constantly received very amusing indeed; he was by no means jealous or pious. Jerry would, no way, give up any of his time for the husbands affected. He knew most of them to be self centred and pompous. *Serve them right!* He thought.

He knew exactly what Tilly was after; he had taken note of the determination and lust written all over her face as she had followed in Jack's wake. He guessed her intention immediately. Perplexed he often wondered *why these women were so brazen. Had they met up with other men on the quiet? He could think of no man on the island who might be prepared for such antics or was it something about Jack that turned them on. Did Jack pay them?* He laughed at that thought, concluding the inquisition for lack of logic.

Meanwhile, Jack turned to face Tilly. Wearing the broadest of grins on his face he said 'Hello Tilly, Nice to meet you', and because mobile phones were unheard of then, followed by 'Do you have a pen and paper?'

Although the most brazen act by an admirer to date, Jack thought nothing of the fact that Tilly had followed him to an actual gent's toilet with a specific purpose in mind; to obtain his phone number and possibly arrange a clandestine meeting between them both. He had become blasé to women literally throwing themselves at him. Their problem, his personal theory suggested, was money. Most of his harem was married to wealthy men purely for their money and/or social status. Jack considered this practice was nearly always accompanied by an enormous price tag i.e. boredom and unhappiness. The majority of the women Jack entertained wanted love because they did not love their husbands. Not one was ill treated either; they all had the option to leave but could not abandon the money and / or status. They simply felt incomplete if their rich fruit cake was not spread liberally with icing on the top. Enter Jack with his multiple nozzles icing machine. Do you want a smooth or rough finish darling? Shall I pipe my sweet covering up your sides or decorate all over your top? Fancy a pattern? Tilly was just another cake.

In fact, so "in tune" to a woman's needs had Jack become, due to his extensive experience, he could identify a very bored and neglected woman in seconds. Only a few weeks previously he had met and enjoyed a cosy afternoon with a very nice but neglected housewife. Jack often found an attractive, but literally forgotten, woman in the form of a "mother-in-law". Have you ever really studied a family unit out for lunch? Most families converse gaily over their dinner, happy to spend time together engaging in lively tales relating to their present and future lives; but there is always one family where the mother or mum-in-law is taken for granted and Jack could spot her easy.

While visiting the island on an actual business trip, Jack found himself deep in discussion, having partaken of a convivial evening drink with Jerry, in a quiet restaurant bar. Bemused by the suggested regulations required for a possible building project, hoping for some form of enlightenment to appear via a possible vision into their drinking vessels they did not notice a family party enter the restaurant. The family consisted of; a young husband (the son in law) and wife (the daughter), the daughter's father (looking bored and tidy but unfashionably dressed, flicking his keys in his pocket) and mother (looking stunning for her age and sexy). The daughter was smartly dressed but appeared slightly tired, probably due to the demands of first motherhood, a new grandchild being the main purpose of the celebratory dinner.

The husband, affable enough, paid hardly any attention to his good looking wife, idly standing back from the bar with an "I'm bored but at least ill get fed" look on his face, while she bought the drinks for the whole party before retiring to their allotted table; Jack however, did notice her. His well serviced radar set focus the minute the group approached the bar, correctly identifying a young couple spending a few hours away from their new baby for an evening with the new Mum's parents.

Jerry and Jack had no other engagements planned for that evening and so, had settled by the bar to imbibe one or two glasses of wine, thereby sustaining their discussion of erstwhile male topics. They both knew Mike, the owner of the restaurant and often stopped by simply for the odd glass of wine appreciation Jack enquired, 'Mike is this one your 'house' red? It's so smooth, beautiful! Can you spare a case?'

Like I said, Jack's beer swilling days had long gone. Without intention, Mr Wine had expanded our northern boy's liquid palette from supermarket 'tinnys' and pints of Tetley to elegant bottles of quality wines and champagnes. Only recently Jack had savoured a few glasses of Dom Pérignon '60. James Bond apparently preferred the '62 in the film, The Man with the Golden Gun. I recon he ceded the '60 vintage to, Jack with the Sexy Bum.

During the course of the evening the elegant mother rose from the dinner table and walked toward the bar in order to obtain more drinks. Jerry, on his return from the men's toilet had stopped and was in conversation with another of his friends who had just entered the restaurant.

Jack bade the woman 'Good evening' as she stood patiently in her attempt to engage the barman's attention. She smiled as she spoke the same words in reply.

'Have you enjoyed your meal? Where is your waiter? He should really take your drinks order' enquired Jack.

She replied that 'Yes, indeed' she had enjoyed the meal but 'I don't seem to be able to attract the waiter's attention for the extra drinks!'

She was, however, very much enjoying the attention of such a handsome man. She thought she would attempt just a few more seconds of conversation before he ended his polite discourse only to be pleasantly surprised that he should appear to want to continue to speak to her for a bit longer. What a refreshing change! Her husband spent most of his time playing golf at Royal Jersey these days. It had been hard work to make him join in the conversation that evening with her daughter and son-in-law. Unless golf was involved he would not make much of an effort. She, on the other hand, had visited the hairdresser for the occasion and chosen her clothes and perfume in order to look her best for her family. Occasionally she wondered why she had married him. *Ah, well, too late now. He was not so bad; he had just become lazy with age. If only he would appreciate the effort she made. Nothing appeared to engage his attention, not even sex. Would she remember how to do it? They had not made love together for some months now.* She sometimes wondered why she bothered. *Well at least that handsome man at the bar had complimented her. Now, if only she could spend a night with him!*

During their brief conversation Jack explained that he often paid a visit to that particular restaurant and, you never know, might bump into her again.

'By the way, I'm a builder; could I give you my card? If you should ever need any building work done I'd be happy to supply you with a quote.'

By the time the barman had returned, with profuse apology, to collate her drinks order she had taken possession of Jack's telephone number. She didn't have to use it, she could throw it away. But it would be helpful to keep, he was a builder but then that sexy look he gave, that suggested something more or was it her imagination? She felt excited, rather like a schoolgirl. She also felt childish and silly. However, in the days that followed that moment, she developed an accompanying shine to the smile more often present on her face. With a feeling of guilt she would admonish herself, *No, it was ridiculous she felt the whole episode was unreal.*

She studied his phone number printed on the card in strong, bold text, producing the item after furtively glancing around her kitchen deep in the expectation that a gremlin spy might leap out of the cupboard and alert her husband to her possible betrayal. She looked at the text again, JACK, followed by his number. It was real all right. Her thoughts turned to her family, inwardly pleased for her daughter and her movement into motherhood. But where did this leave the new grandmother. *I'm a Grandmother!* She had begun to feel old in years lately. *Bet he would not have provided his phone number so easily if he had realised she was a grandmother!* She sighed at the thought of what she felt was her stupidity and placed his card back under her make-up bag in the bedroom however, she could not bring herself to throw it out. She could always telephone on the pretence of some building work, her thoughts explored the reasons she might offer, *and it would not hurt to ask for a quote for something. It would be nice to just see him again.*

One day later that week, her husband returned home from work in what could only be described as a foul mood. She realised that this behaviour had been the norm for quite some time now. Running his business was not easy she understood well, but, *why did he speak to her like it? Why did she let him?* 'What have we got for dinner?' he nonchalantly asked, completely ignoring her tidy smart appearance including hair, nails and perfume.

She made no attempt at an answer; she knew he would not hear it; his daily return to home routine took control of his awareness reducing his attention span. She spoke to herself quietly in jest, 'How are you today my beautiful wife? Had a pleasant day? I've missed you today.'

A nervous smile brightened her face as she made her way automatically into the kitchen to collect and return with a plate of hot food containing the answer to his routine question but her smile continued its journey transforming into a jet of excitement searing through her body at the memory of Jack's complimentary words.

The next day as soon as her husband had departed for work, gathering all the courage she could muster, hands shaking, she tentatively lifted the telephone, and dialled the number on the card.

Chapter 32

Jack, alone with his thoughts, walked lazily along the five miles of beach at St. Ouen's Bay. Unwittingly, he wandered to the exact spot where he had enjoyed sex in the sand, twenty or so years ago, during his first 'lads' holiday to Jersey. He smiled at the memories although the actual conversation spoken at the time lacked clarity in recall due to the inexorable passing of time. Sitting where he considered the impulsive action to have taken place, Jack spent a few moments in reflection; his mind arranging short video re runs of one or two related events.

One of his mates, who had been part of that holiday, had since passed away, a victim of cancer, *poor bugger,* Jack thought. *His widow was gutted*, he remembered, *they had got married after that holiday, life could be a bitch.* But what of his own life, *in which direction was he travelling? Same direction as The Commitments, 'Destination Anywhere'* he laughed at the thought, humming a few bars as he scanned the horizon. He had no worries, surely? He had just made love to yet another new catch, a very attractive but neglected housewife to whom he had given his business card while in the wine bar with Jerry one evening.

She had telephoned on the pretext of some building work but ostensibly in need of his additional 'special services.' Pleased at the thought of making another lonely woman happy, if only for a few hours, he smiled at the thought of her shy, inexperienced touch; Melanie had shaken when he first put his arms around her. Yes, her name was Melanie, surprised he'd actually remembered her name he wondered if she might phone him again.

'I don't normally do this sort of thing Jack. My life has been so meaningless of late. I hope you don't get the wrong impression of me?'

'Of course not, you are fabulous! I'm grateful you allow me to enjoy your beautiful body'

'Is it beautiful? You're just saying that!'

'No, I'm not, how could you turn me on like you have if you were unattractive?' Melanie felt he certainly had a point there. Unable to think of a reply her confidence grew, if only by a minute amount, allowing her to relax slightly. Cuddling into his body she felt his penis, hard against her stomach. Instinct suggested she put her hand down and got hold of it somehow. With a bit of encouragement she, with enthusiasm, managed to perform a couple of acts she had thought long forgotten, Jack's groans of pleasure building her confidence with each passing second.

Years of being a wife and mother could rob a woman of her independence. Marriage required effort on both sides but surely not to the destruction of one or both components? Life was peculiar really.

*

Jack realised his gaze had been fixed toward the distant French coast but he couldn't linger; Tilly was booked in that evening. Her husband was in London for a few days and she had taken the opportunity to indulge herself. Jack thought her spoilt and self-centred but who was he to judge when she wanted him for sex? The taxi was already on order to deliver him to her home later, a bit like 'meals on wheels' really. Jack suddenly realised he had forgotten where he was supposed to be working that week. *Shit! Am I in Jersey for business or pleasure? Sort yourself out mate! Phew! It's okay. I'm here on business but fitting in pleasure. Christ! It's all becoming rather complicated.* Now where had he thought that before?

During the short taxi journey to Tilly's home Jack deliberated whether he should invite her to the 'singles' cruise that Jerry arranged, on occasion, for a select group of his closest friends. Jack's name was always the first to be written on the list and due to the fact he was not actually married to Valerie, this meant he was almost certainly single... the phrase 'in a relationship' would become popular in later years.

Jerry, very single himself and a great believer in life being safer that way, thought it great sport to arrange the occasional, luxury boat trip to celebrate the single status. Many of his friends were divorced, in fact the island had quite a high rate, the responsibility of which should not be laid at Jack's door, I might add.

Jerry had a very wealthy acquaintance, Adrian, who just happened to own an extremely large yacht that was sufficiently equipped to enable him to throw the most sumptuous water borne party. The poor chap had been subject, in recent months, to a very expensive divorce from a complete bitch who had taken the cash and headed back to New York; Jerry wanted to improve his friend's spirit by introducing him to a few of his unmarried cronies, including one or two loose women he might fancy or vice versa.

As mentioned previously, any Jersey social guest list was considered incomplete without Jack. Jerry knew he could be relied upon to select a suitable partner for the occasion from his own personal harem. Inwardly he thought it might be good fun to guess which consort he would bring, even better, he wondered if Jack may possess a spare dollybird, deemed suitable, that he might be persuaded to bring along for Adrian.

When Jerry had suggested the cruise to Adrian he had immediately been delighted with the idea and within only a couple of weeks, preparations for the trip were absolute and invitations had been greedily accepted by the entire guest list. A spectacular voyage had been set, initially setting sail from St. Helier Marina, making a stop for lunch in the bay of La Coupe in the St Martin area, eventually anchoring alongside the manmade jetty protruding from the small beach that was part of Adrian's stunning cliff top home situated a little further along the north east coast.

Jack was peeved he could not invite the BMW and Julie was far too discrete even though qualifying for the trip through being a widow. Although not his first choice, Jack eventually decided to invite Tilly; detail transpired (from Jerry's island information grapevine) that she was not actually married to her partner. This small fact confirmed Tilly's eligibility according to the unofficial requirements for invitation to the riparian event. Under absolute discretion, invitees were guaranteed not to mention the detail of the other participants' particulars. Tilly was delighted the trip would coincide with one of her indulgent partner's many business trips. And so, the excited pair arrived in St Helier harbour early one sunny morning, ready to set sail with gusto.

Throughout the day champagne and nibbles flowed, spirits soared and Jack was able to indulge in a little gentle nibbling with Tilly, 'Have some caviar Darling' 'Why thank you Jack, she said, simpering, and thank you for inviting me'

'It is my pleasure' he replied with a grin.

Champagne is a sexy drink and, accompanied by all the nibbles and nibbling, it was not long before Jack and Tilly were desperate to take some time out together. After the superb culinary luncheon had been devoured the yacht, possibly powered simply by the high spirits flowing throughout the vessel, arrived at Adrian's beachside jetty. The trip was a resounding success with the participants now ready to party well into the evening.

'Damn good idea of yours Jerry and thank you, I haven't had so much dashed fun in years!'

'Glad to be of service Adrian, however your generosity with this beautiful craft has made the whole event possible'

'Think nothing of it, the day has been a brilliant boost to my spirit. Can you arrange another similar party sometime Jerry? I know you can be relied on for absolute discretion, I've already secured a dinner date with that ravishing female smiling at me from over there'

Jerry, laughing, looked across to where a female friend of his stood, engaged in lively chatter with another female. 'Ah, Linda, she's a solicitor you know, lovely woman, devoted to her job and too busy to find a man. No problem, we can make it a regular event but not too often mind, we don't want everyone to become bored'

Adrian suddenly threw back his head in laughter as a thought occurred, 'Jerry! We could assign these little nautical trips a name. You know. Something along the lines of "The Love Boat" perhaps'

'Err, what a fun idea. I'll leave you to come up with a suitable title for amusement Adrian'

Jerry, making a quick scan of the adjacent guests, had noticed one or two now presenting obvious amorous intent. Champagne glass sparkling in hand, he continued his survey to concentrate on the surrounding scenery, gazing as if in a trance whilst performing a study of the beautiful cliffs, now providing a stunning background for the cruiser, glowing bright with light as they bathed in the remainder of the afternoon sunshine.

Well relaxed, full of contentment, Jerry was delighted Adrian was full of enthusiasm, if not sensible suggestions, in his task to identify a fun, official name to promote their unusual dating agency, borne literally via a jolly boating outing. Evidently, their convivial trip had also been blessed by the excellent weather provided.

Jerry's thoughts were abruptly interrupted mid gaze, he grinned within at the cause. Carefully ascending the cliff path toward Adrian's elegant pad, Jerry had spotted Jack and Tilly. Raising his glass to his friend in jest he muttered under his breath, *Jack, you are a legend in your own lifetime!*

Tilly, notwithstanding the bold nature portrayed by stalking her quarry at a wedding (as Jack made his way to the toilet) was in present company a little nervous due to the obvious pairing of some of the guests. Accompanied by such a handsome consort produced, deep within her body, an ardent desire to live and let go with gay abandon, 'I want to fuck you Jack, right now!'

'Below deck is the only, and not ideal, choice at the moment and definitely in bad taste my darling but if you can contain your enthusiasm till we reach Adrian's jetty, I'll give you all I've got. In the meantime, let me get you another glass of champagne, sexy lady!'

His words did nothing to contain her ardour, spoken in such a deep sexy voice; they only served to fuel her zealous desire to get laid. In a short space of time however, her wish was granted.

By mid-afternoon everyone had let their hair down and was having a ball; Jack took the opportunity and signed for her to leave the boat with him. One or two had already taken to the water shouting wildly, like teenagers let loose in Newquay, as they dived or jumped off the jetty. At least half the yacht's guests had disembarked and were now enjoying the beach, sat engaged in lively chatter or exploring the delightful surrounding area. Tilly meanwhile was in receipt of another three course menu, her gasps of rapture carried away to the heavens by the whispering cliff top breeze.

Chapter 33

Jack wondered if it might be more convenient to move to Jersey, that very morning he had flown in yet again, this time neither for business nor pleasure. Jerry had already been alerted to his impending arrival earlier that week.

'I'm accompanying Valerie on one of her short holiday breaks.'

'I'm sure you'll have fun! I'll try to rescue you with a phone call after a couple of days, in the meantime try not to wander Jack, there's something I need to talk to you about. Oh and by the way, Adrian was delighted with his Singles Sailing Shack up'

'What! Jerry what a way to refer to your elegant booze cruise mate'

'It's Adrian's description for what he hopes will be a regular, invitation only event and don't give me that booze cruise rubbish Jack, Adrian's picked a very apt nickname, I spotted you and Tilly, the first couple half way up the cliff in pursuit of a bedroom!'

'We didn't make it to the bedroom mate; she had my gear off the minute we reached the garden.'

'Lord above! Say no more. I won't broadcast your arrival on the island, nor to Tilly either or she'll pester me to let on where you are staying.'

'Christ mate thanks, what is up with these women? And Adrian, what can he be thinking of, Singles shack up?'

'It's boredom my friend, boredom and too much money. Adrian's other effort, by the way, was Amore Ahoy!'

Jack burst out laughing; 'Now that has a ring to it! Can you find some time for a drink in the Wine Bar this Friday? Valerie has a girlie party arranged for the evening'

'You're on, and like I said, I need to talk to you, in the meantime, I'll save ya Olive!'

*

Jack, walking alone on the Saturday morning, totally lost in thought, noticed nothing of the beautiful Jersey countryside, deep in deliberation, trying to make some sense of his life style of late while seriously contemplating the two items of news he had received the previous Friday evening, each from a different source.

Jack, as planned, had met up with Jerry to enjoy a couple of glasses of wine over some genial conversation at one of their favourite venues. Settling back into the leather chesterfield he gently rolled the very fine red wine around inside its glass allowing the aroma to build, taking an initial appreciative sip Jerry immediately set to business.

'Jack, word of your door to door shagging service has reached some parts of the island; one or two recipients of this information have been rather displeased.'

'Really, and who might they be Jerry?'

With humour, Jerry carried on to gaily describe one specific situation where the information had possibly originated from.

'Apparently Jack, two of your harem found out they did not have exclusive rights to you and were none too pleased. Their anger was not with you but with each other! Simon, do you remember my friend Simon? He said it was hilarious! They both nearly flew into a tantrum while partaking of their ladies light luncheon in that new expensive restaurant. I think Simon only overheard a little but it was definitely you they nearly threw handbags over. He had difficulty controlling his laughter at the table Jack; he said both women finished their meal with chilly restraint, trying to keep their cool.'

Jack's face broke into a quiet smile but his thoughts foresaw potential trouble.

Jerry grinned widely as he related his friend's description of the astonished then angry look on the women's faces when they realised the man they were secretly boasting about was one and the same ...Jack.

'Did he say which women, did he know them both?'

'Tilly and Julie'

Bugger, thought Jack, the last thing he wanted was a favourite upset; he was very fond of Julie.

'Jack, you have had a good run I think? But you want to be careful, it might be time to call it a day', Jerry wisely suggested.

Jack agreed, 'Marry or date them they are a constant problem mate, you're right, time to call it a day. I've often wondered how Valerie has never found out considering how close I've flown to the sun at times. She made it easy really, her thoughts have always been on what she could plan to occupy herself with next, and I'm the last thing she considers. Time I sorted it all out perhaps'

'Jack, there is one other thing.'

Jerry, openly irritated by its content, went on to describe a conversation with a taxi driver who had driven him to a meeting a few weeks ago.

'I was dumbstruck Jack! I'd only been in the cab a few minutes, he just asked me straight in conversation, "Is that friend of yours who is popular with the women coming over again soon?" I asked him carefully to whom he was referring and in what way he might describe you as popular? The driver gaily poured forth, "That builder, who does a lot of work over here, is he not a friend of yours? He must be some guy! Early one morning last month I drove him from one woman's home to another! It appeared he'd spent the night with one then went on to the other the next morning. I know both women as the island is not very big, you don't need me to tell you that! I've driven the women and their husbands in my taxi on several occasions in the past. The husbands go away on business often. I noticed that your friend seems to visit when the husbands are away!" the cheeky bugger completed this information with a big grin and a wink!' said Jerry.

Yes, Jack thought, in the past he had flown very close to the sun indeed. Icarus and Daedalus were aware they should have given the sun a wide berth but Jack shook his head at the thought of the two Greek men and grinned. He gave not a care he might fly too close to trouble and destroy his wings. As far as he was concerned he would just fall into the sea......then swim like fuck.

Jack's thoughts turned to the BMW. She still wanted him to move into an apartment where they could be together when her husband was away in America. She had already offered him a luxury apartment on the French coast, everything he could want when he wanted. *Why did he not say, yes?* Jack was of the opinion that he would practically be 'owned.' *He would not be free.* The thought annoyed him. *He had to be free. Free to do what though? The prospect of the rest of his life with Valerie was downright boring. Why the hell did she have to dislike sex? She was a good looking woman.* He needed to feel free. *Shit! I'm not free now. I'm already owned more or less.*

Jack dismissed these frustrating thoughts from his head deciding to waste no more time deliberating over them. The harem had been fun while it lasted. He might still be able to keep one or two happy on the quiet. *I must contact Julie and apologise.*

He had received the first news bulletin from Jerry with an air of humour and flippancy but the second had a far more diverse effect.

Jack's daughter had telephoned out of the blue, just before he left the hotel for his rendezvous with Jerry, excited to tell her father she was getting married.

'Oh, sweetheart, I'm so pleased for you! He better look after you or I shall have to sort him out!'

Contact with his children had been kept lively if sparse, over the years.

'To think I once used builder's string to keep control of you, and your brother's, pushchairs. Where have the years gone?'

His little girl was about to start off on her own journey into the unpredictable world of marriage. He hoped she had found someone with more dedication to duty than he had managed to muster.

As she gaily spoke of her plans for her special day Jack's thoughts were only for her happiness, he was already planning what he should wear for the occasion. *I must look good as I walk my only daughter down the aisle. I must not let her down. How will I feel as I watch her marry the man of her dreams? He better be good! Oh, I hope she has a happy future?*

Unfortunately for Jack, Geanie had chosen this moment in time to wreak her long awaited revenge, taking no heed for those caught in the crossfire.

Unwittingly high-jacked into becoming the vehicle with which Geanie would deliver her triumphant final shot, Jack's initial sensation of joy was violently swept away only to be replaced by desolation within seconds as his daughter, naïve of her mother's retribution, tentatively spilled out the spite filled message, the result of time-honoured, festering anger; born from Jack's decision to refuse to marry her mother.

'I'm so sorry Dad, this is awful, I feel awful but I don't know how else to put this Dad, but….but, would you mind NOT walking me down the aisle? It's a bit awkward for me but Mum wants my stepdad to do it. She said you might not be able to come to the wedding anyway as you are always busy abroad with work.'

Jack recovered well from the powerful imaginary punch, which had momentarily floored him, to reply graciously that 'I will definitely be there on the day my darling and yes, it might be better if your stepdad gave you away just in case. As long as you are happy, and have a wonderful day, then I'm happy too.'

'Oh, Thanks Dad'

Jack felt sick. His stomach gave the impression it had twisted; his mind produced a vision of Geanie stabbing him in his gut, turning the knife as she did so, with a spiteful smile on her face throughout. Never before in his life had he felt so truly gutted. *Geanie, the spiteful bitch, could not stop him going to the wedding at least,* Jack made a note of the date. He would be there even if he had to stand at the back. Something told him he would no way be offered a seat anywhere near the front of the church and the rest of Geanie's family, *did the bastards realise they were not only directing their hate toward him but also toward an innocent young woman who, as a result of their bigotry, would lose her right to walk down the aisle on the arm of her father?* Jack raised his hand to his eyes to deal with a sudden irritation, then realised the irritant was tears.

Chapter 34

Nonchalantly, Jack made his way back to the hotel and the evening's entertainment; dinner with Valerie and some island friends. Ah well, there would be wine, brandy and cigars, delightful little comforts.

Arriving at the hotel, earlier than expected, he walked straight into the bar and ordered a large Brandy in the hope of repressing his sorrow and shock. As he sat beside the bar, surveying the opulent furnishings, his gaze rested upon a tidy looking woman of similar age, her curly brown hair bouncing as she giggled whilst in conversation with friends; enjoying an entertaining discussion, their tinkling laughter held elements of gaiety and happiness. Frustrated by his recent, upsetting memory; Jack thought he knew the woman from somewhere but could not place where exactly, *Bugger! I've shagged so many I can't remember if I've had the pleasure in a distant era or know her from elsewhere.*

As if staged, the woman turned her head with caution to look directly at Jack, smiling as she did so; within a split second her facial expression altered from pleasant acknowledgement to puzzlement. Her friends continued with their group conversation, unaware of their companion's appearance of confusion. Jack held a rye gaze, returning her look of puzzlement; *she's staring at me like she knows me, bugger if I can place her.* He started to feel it might be 'game on' then remembered Jerry's warning.

But his brain continued to strain hard with determination trying to place the face into a memory slot which he knew had been purposely provided specifically for her. *Oh no! It could not be, surely!* Recognition eased into and across Jack's memory. His grin broadened as he finally found the time slot to match the face, now flowing back from somewhere nigh on twenty years ago.

'Is it really you?' she said, as she rose from her chair to approach him, curls bouncing with her every move. Laughing with disbelief, her memory had identified Jack after performing its own mental search through the years of events that had passed during her life to date, she started to blush slightly. Sat at the bar was the original handsome man she had once made love with in the sand, on five mile beach, all those years ago!

Now, laughing together in unison, they both asked how the other was.

'I thought I recognised you but…Christ it was so long ago! How are you?

Are you well?' said Jack.

They could not remember each other's names, forgotten with the passing of time but remembered the sand.

'I remember shaking sand from my knickers and yours!' she said quietly but with a giggle. Her lovely hair bounced as she spoke and her bright blue eyes shone with animation. Of petit stature and looking extremely fit for her age, Jack wondered how he had let this one slip away. Everything about her said 'alive and fun.' Keen to ask each other a barrage of questions, amazed to meet up after such a long time, they both enquired the following:

> Were they married?
> Had they family?
> What work had / did they do?
> Were they visiting the island for a holiday?

There was so much to talk about but their initial questions had established one thing they both had in common, good health.

'Jack, how fantastic, it's so weird we should meet again, well, not in the same place, on the beach, but on holiday and after all this time!'

They spent nearly an hour filling in time gaps, each informing the other of the highlights of their life. Jack however, omitted any detail of his recent nocturnal island activities and also avoided the question 'How is your Mother?' because if he remembered correctly, he had shagged her mother as well; although, in all fairness, not intentionally.

Sarah, her name, she had reminded him in conversation, was Sarah and *she was lovely*. After chatting for a short while Jack remembered the reason he had not pursued the match on his return to England; *yes, he had definitely slept with her mother (was she the one he pleasured while his mate snored?) while on the same holiday*. Which had quashed any intention, Jack may have nursed at the time, to pursue further contact with Sarah once the holiday had finished. *I might have made a mistake there. Ah well, it was long ago.*

They said their goodbyes with smiles, wishing each other well, just as they had all that time ago.

As he made his way up to his room Jack became pensive about his future. It also occurred to him that twenty years ago he would not have given a second thought to his future.

*

Back home in Torbay, their short sojourn over, Jack continued with his building work. His latest project meant he would spend a few months in London, although he would be able to travel home for the weekends. On the Sunday morning he was packed and ready to catch the train. Accommodation was easy; Valerie owned a flat in London where he could stay during the weekdays for the duration of the project.

Saying 'Bye Darling', he automatically kissed Valerie on the cheek, he appeared to have forgotten where her mouth was situated, and not that it was in the habit of responding when he attempted to link his mouth with hers anyway. She responded with the warmth of a cardboard cut-out, had you attempted to make loving advances toward a piece.

'Oh, Jack, don't forget the interior decorators might still be there. Don't start an argument with them if they're not finished'

'Yes darling, I mean, no darling'

'And try not to spill anything anywhere'

'No darling'

With the Taxi already waiting outside, he left his home and literally fell inside, muttering under his breath, 'chance would be a fine thing', glad to escape.

As the train sped east through the rain toward London, Jack thought of the many women he had known in the Midlands, taking no notice as the route passed through the beautiful Vale of the White Horse (at that moment being drenched by the inclement weather), his mind was elsewhere dissecting his two failed marriages. Reminiscing, he wondered why he had found it so very difficult to stop shagging other women while he was married, even though he had enjoyed a sex life with both his wives, well, it had started good with Linda but fizzled out due to life reigning havoc with her body. Shame really, life could be so unfair at times. Sex outside of both marriages had been prepared and laid on a plate for him virtually every week, deeming it rather tricky to engage his will power. This time he had good reason to wander because there was no sex available at home at all.

Unfortunately/fortunately, when performing an analysis of this particular mating he knew he wasn't actually married so there was no chance of arranging an annulment through non consummation of marriage, therefore a parting of the ways was easy, or was it? Jack had a lot of his own money tied up in the home he had built for Valerie and himself. It would have to be sold in order for him to realise his cash. There was no difference in his present relationship to his previous marriages. *So, what was he going to do about it? Forget for now and look forward to meeting up with his work crew in one of the city's lively pubs.*

The rain, sweeping the south and east had stopped temporary, leaving the city's pavements glistening in the early evening sunshine. The atmosphere was electric in The Harp on that particular Sunday, a reminder for Jack of his younger days, spent in the local pub when a Foreman, back home in the Midlands. Jack was not the first person to arrive, most of the work gang were already in the bar, all in fine spirits, having already partaken the imbibing of a few pints, content to socialise while the work plan for the coming week was finalised. It appeared to Jack that the assembled crew were going to get along well. The building faction had distributed themselves at random around one end of the bar, where Jack was sitting with his Foreman, the rest of the group taking over a few of the tables close by.

Seated at a small table next to the jovial gathering were two attractive women, one of whom was accompanied by an appealing well behaved, spaniel type puppy dog, that had serenely curled up beside her feet. The sweet little creature had attracted a fair bit of fuss from two of the gang who were sat at the table immediately beside the women. One lad had bent forward on his chair to stroke and pet the puppy. Meaning no more than honest fun, the lad had already asked the attractive puppy owner a hapless, 'Can I stroke it?' immediately laughing an apology that he was not offering a double entendre. Entertainment was enjoyed on both tables as the women laughed in reply, 'You are sad!' shaking their heads as they did so, in appreciation and acknowledgement of his poor joke. A couple of the other men from the gang offered 'Ignore him love, he lives in the country'

'Will he return soon?'

The women could have reacted with anger but chose instead to make light of the situation, give the lad a fool's pardon and another shake of their heads.

From his elevated position, on a bar stool beside the actual bar, Jack had already noted the women, finding them both attractive; one had a particularly long pair of slim legs extending from beneath a very short skirt, which had drawn his attention with ease, simultaneously, he was also mystified as to the identity of the reason for the steady increase in stifled laughter emanating from three of the work crew sat at the table immediately in front of the two women. With a grin and small groan Jack thought *'simple things please simple minds'* rapidly apprehending the reason behind the girly style giggling.

And it came to pass that neither the puppy nor the 'stroke it' joke was in any way responsible for distracting group attention, a form of treasure was at fault. The booty was hidden, with not much effort, beneath the very tight short skirt. It transpired that the lad who had bent forward to make a fuss of the puppy, could at the same time, easily see its owner's red lacy underwear.

The little dog became popular all of a sudden with two other lads now taking a turn to pet puppy, keen for a flash of red fire. Both Jack and his Foreman exchanged a grin, shaking their heads in resignation of the fact that men can be childish. Jack began to wonder whether the director of Basic Instinct might have been sat in a pub one day only to suddenly witness a similar act enabling him to formulate an interesting opinion of the intrigue men can be capable of when faced with a short skirt and a quick flash of what lurks beneath.

He let his thoughts run on, imagining the Film Director suggesting to his leading lady over a coffee, *"ere Sharon I was havin' a drink in this pub in London last week and these guys were pretending to make a fuss of this puppy dog just so they could see right up its female owner's skirt. How do you fancy we film a scene for the movie along similar lines but with no dog and come to think of it, no knickers either?"*

Leaving that particular thought, Jack became aware of another; *Valerie would be joining him at the flat the following weekend*, relieving him on the first occasion, of the regular weekend train journey home as they had both been invited to a celebrity dinner party to be held at a private house in the city suburbs on the Saturday evening. Valerie had asked Jack to remember to pack one of his best dinner suits for the occasion because a prominent ex Member of Parliament would be present. Apparently he was a very affable chap. However, Jack had forgotten to pack his suit. There had been no real disaster looming as Valerie, in her wisdom, had telephoned to check Jack's memory and safe arrival, after his train journey, later that very Sunday afternoon. Slightly piqued, but glad to have averted a problem, she arranged to bring one of his suits with her when she drove up in her car. Jack thought it might be an entertaining evening, plus the usual little delights he enjoyed so much, fine wines, brandy and cigars, would probably be in abundance. Pity sex would not be so forthcoming. Ah well.

Chapter 35

The first week on site saw the raw crew mould together well. The project flew out of the starting gate like a greyhound, *long may it continue*, hoped Jack, you could never tell; 'expect the unexpected' his old Foreman had warned him, 'always be prepared and have a backup plan ready should anything go wrong, that way you won't lose much time cracking on again, mind you if you've studied the preliminaries well any project should flow.'

It was good to be alone in the weekday evenings with a project of this size, Jack had plenty of quiet time to plan ahead and monitor the work. *Shame there was no comely female to talk his day over with and satisfy his body's natural tendencies, especially first thing in the morning.* Notwithstanding the lack of male satisfaction on his rouse from slumber each morning; Jack's eating habits were very well tended indeed.

The preliminary and first weeks work had gone particularly well, all had been accomplished earlier than anticipated so Jack sent the crew home early on the Friday, always a morale booster when good work had been achieved.

Valerie had already arrived, bright and breezy, to greet Jack on his return to the flat shortly after lunch on the Friday afternoon.

'Hi darling, had a good day on site? Well, what do you think? Does the apartment not look wonderful? I was not too sure about the colour from the chart but I think it has a wonderful warm feel to it.'

Nothing like you then, Jack thought but said instead 'Glad you are pleased with the result and I have been careful with my drips'

'Oh Jack you are so facetious at times, I hope you will be on your best behaviour at the dinner tomorrow.'

'Thinking of food, what are we doing tonight?'

'Eating out of course, I don't want to cook tonight'

You never really do, do you, 'If you had said I would have brought some food and cooked something for us'

'Oh, no, we're in London Jack. Let's eat out'

'Shall we go out and have a drink first?'

'Good idea'

'I'd better shower and change then'

'Why don't you wear those nice trousers I bought for you?'

Out of sight, Jack grinned like a naughty schoolboy, 'I forgot to pack them'

'Don't worry I remembered, I thought you might forget, I checked before leaving home and brought them with me'

Fuck it!

Chapter 36

The black cab, containing both Jack and Valerie, arrived promptly, outside the entrance to the smart London home where the dinner party was due to commence. The guest list was impressive. Jack, always himself, was polite but keen to find someone sensible to talk to before dinner, he had hoped one or two of the guests might be known to him but he established soon after his arrival that he was out of luck. However, the dinner Host and Hostess were equally efficient, both possessing the required skills that would ensure their guests were at ease with one another.

'No dinner will be a success if there is tension in the air' the Host stated to Jack on introduction and in reply to his comment that the atmosphere was warm and welcoming. Put at his ease the minute he entered the elegant property, Jack began to mingle and engage in pleasant conversation with a few of the other guests before the actual dinner commenced.

The menu was superlative, full of culinary enchantment. To his delight, Jack found himself seated between two very slim attractive women, one of which was the Hostess herself; the guests had been arranged around the impressive antique table in a boy, girl, boy, girl fashion. Always admirable in the art of conversation, Jack demonstrated his skill and merit as a dinner table guest, engaging the Hostess in such a manner as to emphasise her lovely 'English Rose' features, however, his troubles began probably because of his unique and delightful approach, which was by no means his fault.

Tamara, quite the opposite of an English rose, try thinking dark hair, eastern, exotic, cheetah; who had been seated to Jack's right, placed her left hand on Jack's right thigh the instant they had sat at the table. At first he thought it was just a swift, friendly foible performed to express her own personal, warm nature in the same way you might touch a person on the arm or face, nevertheless her hand refused to leave Jack's leg, unless left hand cutlery skill was required. The minute any cutlery was deemed superfluous, Tamara returned her hand to its well muscled resting place, with an extra squeeze after each course. Jack did not have intimate knowledge of Tamara as he did of Julie on Jersey and was now concerned as to how he was going to escape from a situation where he had become to feel very uncomfortable indeed. Worried, he realised he had even begun to sweat slightly. *If she was squeezing after the entree what the fuck would she be doing during the dessert?*

After only a short space of time Jack's best behaviour had been expended, the last thing he needed was an unknown woman putting her hand on his leg and cocking it all up...

While frantically contemplating evasive action, he came up with the idea of going to the toilet as a temporary measure to avoid her unwelcome advances. *It might even deter whatever intention she might have on her mind. Did she want him to shag her in the broom cupboard or something? Or did she just like the feel of his leg?* He had no idea of the layout of the house so *where did she expect him to give her one?* These troubled thoughts played within his mind as he excused himself from the table, his mission to seek and locate the rest room, his interim safe house.

After freshening up, in the anticipation this simple action might deter his outlandish table neighbour, Jack returned, settling back into his seat only to receive double trouble. Not only did Tamara's left hand return, complete with a squeeze performed closer to his tackle than was just, his Hostess, seated on his left, suddenly placed her right hand on his left thigh... *Shit, Shit! What was up with them!* Jack could only assume it was the way he spoke; with a slight touch of 'brummie', was it that sexy and attractive? *Did film stars and singers enjoy this sort of harassment? No, they employed body guards. Was he not a body guard once? Surely he could stop them somehow?* With both thighs being touched up at the same time Jack was imminently in danger of becoming sexually aroused. And no way did he intend to round off the sumptuous dinner party, for both of his neighbouring diners, by providing each with the unique desert he had performed on Julie, under the tablecloth, at the Jersey wedding. *What the hell would the other guests think when both of the women, sat either side of him, collapsed off their chairs onto the floor? No way!*

Jack shuffled on his seat a bit trying to dislodge at least one hand but the women had both made their claim and were staying put, their intention absolute by squeezing slightly tighter. After what Jack gauged to be approximately twenty minutes, and now feeling very uncomfortable due to the sweat trickling between his shoulder blades, he rose from the table with an 'Excuse me for a moment please' to escape to the bathroom again.

On this occasion, in mild desperation, Jack hung around outside the rest room for a while trying to figure a way out of the awkward situation he reluctantly found himself in. *He had to return soon otherwise his frequent absences would surely be noticed.*

As he half-heartedly made his way back through the magnificent hallway, en-route to the dining room, he met his Host, now heading for the room Jack had just vacated. He liked and respected the man but was also delighted for the extra respite time, and so, Jack deliberately stopped to speak with him however, before any word could escape his lips his Host said, 'Jack, I've noticed the frequency of your trips to the bathroom.'

Jack wondered if he had observed his wife's wandering hand and was about to challenge him, laying the blame for her behaviour at his feet, or more appropriately, leg, so to speak.

'Is Tamara touching you up under the table Jack?' Jack immediately felt relief grinning as a reply in the affirmative.

'Sorry Jack she is renowned for it! She does it to all our male guests. Take no notice and don't worry as we'll be moving off for cigars in a short while.'

Jack laughed, happy for his short reprieve then exchanged a few more sentences with his Host before heading back to the fingering females. Jack so wanted to say to his Host, 'Okay that takes care of the bird on my right side caressing my right thigh but what the hell do I do about your wife's hand on my left!?

Before long Jack was able to escape his ordeal. And it was an ordeal as Jack would have loved to satisfy both pair of leg teasers with his type of special desert but realised these women were not like the Jersey clique or were they? So relieved was he to be set free from the gauche dinner table situation, in fact, so much so, once the dinner had concluded, Jack made a bee line straight to Valerie, deliberately conversing with her for a short while; on the other hand, no one was prepared for the unplanned entertainment that would round off the evening's events.

One or two of the assembled company were aware that Mr MP was conducting a clandestine affair with one of the guests' wives ('twas rumoured in one or two newspapers at the time) and by the behaviour that was about to unfold during the remainder of the evening there was no surprise the press already had wind of the situation. Whether Mr MP had had too much to drink or what, Jack could not say but his gut feeling was backing the 'or what' because all of a sudden, without warning, a fight broke out between Mr MP and his lover's husband within the expensively furnished drawing room, amongst the after dinner mints.

Jack, his mouth wide open, stared in disbelief. He looked to Valerie for confirmation that his eyes were indeed reporting the slightly violent events, unfolding straight in front of them, correctly. Somehow, a simple discussion between Mr MP, his lover and her husband had turned into a shouting competition but before a good slanging match could ensue, Mr MP had lashed out, punching his lovers' husband in the face. Jack, his mouth still open, started laughing at the mill developing in front of him, mainly for two reasons:

1. His mind flashed back to a local pub in the Midlands, he was around twenty three years old. Many a fight had broken out during a Friday or Saturday evening, but the blokes were never wearing suits.
2. He had never heard the words 'you supercilious little 'bostard' collectively in a sentence before. He was also sure the word 'Bastard' was spelt and pronounced with emphasis on the 'A', surely not an 'O.'

Christ! Jack thought he was mixing in the sort of company where these misdemeanours never occurred, he was tickled pink to find out they did and with the added attraction that the perpetrators wore suits when they fought, not jeans.

His laughter was interrupted by Valerie frantically pleading with him to, 'Do something Jack!'

Faced with a request to resort to a skill used mainly in his glorious youth, Jack went into 'bouncer' mode only to dive in, James Bond style, grab Mr MP and get him out. With long practiced dexterity, Jack parted the warring pair and ushered his now, unofficial charge, away from the drawing room and into the hallway. From there, with the aid of the Housekeeper, who had materialised almost from nowhere, Jack lead the way of escape out through the back of the house to emerge into a wonderful walled, rear garden that doubled up as a second, more discrete exodus in the form of a gothic style wrought iron gate. The Housekeeper now took on the form of Gatekeeper, by producing the key that would complete Mr MP's exit into the well lit London Street. Once safely outside, Jack turned to ask Mr MP, 'Are you okay?' to which the man replied,

'Yes and thank you Jack, I can't thank you enough', with an emphasis on the 'thank you.'

Jack grinned back with a 'No problem.'

After exchanging a few unremarkable sentences together a black London taxi came around the corner in no time at all. Jack ensured his temporary charge was safely stowed away inside, with the destination agreed, before making his own way back into the leafy, and he paused to notice, quite beautiful back garden. Stopping to share a few words of mirth with the

Housekeeper, Jack eventually returned through the serine, tree lined sanctuary to rejoin the now calm guests, along with the two feely fingered women; both had been very impressed with Jack's prowess.

Quite a few 'Well done Sir's / Jack' were offered with respect, accompanied by a very sincere and private 'Thank you' from Mr MP's opposing corner.

Although he was "Mr Popular" for the remainder of the evening, that and the kind comments he received did nothing to brighten Jack's outlook. He knew that this particular night could have ended with a cosy bed down, his body wrapped around teasing Tamara, had Valerie not been present. Her sycophantic 'Well done Jack!' had been uttered with delight (she was enchanted by the flurry of complements she received from the other women present, congratulating her choice of such a fine man) however; this elation on her part would not automatically entitle him to a leg over with her later.

Ah well, at least he was popular for providing something different than sex for a change. However, like his clandestine sexual encounters, this was another affair Jack would have to keep secret!

Chapter 37

Early Monday morning Valerie said her goodbyes to Jack once again but not because of her return home to Torbay. A taxi was waiting in the street outside, destination Heathrow airport; she had arranged to fly out and spend a week with Rosalie in Italy.

'Pity you can't come Jack, they would both love to see you. Are you sure you can't leave the work in the hands of a foreman or something?'

A picture of Rosalie walking into the shower while Jack was splashing about cleaning his todger, popped into his head. He felt automatically worried at the thought and replied, 'Sorry, no way can I leave the preparatory work unsupervised.'

His gut feeling told him to stay well away from Rosalie. He had no idea why, she just seemed like trouble. This was one of only a very few guaranteed shags that would be passed over in his lifetime.

Shortly after Valerie had taken her leave, Jack received a surprise phone call from the Lead Singer.

'Hey Jack! How the hell are you? Heard you were in town. Please let me know when you're here, it's always good to see you mate but actually your timing is brilliant because you might be able to help me with a personal favour?'

'Of course mate, what's the problem?'

'No problem, well I hope not at least! It's my daughter's 21st Birthday in a few weeks.'

'Christ mate, where does the time go? It doesn't seem that long ago that I escorted her to school'

'We've had some fun over the years eh Jack? We've arranged a small surprise party and invited a few of her close friends. We're keeping it secret from her; it's at The Ivy. Could you escort her there for me and linger out of sight in the background till she's ready to leave? We'll tell her you're just escorting her somewhere for a surprise. I'd be really grateful mate; I won't worry if I know you're around. I don't want to be hanging around her like a shrinking violet and ruin her party do I!?'

As he was already in London, Jack cordially agreed 'I'd be honoured; I would feel the same about my daughter.'

Jack also took up the offer of a catch-up between them both one evening the very next week.

Jack was glad the Band had achieved so much. He had travelled to one or two interesting places during his long association with them and had retained quite a few fond memories. While thinking along daughter lines, he thought he better phone his own and enquire how her wedding plans were going. His heart ached every time he thought of the stepfather giving his little girl away. *Geanie, you bitch!*

*

On her return from Italy, three days later than planned, Valerie exclaimed 'It was lovely out there Darling, I just had to stay a few more days. Rosalie was disappointed you were unable to come. She hopes to say 'Hello' when she visits us in a few months'

'Really, that will be nice'

'It would be nice for us to spend some time alone together Jack, but not in London while you are working.'

To do what exactly? He thought with sarcasm.

'How about we take a break in Paris when this project of yours is complete? I know it will be autumn by then but I think it's a wonderful place at any time of the year'

Valerie adored taking short breaks with Jack, mainly to show him off. Wherever they went she knew she was envied because of the handsome man attached to her arm and she intended to display her treasure as often as possible. You don't buy a fur coat and not wear it, do you?

Jack's sagacious decision not to leave the site at such an early stage was a shrewd judgement. Any project of such size required regular monitoring; therefore Jack, as the main stream of authority, should be on site at all times to direct the work and this London job could bring more prestigious work in the future. He was therefore reluctant to leave the site for just one day until it was complete; also, the intelligence report detailing Rosalie's future movements had been well received, enabling him to plan an escape route well ahead.

In relation to the proposed trip to gay Paris, Jack thought it might help for he and Valerie to be together in what was renowned to be one of the most romantic cities in the world and so, assented to her plan. If she was surrounded with the feel of amour, that only Paris could produce, it might encourage her to let him get his leg over for once.

*

A few days later he was on duty for the 21st Birthday party held at The Ivy. The celebratory evening passed uneventfully for Jack who was pleased with the outcome having sat quietly, with a soft drink in the corner, for the duration. The press, luckily, had been unaware the famous man's daughter was in residence, ensuring a relaxed but lively atmosphere. The group of young people were respectful and well behaved but still had fun. *The Birthday girl was a credit to her parents* Jack smiled. Mid way through the evening her manners enquired after Jack's comfort.

'Thanks for looking after me tonight Jack, Dad does worry! Do you have a daughter to worry about?'

'Yes, but I try not to worry!'

'She's lucky to have such a smashing person as a Dad, bet she loves you lots!' Saying, 'I hope so!' in reply his thoughts taunted, *but not enough to let you walk her down the aisle!*

Valerie had many friends, both male and female, all over the globe. Two men in particular; Tam and Cliff, were based in France and she was particularly fond of them both. Their home was a beautiful apartment in Paris; Cliff was a native of the city, and Tam, American. In recent years she had kept in touch with them by arranging a stopover as part of her other travels, diverting via Paris airport to pay a visit en route to wherever her destination might be at the time. Grinning with success, she thought they would easily be enamoured of Jack and think him quite a catch, consequently she arranged to meet up with them as part of their visit.

The two men were both antique dealers and interior designers; they also had a predilection for wine and, like the antiques they travelled the world to gather, could easily spot a possible treasure. Valerie had been introduced to both Tam and Cliff, by her father, whose first acquaintance with the pair occurred during a visit to a French chateau and vineyard. On receiving her invitation to rendezvous they both stressed they would be delighted, especially if her man was to accompany her.

'Valerie, my darling girl, it would be our pleasure, Cliff is shouting, "an enchanting idea", at me. Which restaurant would you like? Shall we choose for you?'

An ice breaker evening, to aid the occasion, was arranged at a superior Paris restaurant, a favourite eatery of the two Parisians.

Following their arrival at the Hotel, both Jack and Valerie enjoyed a relaxing luxurious bath, separately, before setting out on the short journey to the restaurant.

Tam and Cliff, who had arrived a little earlier to ensure a warm reception for their guests, were partaking of a pre dinner aperitif when Valerie and Jack alighted from the taxi. Both men were genuinely pleased the get together had been arranged, it had been far too long since they had last met up and 'Valerie darling, how is your father?' enquired Tam.

Cliff immediately took a fancy to Jack 'such a striking man you have found for yourself my Dear!' eyeing him up in appreciation.

Tam had to agree with his partner however, they were both sentient from the onset that Jack was in no way interested in men, only women.

The restaurant was superior but also fairly popular with the Parisian gay community, this information had been withheld from Jack simply because it was an excellent restaurant and the sexual preference of the diners was of no consequence.

As the maître d' escorted the cheery party to their allocated table, Tam and Cliff glanced toward each other, a coy grin mirrored on their faces, prompt to notice the looks of admiration Jack had attracted, albeit discretely, from at least two of the other male diners in the room. There was absolutely no reason they felt they should mention this to either of their charming dinner guests, allowing the conversation to flow, providing the table with an aura of high spirits and fun. Valerie was well able to converse in both French and Italian, as did Tam and Cliff, but with manners and respect for Jack, all three spoke in English. The food was superb, as only a French restaurant could prepare.

During the course of the meal Jack required a visit to the bathroom; politely he asked to be excused and after receiving directions, left the table to head for the rest room. As he rose from the table Cliff noticed a man, who had caught his attention when he cast a glance of admiration toward Jack earlier, alight from his table and appear to follow as Jack made his way across the restaurant to the 'salle de bain' situated on the other side of the room. Cliff resolved to keep a watchful eye for Jack's return. He was concerned for his newly found friend, he knew no harm would come to him, harm in the sense of being robbed etc. he was just not sure how Jack might react to any sexual enquiries from other men. The last thing required to mar their pleasant evening, was an unpleasant scene.

As you are aware, Jack was astounded when Jersey Tilly followed him toward a men's hotel toilet, such was her desperation to arrange an ad-hoc introduction and the gesture had been amusing for him because she was a woman. The attention he was receiving on this occasion however was in the structure of a gay man, which rather wiped any grin from his face. The chap, a local Parisian, was very insistent in his ardour and Jack, keen not to ruin the evening for his dinner companions, asked him to 'Please go away' in English, as clear as he could possibly perform, supported by quite a few frantic arm gesticulations, considering he had no French speaking skills onboard. The fact that he knew and understood the names of quite a few French wines and champagnes did not qualify him to give directions to a tourist. After a few minutes, with no apparent success, he felt he had no option but resort to the usual fairly worldwide expression of 'Look mate, Fuck off!'

He tried this little catch phrase twice but the chap just did not seem to understand, appearing enraptured by the 'brummie' vision now standing before him. It was also becoming increasingly difficult for Jack to control his temper, as languages apart; it would have been obvious to a snail that Jack was not interested. *Christ! This bloke was worse than some of the women he had known!* Jack was almost near to pleading with the little chap, so keen was he to be on his best behaviour in such a plush place but on receipt of his beau's next gesture, he decided enough was enough. Babbling incoherently, the enamoured, delicately built Frenchman put his hands out toward Jack in an attempt to caress his face. Swiftly, before he could make any contact with the coveted visage, Jack grabbed the man's right wrist with his left hand, erstwhile his right fist gently but firmly punched the man directly, but as gently as he could, in the face.

The temperate force was enough, allowing the man to see stars for a minute or two, without the need to remove the roof. Rendering him temporarily unconscious, Jack caught him as he collapsed into his arms, ironically robbing the little man of a feeling he would have paid a fortune to experience, supporting him while manoeuvring his body in order to line it up with and sit him on the nearest toilet seat, with some sort of decorum.

Ensuring the Parisian was in no way harmed other than slightly dazed, Jack completed his initial task, then having freshened up, left the little man, now groaning, to his own devices. Jack hoped any concurrent visitors to the scene would not automatically assume the Parisian was incapacitated due to the quality of the food.

Returning to the table Cliff enquired 'Are you alright Jack my boy?'

Looking into his face Jack could see he was aware some problem had transpired in the loo. Jack came clean; profusely apologetic he described the events which had just befallen him. His table companions' reaction to the misdemeanour, on the other hand was to unanimously roar with laughter!

Tam, putting his hands up to his face exclaimed 'Oh Jack, apologies my poor boy! That he with the face of an angel should be abused so!'

Jack was not too sure about the face of an angel bit just greatly relieved he had not offended his hosts, thereby he placed his unmolested behind safely back on his seat and breathed a sigh of relief. Cliff, attracting the attention of the *Maitre d'hôtel* both explained and apologised for the misunderstanding that had just taken place in the bog and asked for a bottle of the restaurant's best champagne to be sent over to the unfortunate's table as an apology. Walking away with a discrete smile in play on his lips, the *Maitre d'hôtel* delivered the champagne accompanied by an apology as requested. Word quickly spread around the restaurant encouraging smiles to illuminate most of the faces throughout.

Their Paris jaunt, uneventful but for this episode was soon over and Jack went back to work, extremely pleased to return to Jersey for a restoration project. On this occasion he left his old haunts and female contacts well alone, well, apart from Julie, and the BMW, who were delighted to see him once again. The feeling, of course, was reciprocated. There was no way the Sultan of Solihull would forgo his favourites. Quite some time had passed since his last visit and Jack was determined to avoid any trouble.

Chapter 38

Waking together one morning, Julie, grinning coquettishly, ran her hand over the front of Jack's body then admonished him slightly, 'Where is your flat stomach hiding Jack?' Playfully she asked, 'Have you been overindulging during the few months since I saw you last?'

Jack agreed he had put on a bit of weight of late, 'All the more to wrap round you, you saucy minx! Who cares about a few scratches on the paintwork if your car still does a ton easy?'

Julie giggled then pleaded, 'Oh Jack why won't you come and live with me?'
'I'm surprised you still want me to'

'Oh Jack, don't be silly. We get along fine, you know we do. And I wouldn't stop you building things. I know you enjoy your work but we could have such fun together. We could go over to France on the boat as well' (Jenny also owned a boat and a very large one at that)

Jack pondered whether he should re-class his now, much reduced so called, "Jersey Harem" with a more suitable title such as the Water Girls or even Sea Sirens. In spite of this flippant thought he heard alarm bells ringing, Julie had uttered two phrases in her lyrics that made him wary, he had heard them before, and they were: "*trips here and there*" and "*nice for us to go out together*". They were both two of Valerie's favourite phrases.

Jack suddenly felt tired. Where would it all end? He sighed, 'Let me think about it. I realise you are far too sexy to be living on your own'

Julie simpered at the compliment, he made her feel young again, enjoying the company of what she hoped would be her future live in, lover, a thrill seared through her body, *that answer sounded like he might just be persuaded*, she giggled at him offering, 'I love you Jack' then lovingly snuggled up, cuddling into his body as she put her arms around him. Unbeknown to Julie, Jack had only a few days hence, held a similar conversation with the BMW.

On his arrival at Julie's home her manner had, at first, been cool toward him, she had been very upset due to the boasting of that indiscrete cheeky little cow, Tilly, preening her feathers in superiority.

'I felt such a fool Jack! You should have told me. I would love to have you all to myself but I would have understood had you confided in me.

I can understand the difficulty for a sexy bugger like you! You deserve a slapping!'

'Oh delight! Carry on minx!'

Julie's laughter melted her wounded heart. She was secretly pleased with her performance at the time, she sure wiped the smug smile off that harlot's common painted face when she suggested another woman was in receipt of Jack's lovemaking, the bigoted little upstart wouldn't guess in a thousand years Julie was referring to herself.

Forgetting the annoying memory she turned her attention back to the handsome man now lying with his arms around her, he may have put on a few pounds of late, especially around his waistline but she was still keen to receive his fantastic lovemaking again, unaware it was the last time she would do so.

It would be Jack's ultimate visit, to both the island and his two harem favourites.

While Jack did indeed keep out of trouble during his visit to the island, a new batch of chaos was about to start on his home terrain that would ultimately lead to his nemesis. That well known theory 'it's hard to climb a mountain but once you get to the top it's all freewheeling down the other side' could be used as a description in relation to the development of Jack's sex life (working his way up with the local girls in the Midlands to reach the elitist wealthy women and harem at the top) for at this particular point he was about to freewheel down the other side, but with emphasis on the 'down' because if you cannot train yourself to desist in reckless behaviour there will come a time, usually in the form of a small disaster, when a specific situation is terminated on your behalf, without warning.

Chapter 39

Valerie had become very difficult to live with, well, for Jack anyway. There was probably a man somewhere that would love to jet around the world constantly living the high life. But Jack had become bored with the whole and their relationship was waning, fast. Constantly insisting he accompany her on every short break or holiday booked, she admonished his refusal to visit Dubai for a few weeks with her.

'What the hell do I need to go to Dubai for?'

'I am visiting one of my friends Jack. You've been invited. Surely you would love to come?'

'Valerie what about my job, you seem unaware of the fact that I have a job?'

'You know very well you don't have to work Jack. Just keep me company. I don't really want to go on my own.'

'But how do I earn a living? I can't just walk off and leave the lads to get on with the work on their own. It's bad enough going away for a week but three?'

'Well, actually Jack my Aunt has moved to Australia and I was going to fly on from Dubai and stay with her for another couple of weeks'

'What! Valerie I can't afford to jet around everywhere, plus I'll have no business left after six weeks. Have you no idea? Who would run it?'

'I've just tried to explain to you. There's no need for you to work. I want to see my friend and I don't see why I should not visit my Aunt. I keep reminding you that you've no need to work at all; I don't know why you bother. You know I'll fund you. Why do you have to be so petulant?'

'Petulant! I don't want to be a kept man, don't you get it?

A cold feeling shot through his heart, *Oh my God, I didn't see this coming.* A picture of the BMW shot into his head, *to think I could have been kept by her but I chose this.*

Faltering with the slight shock of reality he stammered, 'I can't, not work. I've always worked. You knew that when you first met me. You'll have to travel without me.'

Valerie's thoughts ran wild. *It would not be the same. She wanted him to accompany her and be seen in his company. Mind you, he had put a little weight on his waistline of late. It would ruin her trip if he wouldn't go!* Angrily she shouted back 'Oh, if you must be so querulous Jack, I'll see you in around six week's time. I can speak to you on the phone and email at least. I expect the time will fly past soon enough!'

On his own for six weeks! Jack wondered why he bothered. *Okay, fair enough, she should see her family when she wanted but if I give up work I'm nothing more than a kept man. I might as well have taken up the offer to be a kept man in France with Julie or the BMW; At least I would enjoy a decent sex life. What the hell am I doing pottering along in this shambles?*

His thoughts protested his ill treatment but his spirits instantly lifted, *why? Why did he feel glad she was leaving him behind?* Mr Mischief brought a cheeky thought, *should he ask who was going to visit each day to feed and water him and perhaps take him for a walk while she had left him on his own? Don't be querulous Jack*, said Mr Sarcastic to Mr Mischief.

Within two weeks Valerie had jetted off, destination Dubai and there was no lingering 'I'll miss you' sex session to top up their nonexistent passion levels before she left either. *Ah well, back to eating at the pub in the evening again,* Jack sighed, *what would he find to do in the evenings over the next six weeks? Find somewhere else to live maybe?*

Just two weeks later, the first complication to instigate Jack's wheels of destruction into motion came onto the scene in the form of yet another, neglected, housewife. Her home was situated within a pretty Devon village, approximately two miles distant from the plot of land where Jack and Valerie had built their second home after selling the first one in Torbay for a large profit.

Her name was Delilah and, she had become resigned to the fact that, every now and then, the occasional idiot would attempt to practice a form of wit at her expense by tunelessly, chanting 'Why? Why? Why? Delilah!' adamant they were being funny. She was rather sweet and had, since an early age, endured, or rather more accepted, each repetitive, stupid comment from every moron who just had to sing the line from the song, so certain were they in their thoughts of being the first idiot to remember the famous hit record.

Whilst in her teens, in an attempt to escape the constant repetitive barrage of insults to TJ's singing, Delilah had asked close friends if they would please call her De-De. This request had been quite successful and enjoyed the added bonus of having a rather trendy ring to it; the name had also been made fashionable by the Pans People dancer.

Bizarrely, ever since her birth, when her Christian name had been announced, her Grandmother had insisted on referring to her as Lily, which annoyed her parents no end. The determined old dear had not been overtaken by the wicked Alzheimer's disease; she just thought the name stupid and, being a grandparent, felt she could exercise an unofficial right to behave as a matriarch. By the time she had reached her teenage years, as far as De-De was concerned, any name was better than Delilah.

Jack would hear all of her problems, complicating matters by not only becoming her lover but also lovingly referring to her as Dilly.

'And why, you sexy man, have you decided to call me that?' she asked as she bit her lower lip in the fashion of a shy schoolgirl.

'Because you're delicious, Delilah, De-De, Lily, Dilly!'

She laughed heartily, *oh, he was so refreshing and, slightly on the wild side. He was also very tempting and very, very sexy.*

The pair had met through an exchange of appreciative glances while attending a local neighbour's birthday party. The minute their eyes made contact, Jack realised he wouldn't need to travel across the English Chanel for sex any more in the future. She was a quiet, almost dainty sort of woman who after providing her husband with four children, just wanted affection and a little more attention than was gathered from her occasional visit to the local hairdresser while having her hair streaked with a complicated shade of auburn. Enter Jack stage left to ensure she acquired a little of what she desired, especially until Valerie returned from Australasia. Not that that would alter anything.

But when Valerie did return, far from concluding, the affair continued to build eventually expanding into a full blown concern. The majority of their seductive meetings were performed during visits to the occasional B&B, situated near and around the Devon seaside, when Jack was supposed to be in London or elsewhere. But, after only six months at home, Valerie jetted off again, this time to visit Rosalie, who had recently moved from Italy to Los Angeles.

'Come stay with me for a month or so Darling! Tell Jack he is most welcome.' *Bugger that*, Jack bit back this tart reply offering a considerably more temperate 'I'd love to visit Los Angeles but a month is too long because of work Valerie, sorry'

'What about flying out and joining me for a week then?'

'Err; it's hardly worth the long flight for just a week is it? Perhaps we could go to Paris again later, it's not so far and it would be easier'

Valerie, brightened by the very thought happily packed her bags once again. Meanwhile Jack blew a long whistle of relief; *good I can spend time with Dilly and relax.*

During this time Jack and Dilly even visited one or two local restaurants for dinner together, sometimes making a foursome with another married couple, both were friends of Dilly's and sympathised with her situation. The affair might have lasted much longer then, one day, Dilly announced to Jack that she was pregnant.

Chapter 40

Temporarily diverted with a new flame to flit around, Jack's spirits were bobbing somewhere close to high and happy. This level dropped only slightly toward the 'un' part of the happy chart due to the impending arrival of his daughter's wedding day, patiently awaiting its planned staging the very next weekend, however, a damper had already been hung over the complex proceedings. Jack's initial expectation to receive at least one small consolation from the day had been obliterated on the discovery that his parents had not been invited.

'Hi Mum, I'll be up to stay with you on Friday night okay? We can travel to the church together'

'What church Jack? Are you getting married again? What on earth for, you know it doesn't suit you!'

'Mum! Mum! Not me, it's your bloody Granddaughter's wedding, have you forgotten'

'How do you mean forgot? We had no idea. Haven't seen her for ages'

'Not seen her, not invited?!'

Jack began to feel both angry and dismayed concurrently, *that fucking Geanie! This was her doing. Spiteful bitch!*

'I understood you were going to be invited. I'm not having that; I'll try to sort something out'

'Oh Jack don't bother, I don't want to see that bitch again, the conniving little tart. Got pregnant deliberately she did and the other one!'

'Alright Mum, don't go on. It was years ago, let it go.'

Well aware his attendance at the celebration would be considered unwelcome by the bride's paternal family; all Jack wanted to do was be there on the day to support his daughter. He realised there were plenty of times in the past when he had not been on hand for her. The last thing he wanted was to stir up trouble on her special day.

His thoughts were, albeit temporarily, diverted from the consequences of his mother's upsetting information by spending a couple of hours, earlier on the Friday afternoon, licking Dilly in all her most ticklish places encouraging her body to contort in raptures. Their refreshing liaison over, Jack put his best suit in the car and set off on the four hour journey to his homeland.

*

The uneventful drive completed, Jack arrived to broad welcoming smiles from both his parents. *Weird! It feels good to be home*, he thought, putting his arms around his mother, crushing her gently in a bear style hug. Looking to shake hands with his father, Jack was shocked to notice they were both advancing in years.

In an attempt to lie convincingly he offered, 'Mum, Dad, so good to see you. You both look fantastic!'

'I'm not one of your pickups my son, don't lie to me!'

'Christ I can't win whatever I say can I!'

Wondering why his father was hesitant to shake hands and about to ask for his help in jest as a retort to his mothers comment, Jack became puzzled, his father was paying no attention, looking altogether in quite another direction.

'Dad, are you okay?'

The 'Eh?' he received in reply stunned Jack into instant confusion.

'Jack, don't stand out here, come inside, I have to tell you something about Dad.'

Alarmed, he immediately asked 'Is something wrong, is he ill?'

'Just go on in Jack, Dad come back inside the house love.'

Jack, totally bewildered, wondered why his mother was taking his father's hand in order to lead him back into the house like a horse.

'What's wrong with Dad? Dad, are you okay?'

'Jack, your Dads' got Alzheimer's.'

'What! No! He was fine last time I saw him.'

'That was last year Jack, the Doctor said it could appear all of a sudden, he'd been forgetting things for ages, we didn't realise it was the start of it. It might clear in a minute and he could come back to the present, he sort of drifts in and out. The Doctors said eventually he will go right back in time, might even think he's a child again.'

Jack was speechless through sorrow and disbelief. What a sad start to his return home. Already expecting an awkward day tomorrow, the present one had now been ruined by the shocking news of his father's defeat to a wicked disease. 'Mum how will you cope with this?'

'Don't you worry son, I've all the help I need from your two Aunts. Dad, come sit down here my love while I get Jack a cup of tea.'

Sitting patiently with a serene smile on his face, his father appeared quite happy, wherever he was.

'I'm surprised you've come up for the wedding'

'Mum it's my daughter'

'Well I didn't think you saw her that much, still it will be nice for you to do something in the role of a father and give her away'

Oh shit, it gets worse, 'Her stepfather is giving her away'

'What! That idiot! Oh Jack, why do you let it happen to you? That's her bitch of a mother's doing!'

'Yes, that's obvious to me, and I'm not ruining her day by letting her mother get away with everything'

'She was such a happy little thing with her brother when you brought them both here when they were children', Jack held his tongue remembering how grumpy and difficult his mother had been at the time.

'Yes well, I'm sure she's happy now. I just need to be there tomorrow and don't say anything about the past. I know I've not been around for her and that bitch has done nothing to help; she's done her best to drive a wedge between us. She will win if I don't go.'

From the front room they heard his father shout, 'Mum, is Jack getting married again?

*

Jack found a space to sit, near the back of the church but next to the aisle, having just dodged a glance, loaded with hate, thrown directly toward him, in spite and anger, by Geanie. *Christ! if looks could kill he would have collapsed and died on the church floor right there and then.* He had not recognised her at first; she had changed much in appearance, the lively, spiky blonde hair of her youth had turned grey since they last exchanged words. She also appeared old for her years. Both of Geanie's parents had thrown similar glances toward him, emulating the three Erinyes with their collective wrath. Age old anger still festering away, Jack had received other negative glances from the few remaining family members aware of the history, most appeared loaded with a mixture of disbelief or disregard. Dismissing their resentment Jack patiently awaited his daughter's ultimate entrance.

Bugger the lot of you, he thought, then turned to look toward the back of the church, in unison with the rest of the congregation, at the organist's loud start of the Wedding March, "*Here comes the bride!*"

Jack, in the next few minutes, would experience both the best and worst feelings in his life, ever, simultaneously. Turning his head to observe the Bride make her way down the aisle toward the alter Jack's eyes were transfixed, absorbing every detail of her beautiful, ethereal appearance. But, as his little girl commenced her procession he felt a knife stab his heart. Proceeding gingerly but with grace she gave her stepfather a quick, sideways glance accompanied by a nervous giggle which lit up her pretty face, already favourably illuminated by the excitement and enormity of the occasion. Glowing with pride (a feeling hitherto excluded from his repertoire of emotion) at the sight of his daughter in her white, gossamer dress, Jack's body was synchronized in anguish. A large measure of jealousy had been thrown in for extra torment.

She was so beautiful! She should have been on HIS arm! That man was not her real father! Geanie you absolute Bitch!

Never before had Jack felt so high and so low at the same time, literally torn apart by his inner feelings. He so wanted to hug her. Tell her how proud he felt. Laugh in unison with her. The enormity of the realisation that he could look at but not touch his own daughter filled him with grief. Tears sprang unannounced from both his eyes to flow unhindered over his cheeks. Wiping them hastily away with the back of one hand he prepared himself, using all the inner strength he could muster, to endure the rest of the service. As his little girl swept past his pew Jack could smell her light perfume like a breath of fresh air. She was totally unaware of his presence and untouchable. He cried. Jack was gutted.

Confetti danced through the surrounding air, whipped around in asymmetric patterns by the playful breeze. The torture of having to watch a complete dick walk his daughter down the aisle over, Jack now had to tolerate the endless photograph taking, from which he was also excluded. While scanning the churchyard at the various Jersey weddings he had attended, Jack had always managed to find an amiable soul or souls to pass the photograph section with either that or he simply headed straight to the reception for alcoholic reward; here however, he felt outcast in his own homeland, totally excluded from the lively collective chatter, hat holding in defiance of the breeze and general excited aura generated by the assembled guests. But he never gave up.

About to make his way to the wedding breakfast his attention was caught on hearing the words, shouted loudly, almost in panic 'DAD DAD!'

Turning in hope, he was momentarily rewarded; his daughter was calling to him.

'Dad, come and have your picture taken with me please'

All smiles, despite the fact her new husband had buggered off, obviously not wanting to be seen alongside him, Jack promptly walked, his heart beating wild inside his chest, toward the only woman, he now realised, he had ever truly loved.

Chapter 41

Valerie returned with a shower of apology, 'Sorry I was not able to accompany you to your daughter's wedding Jack. Why didn't you remind me? I would have loved to come with you. I would have rescheduled my trip'

Her apology diffidently accepted, Jack said 'It was difficult and you would not have enjoyed it, forget it'

Mildly surprised, but unwilling to lose sleep over a past event, Valerie let the whole issue meander away into the darkness.

In the meantime Jack's affair with Dilly had continued to build. Dilly had escaped her wife /mother duties temporarily by using the excuse, 'I want to stay with my old school friend, Jane, who is unwell. You remember Jane? I thought it would be nice to stay with her one weekend a month or something and be of help. She never married and lives on her own.'

As she spoke the words she felt not only guilt but also annoyance. Had she actually asked her husband's permission? Come to think of it, she couldn't remember the last time she made a decision, that concerned her own life, independent of her spouse.

Her husband smiled 'Go on little Florence Nightingale, but don't make yourself ill. I'll look after the children this time but your Mum may have to help out next time as you know my contract requires me to work a certain number of weekends per year'

'Surely you don't need to work every weekend do you?'

'Let me know when you want to go and we'll see when the time comes'

Dilly knew she was expecting Jack's baby because she now rarely enjoyed sex with her husband, they had both literally forgotten to tend this part of their marriage. His job had come to dominate his life leaving Dilly to look after the children and manage their lives; having provided her husband with four children during their marriage, one baby every five years or so since her twenties, the youngest child was now only five years old.

As she had never needed to work, having married soon after leaving school, she had eventually become trapped within her own home. She dreamed of leaving her husband, who was by no means a bad person, but she yearned for some excitement in her life. She knew, because of the children, she would never leave him and, as his income was large, it was financially a lot to put aside, plus the upset for the children, so she chose to conduct her life, short changed, stealing the occasional secret session with Jack.

News of the developing baby was a shock to both of them: Dilly had not thought she would be fertile enough, even though only in her forties and Jack, now well into his forties, had not changed the habit of a lifetime, giving no thought to birth control.

After much serious discussion it was decided the most sensible thing to do would be to abort the baby although in all fairness Jack would not have minded if she chose to keep the child. His thoughts ran back to the Midlands of his twenties, revisiting some of the heated arguments he had undergone with Josie and Geanie. He wished his lifestyle had allowed him to be a normal father. Even now, although it seemed a last chance had been issued him, he knew deep inside it was not going to happen. Everyone is supposed to be happy when you announce the impending birth of a baby, but of course that only depends on the circumstances in play at the time.

He realised the unplanned child could cause chaos and mayhem but he felt the final decision should be with Dilly, if preferred she could always pretend it was her husband's baby but they would both know it was Jack's. Could he watch a child grow up within a neighbouring family knowing it was his and say nothing? That was not really his style.

Eventually, after much deliberation, both Jack and Dilly decided it would not work for them to move in together.

'Jack I'd love to live with you but it just would not work and I have to think of the children. I'm busy with the four I already have! Oh, why did this have to happen now! I can't pay out the money for an abortion on my own Jack, my husband runs all the finances, he'll find out because he would question the amount. He checks everything as it is. Not nasty mind he's just thorough.'

Jack was insistent he would pay.

'I've got you into this mess, it's my responsibility to get you out, don't worry. Honestly though, we could make a go of it. You only have to say the word.'

'Thanks Jack. I do love you, another place, and another time? I wish above everything I could be with you, it's just not meant to be.'

Dilly felt there was no other option and that their destiny was under the control of others.

When the termination date had been arranged and confirmed, Jack felt rather low but he could not work out why. Within a few weeks their affair had petered out, probably in sympathy with the baby. After all, they had no intertwined future to live for anymore.

Never one to waste time in pensive thought, Jack carried on; throwing his energy into his work, plus another bastard customer had not paid him the balance of money due on completion of the work. He'd have to engage the services of his solicitor again. The cost was hardly worth the return. The scheming gits should be made to pay up. You wouldn't be allowed to leave a supermarket without paying for your shopping would you? He contemplated paying a visit to the customer's house with a sledgehammer and knocking seven bells of shit out of the conservatory he had just constructed. When were the Government going to sort out customers that didn't pay?

*

Now Jack was far from stupid but sometimes, when chaos reigns, we don't think with caution. Jack paid for Dilly's hospital visit with his credit card.

A month or so later Valerie's accountant was collating Jack's quarterly VAT. Puzzled by an entry for a hospital charge she asked, 'Valerie, is this hospital charge a mistake? Have you any idea what building job this amount, for four hundred pounds, relates to?'

Informing her of the mystery amount on the statement, Valerie, in the first instance was concerned Jack may have some medical problem. Immediately on his return home she asked after his health and whether he was aware of the mystery amount on his statement.

'Is everything alright Jack or is this a mistake. You can never be too careful. Has someone got a hold of your card details only to use them fraudulently?'

'Eh?'

'You have made a payment to the hospital with your credit card.

Fuck it! Stall for time. 'What?'

'Linda was collating the accounts and noticed the charge; she thought it didn't look like building work.'

Nosey cow!

'Are you alright Jack? You look a bit pale. You would tell me if anything was amiss?'

Something definitely is amiss and I can't sidle out of this one. Not this time.

Realising he was surrounded, in far too deep to escape detection and never one to lie when approached direct, Jack released the reason for the charge.

He ducked as the heavy glass ashtray flew past his head.

'YOU BASTARD!'

Remember, he had been along ashtray highway before, Jack knew just when to duck to avoid one hurled at his head. Waiting to find a gap for speech in the barrage of glassware hurling his way, a single ashtray was simply not enough ammunition when you were to consider the magnitude of this particular misdemeanour, Jack, eventually, when all throw able glass ornaments had been exhausted, stated 'For christ's sake, I'll pack immediately and leave.'

To his amazement and, it has to be said, quiet disappointment, Valerie broke down, 'No! Please don't go, please. I want you to stay.'

He knew it was all wrong, their relationship could surely not last much longer, but, for the moment, he would put it all away and carry on as normal, whatever that was.

A few weeks later, her temper having subsided with the passing of time, Valerie announced it would be good for them both to visit Paris again, she had decided the short break would help their relationship and as Jack's latest project had just completed they packed their bags and flew out almost immediately.

Jack felt uninterested even before they had left England, finding it difficult to work up any sort of enthusiasm for the trip but what the hell; Valerie had arranged for them to meet up with Tam and Cliff again which was about the only itinerary item Jack was actually looking forward to and it was certainly no hardship to consume the superb local cuisine. By complete surprise, they had all met up in Italy while on a holiday / vineyard errand for Valerie's father, the year before; Jack liked them both for their intelligent conversation and warm manner and was keen to catch up with them. He was also rather confused and slightly worried; it occurred to him that he was more interested in a reunion where he would be conversing with two gay men rather than Valerie, strained as their relationship had now become.

Paris in the springtime! Forget it. There would be no romance for Jack who, in all fairness, could appreciate the depth of Valerie's wrath which had, since the declaration of his affair, easily been detected due to the constant presence of anger intertwined with her voice in part of her answers to his polite enquiries and attempts at conversation, and spoken in monosyllables. *Why the hell had she insisted on the trip if she was going to treat him with indifference.*

Dilly did not disappear from their thoughts so easily. It had been most unfortunate for them to bump into her while they were filling up the car with diesel en route to the airport. Jack noticed her right away and spoke without embarrassment across his pump to her, 'Hi Dilly are you alright? Have you recovered okay?'

'Yes, I'm fine Jack, don't worry, you okay?'

Dilly noticed Valerie head toward the payment kiosk from the corner of her eye; shrinking slightly in stature she tried to become invisible while maintaining her concentration and continue her conversation with Jack. He had telephoned her on a few occasions since their decision to part just to make sure she was alright and in good health but this was the first time she had seen him in person and she felt quite unsettled.

Jack boldly continued in conversation, caring not one jot. 'No, I'm far from okay but that's up to me to sort out, you take care of yourself and, call me if you ever have a problem.'

'Thanks Jack.'

He got back into the car the same time as Valerie returned from paying at the kiosk.

'What's SHE doing here?'

'Buying fucking petrol like everyone else, Let it go!'

It was not really the actual affair with Dilly that had dismayed Valerie, she was not so immune to her milieu, well aware that Jack was an extremely handsome man and as such, quite a catch; she had known right from the start of their relationship that women would want to steal him away whenever possible and if their attempts to woo did not succeed completely, then, they would possibly try to borrow him for a bit (no pun intended).

The source of her angry resentfulness was? Jack had bestowed upon Dilly a gift unreciprocated to her. This is where the practice of the harem demonstrates its equality, if you give a baby to one wife you must not insult another, she must also be provided with the gift of a baby, a new car or handbag, given by proxy, would be quite out of the question.

Valerie had no intention of allowing Jack to give her a baby but this small detail was not relevant, she did not want his child, therefore, no one else should have one either.

She had known for some time he was meeting other women but was happy to ignore the obvious as long as he kept these peccadilloes hidden from her; sex was messy, messed up your hair, make-up, sheets etc, Valerie had other, far more interesting treats to enjoy such as meeting friends for lunch while wearing designer fashion; all nice and neat.

Jack, unaware of the term polygamy, had quite unintentionally favoured both women where Josie and Geanie were concerned; he had also overlooked one or two other points that were required for a successful plural marriage;

1. It helps if you are married to both women. However this situation is difficult to achieve, polygamy not being standard practice in the UK, another word is brought into use under English Law if more than one wife is taken, Bigamy.
2. Jack also faced ascending a rock face similar to north of the Eiger in any attempt to ensure harmonious discord between his women; this was simply called, 'Sharing.' Geanie had no intention of allocating any of Jack's special parts for use with any other woman and it has to be said, he couldn't be too sure about Josie either.
3. He may have been on a winner with the third point, Religious practice. There are one or two religious groups that would accommodate his wish to change his faith and therefore avoid being branded a Bigamist in the UK, on the other hand, Jack had no wish to believe in the teachings of another, only his own. So he was buggered really.

Occasionally he allowed his mind to wander aimlessly into forbidden territory, thinking about what may have been; as an absent parent in his twenties, he now, with a maturity of sorts, realised he had missed out on a lot. Could he have made parenting work with Dilly? What an almighty fuss the attempt would have caused. Did he love her enough to ride out the storms of outrage, birthed by scorned spouses, sent to destroy their tentative future?

He was very fond of her and strangely enough, since the baby had been terminated, he thought of her in an entirely different way, with much fondness but not fond enough to endure a tempest.

*

Spirits were high, as always, when Tam and Cliff were around, they had booked a table in the same restaurant where Jack had smacked and deposited the unfortunate love struck Parisian in the bog two years earlier. Jack hoped the memories retained by the staff within, short and the episode long forgotten; the chance of the same little man dining in the same restaurant at the same time was surely remote. On the other hand, he had underestimated both Cliff's, and the elegant establishment's sense of humour big time.

Tucking into a dish of oysters with relish, grinning simultaneously because his thoughts had temporarily flown back to the BMW, yachts and Majorca, an announcement was politely broadcast to the assembled diners over the restaurant microphone. Jack took no notice; his thoughts wavering *get a grip Jack!* Concentration was difficult, he tried hard not to laugh while attempting to squeeze a few drops of lemon distractedly over the shellfish, and, as the information was given in French and his thoughts were still stretched out on the sun lounger of a fast cruiser, he paid no heed to the foreign proclamation. As the French speaking drew to a close every guest in the restaurant erupted into laughter, instantly turning to look in Jack's direction. Whatever had been announced certainly appeared hilarious to the French clientele surrounding him, Jack perplexed, looked to Valerie for a translation.

Forcing her mouth into a smile for the benefit of manners toward Cliff and Tam, instead of offering an English rendition, she simply glared angrily toward Jack the minute their companions turned to acknowledge and share their enjoyment with the rest of the diners within the room, refusing to vocally respond to his query.

What the hell have I done now? Jack had to admit Valerie had not laughed much since the day his credit card statement had been scrutinised by Miss Efficient in the office. He knew they must both discuss the affair and clear the air if possible or there was no point them staying together.

Before he could press her to explain what was obviously a very funny ditty; Cliff, bending his hand in a stationary wave, full of camp mirth, obliged.

'Jack my boy, the Restaurant Manager has just informed his guests to please leave the straight Englishman alone unless you want to be punched and sat on a toilet!

Jack laughed out loud. He thought how civilised Paris was in relation to its gay population.

As the laughter died back and the convivial foursome returned to the enjoyment of their food, Valerie still gave the impression of thunder about to erupt. Ignoring her resentment, Jack turned his attention back to the oysters.

His memory suddenly switched on, then flew back a long way both in remembrance and mileage, to New York and the first time he had encountered a gay man; if there had been any around during his youth in the Midlands they had kept quiet.

Jack had been approached by one or two gay men, in the hope he was of the same denomination, on a couple of occasions in his past, both during visits to New York, when he had flown out to join the Band just because they were bored, fun times! Kit would telephone 'Hi Jack. How are you? How'd you fancy flying across the Atlantic to spend a few days with us in New York? Stay longer if you can spare the time, all expenses paid, we miss you!'

Jack was honoured; they treated him as part of their extended Band family.

During one of these impromptu visits, Jack had spent most of the daytime helping the crew set the stage for a scheduled concert. While performing one of the tasks allocated him he began a conversation with a very handsome guy who was working as part of the stage crew; his forte was electronics and sound.

Over general banter, Jack asked if he had a girlfriend, was married etc. With no embarrassment he replied his partner was a man. Jack, bold as ever, stated he must surely be pursued by women owing to his striking looks 'Not that I fancy you mate but you must disappoint quite a few.'

Laughing, the chap admitted 'Yeh, I have broken a few female hearts, though not intentionally.'

'It must be difficult for you to meet other men; they must think you're straight surely?

He shook his head slowly, a look of complacency on his face, 'No Jack, there's a way of knowing if another man wants you or not and, if I should happen to be in a place where I need to find a similar spirit I have my own little Bible'

In answer to Jack's gaze of puzzlement he offered up a little information in relation to a book he owned, 'Jack, it's literally a worldwide guide to toilets frequented by gay men and where they are situated, I'll let you borrow it if you need help to meet some new friends while you travel with the Band?'

He glanced toward Jack with a grin, quite sure that he'd take the joke and not be offended.

'I'm sure you are aware that's not my cup of tea and anyway I've enough trouble with the women I meet already'

'Perhaps that's your problem Jack'

'Eh?'

'You're drinking tea when you should try coffee!'

Jack managed to raise his eyes and shake his head, he thought him a nice guy regardless, managing to refrain from using "fuck off", as a reply.

His thoughts returned to the present and the excellent French cuisine set in front of him. Apart from the food and the presence of Tam and Cliff, he felt as flat as a pancake. *What was he going to do about his relationship with Valerie?*

They say nothing lasts forever. The short, Parisian break had been conducted, literally between strangers. The only time a look of something close to animation appeared on Valerie's face was while she was shopping. Jack, bored, accompanied her as if on normal bodyguard duty. He wondered if that was all he was or ever had been to Valerie. Now approaching his fifties, he realised he'd put on a few more pounds of late than he had carried in the past and *was his hair looking a few shades lighter when illuminated by the brightly lit shop display windows, was it grey hairs he could see squeezing through at his temples?, who cared!*

Maturing as gracefully as an esteemed bottle of vintage wine, Jack was still very handsome and of course, he still had his greatest gift, Charisma. Amazingly, women of all ages were still falling for it. He glanced at one or two Parisian women as he escorted Valerie into Chanel, *French women were born complete with elegance*, he was pleased to notice that both women had returned his smile of appreciation with their own, of him.

Mind you, just lately he had become aware that he required a lot more puff to perform sex a second time, being unable to spring back quite as quick as in his youth. A short rest was now required in between to catch his breath but the quality was, as always, one hundred percent leaving his conquests in a parallel state, contented and breathless. However, unbeknown to Jack, his next 'joie de vivre' would be his last.

Chapter 42

It took around a year for the Dilly disaster to fade from Valerie's immediate memory, just when she thought he might at last settle down and be done with sex, Jack's path crossed with that of a young single, local woman; she had a part time admin job at the local swimming baths and cleaning the homes of a couple of wealthy clients kept her busy the rest of her working week.

Their eyes met through the regular Friday night cigarette smoke, found billowing delicately around and throughout the nostrils of every inmate of every local pub. Jack was participating in his habitual end of week wind down discussion with some of his workmen.

'Will they really ban smoking in pubs and restaurants?'

'Nah, people wouldn't stand for it, mate.'

Returning to the bar for drinks top-ups at the same time, Jack stood politely beside Sandra. Perhaps they both sensed the kindred spirit that persuaded them to turn and observe each other.

Barbara Cartland used the word 'masterful' to describe an impressive man's attractiveness to a woman in several of her books. Whether their content brings reminiscence, delight or dismay when read, that particular descriptive word was relevant in relation to the spark that instantly set the direction of the final chapter in Sandra's life.

Glancing up into the handsome face of the big man standing so close beside her at the bar Sandra felt small and just a little breathless. Smiling warmly into her wide, bright blue eyes he offered, 'Would you like a drink?'

'Yes please, thank you. I'll have a rum and coke.'

The drink sealed an unspoken pact. For the rest of the evening Jack divided his time between his workmen and Sandra until her boyfriend, a tall, rangy, sullen faced youth walked in, scanned the pub for her whereabouts then, spotting her as part of a small group of women the other side of the bar headed toward her, regardless of the assembled punters enjoying their individual pint, shouting in rather an accusatory tone, 'Why are you still in here? Why didn't you come straight home from work?'

'The girls in the office asked if I wanted to join them for a drink after work.

It's Naomi's birthday'

Naomi suddenly felt guilty, wishing it was someone else's birthday at that particular moment.

'I did tell you.'

'I don't fuckin' remember!'

Jack, having just returned from the bar with a birthday drink bought especially for Naomi, walked away, his anger bubbling over, *gobby bastard.* Great was his desire to punch the lanky twat in the face on account of his vulgar, disrespectful answer but he had managed to cultivate a small helping of patience over the years. Plus, you couldn't go around punching people as easily in the twenty first century as you could in the nineteen seventies.

Jack was very aware his own treatment of women in the past might be described by some as cavalier but he had never felt the need to speak to any one of them with such ignorance and could not sit idly by and listen to the bad-mannered youth pour forth such offensive disrespect. But, at the end of the day, he could not interfere if Sandra chose such a wanker for a boyfriend.

A week later, Jack was once again to be found in the same pub, chilling out as part of the regular Friday night wind down, however, on this particular evening, rather than stand at the bar, he had found a table where there would be room for him to sit and eat.

Valerie did not have a regular "nine till five" job but would often arrive home late from either shopping, chatting or visiting friends and family. Jack had become a fairly passable cook over the years and would often chip in through necessity or just general pleasure, but due to the absence of a "whose turn is it to be chef tonight" rota system, Valerie would frequently return home late and not feel like cooking at all, only to suggest they both eat out on the spur of the moment. On most of these occurrences, by the time they had arrived at their selected pub or restaurant, which may already be full to capacity, they often found themselves not actually commencing their meal until almost nine thirty. Jack's inner workings, once happy, especially in his younger years, to contend with irregular eating times, were now starting to complain at this treatment. However, in relation to this particular Friday evening, arrangements had been planned with some efficiency earlier in the day. Before he left for work that morning Valerie had, with an 'Oops I nearly forgot!' asked Jack if he wanted to eat out later, by joining in a pre arranged meal with some of her friends, he declined, preferring the end of week wind down with his workmen, and so, shortly after entering the pub, he found a table and ordered some food.

In recognition, as Sandra passed his table she stopped and said 'Hi! Had a good week?'

Jack smiled in reply 'Yes fairly, how about you?'

'Busy, but I'm now ready for some relaxation'

'Good for you' retorted Jack, then bold as ever, 'Mind you, I don't know how you expect to find any relaxation with that foul mouthed git you've chosen for a boyfriend'

She laughed in reply 'He can be such an idiot! He and I used to have a right laugh but just lately he's become rather possessive. I'm not sure whether to ditch him or not'

'You'd be better off ditching him, believe me, it's not good to be possessive and no one should speak to you like he does'

'My word, she said playfully, I think I've found a gentleman! Can I enjoy some polite conversation with you for a while?'

Jack's legendary grin appeared, 'Of course, my pleasure. Here, take this "tenner" and get yourself a drink, I'll have another pint.'

And there you have it, simple introduction leading to eventual chaos...

'I don't suppose you fancy a midnight swim?'

'Eh!' Jack, slightly flummoxed, gabbled a reply that 'Yes, he would love a midnight swim, in Barbados or somewhere warm but Torquay, in winter?'

They had spent the majority of the evening together, Jack having bought Hunters Chicken for Sandra to devour (she had not eaten her evening meal before entering the pub) as a first course, followed by Toffee sponge and custard, 'I can't sit here and eat alone in front of you', in between chatting to his workmates. One or two exchanged wry glances, well aware of their Boss's fabled sexual prodigy.

In a short while he was completely hooked, *where did this woman intend swimming and at midnight?*

Torbay, although described in holiday brochures as an "English Riviera" did not, regularly, possess the persistent sweltering temperatures that its

French counterpart could boast. And, there had never been a report, to date, declaring how the Local Council in the South of France had found it necessary to wrap their palm trees in hot water bottles during the winter in order to keep them from catching flu and deteriorating.

'Warmth is no problem Jack; I hold the keys to the local swimming pool.' 'What! Is your boyfriend going to join us?' he asked tentatively, ready with a 'no' as reply if she answered in the affirmative.

'Oh bugger to him! He doesn't own me!'

'If he treats you anything like he speaks to you, I wonder why you put up with him!' a broad grin spread across his face as he retorted. Her suggestion, however, was outrageous! She was certainly not backward in coming forward.

Jack hardly knew the girl but he had done nothing outrageous since supplying Julie with an orgasm whilst in the middle of a crowded hotel dining room, sat at a table approximately three feet away from another wedding guest.

'You're on', he laughed with a grin reminiscent of his twenties.

They left the pub just before closing time and made straight for the pool, covering the short distance on foot. Jack, unaware of the normal timetable arrangements of the local swimming pool, having never before entered its domain, had assumed, incorrectly, that the local baths were now promoting the unusual, a midnight swimming session.

Making a visual check that there was no one, with curious eyes, lurking in the vicinity; Sandra let them both, very quietly, into the building using a side entrance, with her own set of keys. There was no one inside and due to it not being the sort of establishment that required night shift work; they made their entrance as if invisible.

'Sandra what are you doing?'

She giggled in reply.

Heading directly to the pool room, there was one more door for Sandra to conquer. Her key opened the door in time with her voice 'Open Sesame!' and they walked into their private domain.

Surprised at her boldness, she was already pulling off her t-shirt top; Jack moved to stand in front of her and helped pull the remainder of the material over her head. Putting his arms either side of her waist and around her back he undid her bra fastening, kissing her as he pulled her in toward him.

'You are wild! He laughed. It had been a long time since he had encountered such fun.

Pulling away from him she bent down to pull her jeans over her feet then, straightening up elegantly and with a hint of tease, after noticing his grin, a reaction to her absence of wearing any knickers, walked carefully toward the edge of the pool and with a fleeting, saucy look back, rose her arms above her head to drive, in the shape of a beautiful arc, into the deepest end of the pool.

Water nymph was all Jack could think of as he tentatively made his way, due to the lack of sand underfoot, so Health & Safety must be adhered to where walking on damp tiled floors was concerned, to join her with a laddish jump into the water.

She had almost reached the other end of the pool such was her proficiency in water. 'Come on baby, catch me!' she laughed back at him, wiping her hair and the residual water from her eyes.

Jack was in water heaven, he had not felt so alive since diving into the warm Mediterranean waters around Majorca. Okay, there were no yachts or fast cruisers moored up nearby and the poolside refreshments could do with some improvement but what the hell! The water was warm, notwithstanding the faint aroma of chlorine and the omission of the ocean's natural salty taste but, happy to play with him in it, was a pretty, nude woman.

After leisurely swimming about for a few minutes Jack deliberately caught up with her near the shallow end. Taking hold of her hands he pulled her slim body into close contact with his, wrapping his arms around her as he bent his head down to kiss her. Laughing at the watery kiss, she put her arms round his broad shoulders and hoisted both her legs, one either side of him, in an effort to cling to him monkey style. She giggled as he lifted her away from his body, his hands under each thigh, to sit her on the side of the pool. But when he put his head between her legs to explore with his tongue she gasped in pleasure and excitement. Putting her hands to her sides for support she laid back to enjoy the elation. After only a few minutes he brought her to a lingering orgasm.

'Oh Jack!' catching her breath she seemed amazed. 'You took my breath away. I've never had anything like that before!'

'I haven't finished yet!' Grinning he lifted her back into the water and onto him.

The water thrashed around them, displaced into frothy mini waves by their rhythmic movement. Jack, starting to feel the restrictions of his fifty years of age, aided by several suspect cigars enjoyed in the past, told her she was fantastic. He meant it. For the first time in ages he felt alive.

'You are crazy but absolutely lovely.'

She laughed back at him 'There's plenty more where that came from baby!'

When their sexual appetite was in spate she acquired them both some regulation towels from a linen store. As they dried and dressed their next meeting was arranged.

Jack arrived home with the same grin still lingering round his mouth. He had not experienced such a whacky situation for quite some time.

For Sandra, the encounter brought satisfaction of an alternative kind and one she felt indebted to fate for. The experience she had just undergone had exceeded one of her definitive dreams. Euphoric from the feeling of supreme ecstasy radiating within her body, not only from the sex she had received but also by being alone with such a handsome "real" man, Sandra, in joyful elation of the moment, had omitted to perform a crucial "off" "on" procedure concerning the swimming bath's premises.

The consequences of this simple lack of attention to detail were observed the following Saturday morning when the administration staff arrived for, what they thought would be, another boring weekend shift at work listening to the general public as they splashed and played in the warm water.

Drunk through lust and longing, Sandra had omitted to turn off the night time security CCTV video. The silent sniper had observed undetected as the pair frolicked naked, methodically shooting the evening's carnal action, the result of which meant a replay was on offer for anyone who might care to watch.

Chapter 43

Libby, Tyrone and Sarah, the three weekend duty office staff, were discussing their previous Friday evenings' entertainment while performing the routine admin "start-up" procedures before opening the pool to the general public. Nonchalantly rewinding the tape for signs of any unusual behaviour or break-in, Tyrone gave a gasp mid-description of his conversation at the pub with his girlfriend the previous night, 'She asked me "when are we going to get engaged", I said ...what the fuck?!'

'What! Why did you say that to her?' exclaimed Libby.

'No, no! Not that, to her. Look! Look at this. I don't believe it! Look at this!'

Tyrone rewound the tape a few seconds then pressed the replay button as Sarah and Libby turned to see what had caused his astonished outburst only for both their mouths to drop open in disbelief.

'Tyrone, are you trying to be funny? What tape have you put in there?'

'It's not my tape it's our tape'

'What! You and your girlfriend's? You complete tosser!'

'LISTEN both will you! LOOK! It's not me. It's this pool here. Last night. This lot is on last night's tape'

'What! Who the fuck is that?! How did they get in' said Sarah.

'Oh my god, I don't believe it!'

'What Libby? What is it' asked the other two of the detective trio.

'I know who it is!'

'Who?' They both asked in unison.

'Look. Look at the woman. You both know her.'

'Fucking hell!' Tyrone offered in awe.

The dumbfounded trio started their day with a sneak preview of a recorded display of what one could only describe as the nautical joys of sex (Tyrone made a mental note to have a bash at one particular act with his girlfriend that very evening if she would let him). "Smile you're on Candid Camera" and "You've Been Framed" never received Jack's only unconscious effort of a blue movie. The assortment of riparian positions and acts recorded in the pool was worth far more than £200 quid to some in the business.

Sandra, of course, lost her job. Her employer had no alternative really; Nocturnal Water Sex Games were not what the Local Council wanted to offer in order to draw in the general public as part of its "wide and varied" swimming programme for the winter season, however, the final damming judgement against Sandra arose due to the nuisance factor. The swimming sessions for the whole weekend had to be cancelled while the pool was drained for hygiene purposes.

As the video did not go on general release the whole affair was kept quiet. Jack, initially concerned for Sandra's lack of employment, felt it would be in their best interests to take the odd trip to a seaside B&B, which could also provide a swimming pool, in future in order to enjoy waterborne sex throughout the winter. Unbeknown to Jack however, Sandra had an agenda of her own, the job didn't matter she assured him, she would earn enough.

'Why work full time if I don't need to?!' insisting she had not lost out in any way over their reckless behaviour.

Over the winter Jack's daytime thoughts often wandered off to linger, mainly over bewildered scenarios relating to Sandra's strange outlook on life. Of all the women he had known this one seemed hell bent on some sort of crazy crusade. He accepted he had pushed the boundaries with his own risqué behaviour in the past but this woman was putting her own reputation on the line. *Why? Why should he worry?*

Because an experienced well worn feeling told him something was very wrong, *but what?* Perhaps old age was slowly creeping up on him and, after all; he had to face up to the inevitable.

A few weeks later he booked them both into a nice bed and breakfast, on the South Devon coast, for the coming weekend. More lies for guaranteed sex, but Oh! To sit down after working all day, with a woman who made you welcome, that you could converse with over a homemade dinner. Ah well, it would all come out in the wash, as his Mother used to say.

The final act that would break the camel's back, (to sum up the whole affair with no intention of suggesting Valerie was a camel) was consequently a sexual one, the outcome of which would finally terminate Jack's empty shambolic relationship with Valerie. The ultimate piece of action to come under scrutiny was brazenly performed in public and, on this occasion, there was no camera silently recording the risqué pair. In spite of this the act had been spy /eye witnessed then reported verbally, direct to the dromedary.

Chapter 44

One crisp morning, subsequent to Jack leaving for his day's work, Valerie received a cryptic telephone call from a Mr and Mrs Good Neighbour (GN) to inform her of a shocking to do which they could not possibly discuss over the telephone; you never knew who might be listening in did you? Valerie, puzzled, innocent of the disaster about to unfold directly into her lap, bid them welcome to visit and tell their tale, if possible, please within the next half hour as she had an appointment in the town later that morning.

Like two reprimanded children summoned to a Headmistress, such was the sentiment they would experience as they now found themselves sitting bolt upright on an expensive chesterfield settee, Mr and Mrs GN felt extremely uncomfortable, struggling to part with the information, now burning their tongues as they attempted to impart the sordid details of the grave misdeed they had both borne witness to. Valerie could only look at them in wonder, *what on earth had they seen to cause such consternation on their part? Were they slightly potty? Best humour them and hope they will leave as soon as their mission has been accomplished.*

Between alternate mouthfuls of coffee and biscotti, interlaced with a large spoonful of embarrassment, Mrs GN offered a halted, somewhat censored description of the action offered up in their very street the previous evening, as an alternative to regular Saturday night TV.

Coughing discretely into her hand, Mrs GN, fortified by the strong quality coffee gathered courage, then launched herself, literally off a cliff, into a description of, in as low a voice as possible, how they had witnessed Jack receiving, what she could only vaguely describe, as a sexual act, while laid part back / sitting over the bonnet of a neighbour's car, in the street directly outside their house.

'Of course, it was dark and the street lighting was not too bright. We just happened to part our curtains in order to look out into the street as we heard a noise and wondered if it might be vandals or something.'

Valerie started to feel cold. *How could he embarrass her like this? Bastard! Who the hell had he met up with now? One minute he was giving a baby to some tart rather than her, now this!* Valerie had been deeply insulted by the Dilly, baby incident, it kept returning to her memory, taunting her. Mrs GN, her witness statement now gathering momentum due to Valerie's silent manner, the result of both shock and concentration, was starting to patronise and annoy.

'We could hardly bring ourselves to watch, could we Martin? It went on for quite a long time you know!'

Valerie wanted to scream at her in protest! Managing to use restraint, thinking instead *why couldn't the nosey cow have just shut the curtains and returned to the episode of Benidorm or whatever they were watching on TV, no, she found the antics in their own street more entertaining. Damn them for being so nosey. And then to ring up and complain! Oh what a mess Jack had provided for her now. How could he? He really had gone too far this time. Everyone would know. These sorts of people made out how embarrassing the whole thing was, then happily informed anyone who would give them false sympathy.*

For someone who had given the impression of being affronted by what she saw, Mrs GN gabbled on, detailing with glee how she had watched Sandra back Jack onto the bonnet of their neighbour's car, proceed to unzip his jeans, take out his penis and perform one of the longest blow jobs possible, omitting to use the words "penis" and "blow job" which were substituted by "thing" and "use her mouth".

'Well, I never!' said Mrs GN.

No you wouldn't, thought Valerie, flushing as her conscience sent a reprimand, she had not performed this act for Jack EVER, *but you'd watch, you nosey cow.*

Jack and Sandra, oblivious to their inquisitive audience, gave not one thought that anyone living nearby might want to watch anything other than was provided by their TV set on a Saturday night.

Valerie confronted Jack on his return from work that evening, verbally throwing the damming information toward him.

Flippantly he retorted 'Why were they so compelled to watch?'

Valerie screamed at him in temper and frustration, 'I've had enough of your bloody affairs! How can you be so cavalier? You're a complete bastard!' Snatching at one of the framed photographs on display, strategically placed within her arm's range on the wall unit, she hurled the picture in fury, without aim, across the room to hit and smash against the wall close to where Jack stood, thereby breaking the glass in several pieces and tearing the picture within. The photo had been presented as a gift and reminder of Jack sharing the Jacuzzi with the twelve calendar girls.

'I suppose you fucked all of them as well' she screamed with burning wrath.

His reply of, 'I never got the chance', only served to fuel her vehemence.

The house that Jack once built was now crumbling all around him, in a pattern similar to how snow might fall.

Unlike his actual building work, his private life had never been built on solid ground. Cracks had slowly appeared in every room, a result instigated, in part, by the Dilly disaster; Sandra, "the roof" had now collapsed, leaving the foundations swiftly to follow, disintegrating into crumble and eventually powder. No foundations, no home, is a popular phrase.

An additional complication, which only served to exacerbate matters, arrived in the form of Sandra's very affronted, angry, sort-of boyfriend, who turned up in the pub, seeking revenge from the burden of carrying the complete weight of the information relating to the act, provided from a mate who could not stop laughing as he gleefully spilled the sordid beans to a bloke, he had never really liked, the following Friday afternoon.

Jack always paid his workmen on a Friday afternoon, over a pint in the local. All the erstwhile relaxed customers turned to stare in mild alarm as the savage young man stormed into the crowded public bar shouting toward Jack, 'You've been shagging my girlfriend you bastard!'

Where had Jack heard this before? He suddenly felt very tired but not tired enough to stop planting the twat with a punch straight into his enraged, furious face.

The boyfriend kept shouting obscenities, to the glee of Jack's workmen now wrapped in collective stifled mirth. Entertainment had begun early that weekend! Jack did the usual, controlling and ending the fight before the Landlord could protest, advising the boyfriend to 'Fuck off, out of it!' Which to the relief of the other customers and the Landlord, he promptly did.

You could enter the pub by one of two doors situated either end of the long rectangular bar. While Jack escorted the rather dazed boyfriend out of one door, with the help of a workmate, Sandra haplessly entered from the other. He turned to make his way back into the bar, noticing her smiling unawares, as she made her way toward him. Jack walked quickly through the amused crowd straight toward her. Grabbing her arm to usher her back out the way she had just come in he said in a more serious tone than she had thought him possible of showing, 'Don't come in here just now!'

For once his trademark grin was not lighting up his face. Jack, for once, realised that now, enough had become literally enough. It was time to pack it all in. There would be no shaking of the head and laughing when remembering this episode.

Chapter 45

The Friday night incident in the pub, concerning Sandra's boyfriend, had been quickly forgotten in time with the weekend, as it had unfolded. After escorting Sandra outside the pub, Jack had arranged to meet up with her later after closing time so they could discuss their future and, if indeed they had one.

'Sweetheart, this situation can't go on. I must either commit to you or let you go. I don't know if I'm the right man for you either. You should be with someone younger and kind, not like that twat you have now. You won't stay with him surely?'

Sandra smiled at him but replied only 'I'll see you later; we'll talk then, don't worry handsome man.'

Jack felt uneasy throughout the rest of the evening, she was so young and her behaviour was definitely eccentric at times, and the way she spoke, in riddles emulating a soothsayer; his normal Friday night routine had been disrupted leaving him unsettled. He had a sinking feeling that the same now applied to his future life.

Liaising with Sandra in her car later that night, Jack admitted he had decided it was time to leave Valerie but didn't want to jump straight from the fat into the fire.

'I need to find somewhere I can call my own. I need to give my future life some thought. What will you do about your boyfriend in the meantime? Surely you don't want to stay with him considering the way he treats you?'

She sat quietly, smiling at him like a social worker, allowing him to run on.

'Sandra, we can keep in touch with each other for the present, I can take you out now and then but the next few weeks will be difficult while I find somewhere else to live, arrange to pack and move home etc. Christ, there's so much to sort out with Valerie; after all I've been with her ten years now. Why did I let it go on for so long? It's all a complete mess and I don't want you caught in the middle.'

Sandra, put her arms around Jack in a style not dissimilar to a mother comforting a child, then spoke steadily to him 'Don't worry Jack, everything will be alright. I'll go along with anything you chose to do.'

He studied her serene expression, *what was this woman like?! Someone should take care of her, love her. I should take care of her.*

She was vulnerable and sweet natured, regardless of her unpredictable tendency to reckless behaviour. No. Jack would not be rushed; he needed time to think it all through. His track record to date had proven him far too eager, rushing head first into every previous relationship. *Where had it got him? It was time to square it with Valerie.*

Boldly selecting as decent a time of day as possible to inform her of his decision, Jack sprung to his mission after work and on her return from a family visit two days later. Difficult enough as it was for him to face up to reality and attempt to take action; Valerie immediately crumbled his resolve by pleading with him to stay.

'There's no need for you to go Jack. Please don't go, don't leave me please!' He looked at her with a mixture of bewilderment and relief. *Christ! He'd impregnated one woman and performed sexual antics for video camera and the general public, with another, plus countless other affairs of which he had no intention of collating a total. How could she want to stay with him? And why did he now feel relieved?*

He didn't really want to stay but what an upheaval to arrange for them to part. He mulled it over; it would be so inconvenient, all the packing. It would interfere with his work.

'Let's go to Paris, Jack. You can wear those new clothes I bought for you.' offered Valerie.

What was he, a bloody Barbie doll! What was the man doll called.....Ken. He was just a human Ken. No it had to stop and right now. 'Valerie! I don't want to bloody go to Paris for Christ sake'

'Okay, I thought you might feel better if you had a break but please there's no need for you to leave. We've been together so long it would be a shame to throw it all away.'

Throw all what away? He chided himself, *come on Jack, tell her it's over. Was she under the impression that theirs was a "normal" relationship?*

She took his silence as green for "Go" just one more plea on her part should do it.

'Jack, I love you so.'

He gave in. *Well, stay here a bit until you find somewhere that suits you.* He had to weigh up his options carefully. *There's no need to rush out.* They agreed he would stay in the house till he found somewhere suitable to live.

A few months later Jack was unsurprised to find himself still in residence having made no attempt to seek out a new habitat. After allowing some thought for his future he concluded there was no need for him to move out at all really because he and Valerie already lived their own lives under the same roof. He had never stopped her jetting off to visit family or friends, if he had accompanied her he would have been a sort of partner, if he stayed at their home he could almost be classed as a lodger.

A few months after the Friday fracas, Jack received a surprise telephone call from Sandra's sister, Suzie, whom he had met on a few occasions. He had spoken to Sandra on the telephone a few times since their "decider" meeting, mainly non-committal "hope you are okay" type conversation but no secret sexual assignations had been arranged to follow and he had not seen her for nearly two months at his reckoning. Jack felt it might be easier if a cooling off period was arranged and with no particular timescale assigned. Sandra's sister was, *a nice girl,* he remembered. *Why is she phoning me now I wonder?*

Before he could inform the sister of how he had not heard anything from Sandra lately and ask how she was, plus he had been working in London again so had been concentrating on his contract and what could he do for Suzie now she had telephoned him?, Suzie delivered her announcement, direct and with earnest. 'Jack, I'm sorry but I don't know how else to do this, I know you're in an awkward situation but I've got to tell you what has happened, Sandra, my sister has died.'

All Jack could offer was 'WHAT! NO! No Suzie, what has happened?' His words exploded like a cartridge from a sawn off shotgun.

'I'm sorry to tell you over the phone Jack but I don't know your address and wanted to speak with you face to face really; Sandra had ovarian cancer, she had known for over a year. She told no one, only I knew. I would rather say all this face to face like I said but you can imagine; how would I be able to wait until we met up by chance to tell you? And I felt you should know'

Jack mumbled a reply of condolence; his thoughts were confused and incredulous. Of course he understood she had no choice but to tell him this way. It was good of her to be so kind. She must be heartbroken.

'Jack, did you know she kept a diary?' Jack, his mind reeling from the receipt of such tragic news, was unprepared for the enormity of this fact.

'A diary detailing everything she had done ...with you.'

'What!'

'Yes Jack, she had logged all the places you visited together, detailing literally everything you had done.' She giggled ever so gently with embarrassment, 'She even wrote in a description of your fun at the swimming baths! Jack, I just wanted you to know that you made the last months of her life on this earth so happy.'

Jack was stunned into silence.

Suzie went on to say, 'On one page in her diary she wrote, "*Jack is my reason to live as long as possible.*" I said to that idiot she was living with, that he should let you have her diaries.'

All Jack could limply reply was, 'That twat has the diaries?' his muddled thoughts were still disbelieving of the shocking statement Suzie had just reported to him. Jack was devastated and told her so.

He had not loved Sandra but she had been full of fun. He thought of the episode at the swimming baths which had lost her the job at the time. *He wished she had told him about her illness. The situation would have been very different. He would have moved in with her, could have helped her. They could have spent her last days together. Why the hell did she not say anything?*

A few days after Suzie's phone call, the Boyfriend, proving he really was the prize twat that Jack had originally described him, did indeed pass over the diaries; he sent them through the post addressed to Valerie, who, after reading one or two selected pages, promptly destroyed them without Jack's knowledge.

Jack irrevocably packed his bags and left Valerie after being informed of the destruction of Sandra's diaries and mementoes.

'I didn't think you would want them Jack! Surely you wouldn't want them!'
'Had it not occurred to you that that was a decision for me to make and not you? Just because you tell me what clothes to wear does not mean you can choose what I read.'

Jack was very angry. Outraged, that the decision to destroy the diaries had been hers, not his. *To hold and read, then destroy them without his knowledge! It was none of her bloody business. Poor Sandra, she didn't deserve her fate. Why didn't people keep their bloody noses out of other people's business?*

The diaries could have almost been her last words to me, in private.

Jack, moving as slow as a snail, came to realise that his life of late had been ruled, quite without his knowledge, so wrapped up as he had been in his playful pursuit of women to sleep with. After all that had occurred in the past, in this particular case, he now had the momentum to leave.

Valerie, incredulously, still yearned for him to inhabit with her, possessing enough complacency to act out some form of relationship regardless of his seemingly endless catalogue of infidelity.

A strange feeling dug deep inside Jack's body when he thought about the times he had shared with Sandra, *she had always been laughing; to think that all the time she knew she was dying but kept it to herself.* Jack thought her a brave woman. To destroy the personal diaries that had brought a, deceased, woman some measure of happiness was childish. *How could paper be a threat now?* Jack was furious; his anger rendered him silent while Valerie pleaded with him to stay. He stood still for a moment, just staring at her, thinking how he had been literally paraded like a prize bull, by the ring in its nose, *what had his Mother likened him to, a trophy.*

Decision made, Jack headed straight for the master bedroom. Grabbing a travel bag from the top shelf of the built in wardrobes, he proceeded to ungraciously stuff the bulk of the clothes, and the few remaining possessions that were actually his, inside. He left his dinner suits behind, was this act an acceptance of a very different future looming for him on the horizon?

'Please don't go Jack', Valerie sat on the side of their bed.

From the corner of his eye he noticed where she sat. He yearned to throw an accusation at her, *do you realise that bed has never seen any action between us?* Valerie sat watching his movements quietly, hoping her eyes, full of remorse, might just change his mind.

Impervious to her silent strategy his rigid concentration tackled the task in hand, sorting his clothes by a simple method of evaluation; useful, throw in holdall, impractical, chuck back into bottom of wardrobe. Any clothes deemed useful that would not fit into his bag were shoved into a couple of black bin liners. The remnants, left in the bottom of the wardrobe, most of which had been provided by some of the more desirable gentlemen's outfitters, Jack summed up and decided their fate with one sentence.

'You can give that lot to a charity shop'; with one short glance around to ensure he had forgotten nothing important, he walked out of his home, true to past form, with nothing much. For a third time, Jack would leave his house and its contents behind. Third time lucky maybe?

Chapter 46

The building boom had long gone and new work had become scarce, Jack had no other option but to close his company. Many of the men that had worked for him asked if he would contact them, should he ever start up in business again. One ex-employee said, 'Not only was the work varied Jack but the Friday afternoon, end of week, pub meeting had come to be pure entertainment. No other employer, I have worked for, could match it'.

Meanwhile, notwithstanding his ability to entertain his employees with his love life, Jack knew he would have to conduct a sort of job-search in order to find something to do; he had very little savings to float on, so what does a builder do when there is no actual building work?

Smiling, as his thoughts returned to the hedonistic times he had spent on Jersey, he wondered if he should seriously attempt to contact an Escort Agency. *It would be a novelty to actually be paid for his services. Cripes! He might be sent round to one of the women he had entertained for nothing in his past. That would be hilarious! And, he would need to retrieve his dinner suits from whichever charity shop they had been gifted to.*

He was well aware of the privileged life style he had enjoyed; there had been many an occasion when his treatment had been similar to that of a King. A pleasant scene surrounding the BMW, a worthy Queen, flowed into his mind; *I wonder what she's doing now. I could contact her? Would she help him like Richard Gere's character, Julian, in American Gigolo? He was helped by a client. Shit Jack, you're becoming fanciful and anyway you haven't been framed for anything. No, he must not go back there in particular. He must move on.*

He thought of one or two other women he had known. *Julie. She was fun. No! He was too old for all that malarkey now.* He laughed at his feelings, realising he could not actually be bothered any more, some women were just too much trouble! But he must make haste to obtain a job. The local superstore always had vacancies. He thought of being a cashier on a checkout but the picture that popped into his head made him laugh. *His huge hands and fingers would push more than one button on the Till at a time! Who knew what chaos he could cause there? It might not be too bad; everything was bar-coded now anyway. He could flirt with the female customers. No, that would be rather sad, not my line at all* thought Jack.

And so, it came to pass, that Jack eventually found himself living in a charming but damp flat, hidden amongst the Devon countryside and.....all alone.

Chapter 47

Ever get the feeling that something has peaked and from now on it's all downhill? One morning (now in his mid-fifties) Jack, awakening from his previous evenings slumber, slowly scanned his immediate surroundings, a regular act that was in no way different to any other day, but on this particular morning his eyes perceived the reality of his present situation beyond that which was held within his bedroom walls.

He realised he'd been staring into space but at nothing in particular. He actually studied his bedroom, one of just two rooms making up a pretty, but damp, flat (Devon is well renowned for its valley mists), the accommodation supplied with the job he had managed to procure.

He precipitously apprehended that his life, so far, had been based on what could only be described as a sexual odyssey. In comparison with Odysseus, he had returned to his home only to find chaos. Jack's life to date had left him with nothing but memories; some of which, just like the King of Ithaca, were fabulous. A plethora of women, some very beautiful, some very wealthy but in the main connected only with hedonistic times. His trademark grin lit up his face as he recalled a few thoughts from some rampant times related to his past. *So many women! They had just thrown themselves at him. Why should he say no? Any man would have done the same, given the opportunity.*

But rarely had true love been allowed to spring. Jack, in study of his face seemed almost wistful. On the rare occasion that love might have been allowed to brighten his life or tempt him to be faithful, it had quickly fallen on barren ground. And, with the constant passage of time, the actual detail related to certain incidences making up his journey through life had become hazy; so many wonderful memories had been lost in misty time barriers too far back in the past, with no chance to rekindle.

His awareness of the reality of his present existence hit Jack hard; it was quite evident now that everything he had experienced in his life had only really lasted for the brief time period to which it belonged.

During his crazy, fun times with the Band he had rubbed shoulders with the rich and famous, would they remember him now? He doubted it. He smiled with sadness in appreciation, reminiscing over the beautiful voice of Annie Lennox, his favourite female singer; he had met her during one of the Band's recording sessions many years ago. He had felt privileged to hear her sing, not in concert but even better, in the private recording studio of another famous musician; as part of a practice session and in a relaxed atmosphere, she had sung with raw energy; the sound had been beautiful, literally music to his ears.

His thoughts returned to his home ground. As part of his lifetime achievement record, there were no gold stars for Jack, he had accumulated no assets of any real value, not much of an attraction to a prospective future partner. The houses he had bought or built for each accompanying marriage or relationship, he had happily ceded to every corresponding scorned female but, slightly more of a concern to him was the fact that, at some point along the raunchy ride his life had eventually become, Jack had mislaid his Rolex watch and, of slightly more concern, his leather Valentino coat.

Wistfully he sifted through one or two fond memories of his visit to Rome with the Band. He could still remember the actual year and the very prestigious place where the coat had been purchased. Then his thought turned to panic. *Why had he only just realised these two possessions were missing! Where and when the hell had he lost them?!*

Frustrated, he tried to remember the last time he had worn his Rolex watch and *where the hell was the coat? Shit!* He always took off his watch and placed it, while sleeping / shagging on the bedside table or floor beside whichever bed he had literally jumped into at the time. Had he left it in a woman's bedroom somewhere? *If so which one? Shit! How could he not remember! What if a husband had found it?*

'Oh it's a surprise gift for you my darling husband', he imagined one or two of his harem offering for an excuse.

He had allowed his life to hurtle out of control. *What was he going to do about it? Where would he go? Just stay here in Devon for the rest of his life?*

Most men would surely envy him his new job; managing a fishery and teaching people to fish. Surely an Odyssey in its own right for many men! But Jack would never be Jack without a woman. His very existence had always depended on some sort of a relationship with the opposite sex. However, there appeared to be no available, compatible or game female within a twenty mile radius that he was aware of. Fancy! It appeared he was completely buggered.

What is the saying? "If the mountain doth not come to you..." well, it would definitely have to go to Jack, because, while describing this tale of fun and frolic I have omitted to inform you that he no longer possessed a car, if he was going anywhere it would be on foot or by bus. He had to exist on a frugal income these days so taxi journeys were now slightly out of his price range.

Looking out through his bedroom window he made a short survey of the beautiful rolling, Devon countryside. If nothing else, he at least felt at peace, well, once he had got out of bed and that specific morning's erection had subsided, anyway.

Jack so missed female company. But, apart from this one thing, he was grateful to live in such a stunning area. His two room flat, provided with the job, was situated at the edge of a wood, adjoining to which were grass filled fields sloping gently away into the valley. Many a morning he had woken to peer carefully through the bedroom curtains and been privileged to spot one, or maybe two, roe deer nibbling daintily at the farmer's precious grass in the field next door or wake to the cry of the baby buzzard circling high in the hope of spotting a tasty meal for breakfast, perhaps a vole or field mouse, negligently breaking its safe cover from beneath the undergrowth.

His nearest neighbours lived in a scattered spatial geographical layout, mainly on remote farms or cottages, and were delightful. Often they would telephone and enquire if Jack would like a lift to the nearest village or town whenever they might need to visit. Settling into his new life, his thoughts occasionally returned to selected chapters in his past, the most recent of which appeared, on the whole, the most vivid.

He knew the opportunity to open and consume bottles of "Chrystal" champagne, as he had done on many an occasion in the past, would probably not arise in his future life, bleak as it now appeared and, almost certainly not if based on his current financial position. Still, Jack was not one to dwell on sad thoughts and he clearly understood how he had arrived in the position where he now found himself. He had been content to enjoy the high life while it had lasted and thrown his entire being into every opportunity that had come his way but in the meantime he had a fishery to run; putting his pleasant thoughts of the past away, temporarily, he made a conscious effort to ready himself for the day before him. Bacon and egg for breakfast, smashing! And, he never knew who he might meet today.

Through his kitchen window Jack saw the first two fishermen of the day arrive, via a Range Rover, in the car park; he studied them as they exchanged their shoes for designer wellingtons, one chap, he noticed, wore a very superior, and expensive, wax jacket. Jack remembered he had once owned one of the same, *now where the hell did he leave that? It would have come in handy now.* A random thought, sent from Mr Mischief, rode roughshod through his mind to tempt him like the sirens sent to destroy Odysseus, *take the easy route Jack; you don't have to stay here. You can have all these nice things again, go back ...go back.*

Epilogue

A couple of years before I started this literary piece, I boldly decided to head off for the day, alone, into the backwoods of deepest Devon. Due a week's holiday from work, I decided to spend a day learning to fly fish. I had always wanted to learn how to fly fish and was delighted to have come across a free voucher which would entitle me to a few hours, plus tuition, for a reduced price at a local fishery.

My father never had any interest in the sport, although he would have taught me if he could. As a successful ex-heavyweight boxer the fact he'd been presented with me, a baby girl, the only child by my Mother, didn't help much either. Girls didn't learn to fish did they? And they definitely did not box, not in my father's day anyway.

Born in Devon I have no fear driving through its notoriously small lanes but my destination for that particular day lead me into ever decreasing pathways that were just wide enough for a car to pass. I had only just got my licence back after six months duration, due to being temporarily banned because of my health scare so I was still a bit nervous of driving. The event that had befallen me the previous year had stripped me of confidence, not capability. It had also affected my self-belief in relation to a lot of other personal pursuits; especially sex. Not only was I in my fifties I was also single; how would I meet anyone of the opposite sex to go on a date with and who would want to sleep with me anyhow? Sorry, I digress.

So, such are Devon's lovely lanes; built for the traditional horse and cart most have now been forced aside widened over time by tarmac and diesel powered machinery, the tyres of which pare the natural hedges as they traverse. As I advanced however, I became concerned, as the lanes, although easily passable for my vehicle, grew narrower as I approached my destination, if I did indeed draw near to my destination. I couldn't be too sure of my progress because I couldn't see over the hedges on either side of my vehicle. At one stage I thought of giving up and feared I might even be lost. No way could I turn back, I had inches to spare either side of my car, there was no room for any direction other than forward. My imagination grew wild. Perhaps the lanes would just swallow me whole, never to be heard of again. I heard my family discuss my demise. *"We told Mum not to go there on her own!"* The local gossip would carry on for millennia, *"er went missin' in them lanes you naw...."* The enduring speculation would be on a par with the so called "Beast" of Bodmin moor.

For one split second, as I approached a fork in the road (for the purpose of clarification, no one had actually left a garden fork lying in the road, the road split to offer two directions in which you could travel), I nearly turned back, which way should I go now? I had not spotted a directional sign since turning off the A361 and I didn't fancy retracing my steps the way I had just come. To use an old cliché, a "feeling" compelled me to continue by taking the road leading to the left, however, I had disgracefully lost faith in my instinct mainly due to the height of the lanes; I was literally driving in a maze with no sense of direction. At this particular point I wished I had read the instruction manual for the Sat Nav. I've never really bothered preferring to rely on the age old skill of reading a map, plus it is well noted that women are extremely good map readers.

I finally gave in to technology; after three calls on my mobile phone to the fishery owner (lucky there was a signal) I reached my destination, albeit slightly in disgrace through my own lack of competency; how is it possible that a Devon born girl could be bloody lost in her own lanes?

Stepping out of my small truck, I felt rather relieved if not a little self satisfied. Through a mixture of luck, technology and the aid of an out of date AA road map, I had eventually arrived at my intended destination.

The Fishery owner appeared, as if on cue, from behind a nice row of (sadly) unused stables to greet and congratulate me on my navigational skills.

'You made it then!'

Cheeky git.

After exchanging the usual pleasantries, offered upon greeting between most humans, he encouraged me, 'Okay my love, when you are ready just take yourself on over to the Clubhouse and make yourself a cup of tea, do you see the new timber building over there? My Manager will get you started. You can't miss him he's a big guy. His name is Jack.'

As I, and it has to be said, nervously, walked toward the very neat log cabin style clubhouse, a man, in possession of not only an extremely large fish but an even bigger grin, came around the corner, 'Hello' he said, 'Good luck'

I thanked him in the hope another woman might materialise. No chance. I was on my own here. By the way, did you know that the record for the largest salmon ever caught in Britain is still held by a woman - Georgina Ballantine who set the record in 1922 for a salmon weighing 64lbs landed on the River Tay. Ah well, the male fishermen within the vicinity appeared a friendly bunch and not too surprised to observe a woman on the scene.

Having almost with a giggle, smiled a 'Thank you' in reply, *what the hell was up with me? Nervous I suppose,* I prepared to take my next footstep toward a cup of tea when all of a sudden; from around the back of the stables, a huge man appeared. *Shit!* I thought. *I wouldn't want to upset him!*

I was immediately aware of his large solid frame which suggested "don't mess with me" but bizarrely, the top of his head was covered in curly, pale sandy coloured hair that offered, at cross purpose, "I'm quite a pussycat really".

A smile, or perhaps something you might describe as closer to a grin, spread across his mouth. 'Are you fishing?'

'Err, attempting to, yes'

'Oh, well done! We get one or two women here but not very often. Glad you came'

With the admission of these words he instantly dismissed the feeling of unawares that had previously encouraged me to feel nervous because the man now standing in front of me was huge, generating an appearance far more imposing than any random action of entering a wholly male dominated environment could procure. I guessed his weight at around eighteen stone, my expertise in this area brought about due to his apparent similarity in stature to my friend's husband, a rugby player whose position on the team had been generally described as "loose prop" or "prop head" or some other strange reference; possibly describing his ability and capability to mangle anyone in his way. The man now standing before me could certainly mangle anyone in my opinion. My thoughts translated themselves into a random statement for some strange reason. I felt compelled to blurt out, 'I bet few people mess with you?'

'Oh one or two in the past but as you said not many. Come on then, let's get you started. Have you done any fishing before?'

'Yes, a little but a long time ago and I've forgotten most of it'

'No problem. You'll have some idea at least'

He grabbed a rod which had already been tackled up, 'Have you had a cup of tea?'

'I'm fine for the minute'

'Well, feel free to go into the clubhouse any time and help yourself. It looks like we will get some rain. Take a break then if you like but please help yourself okay?'

'Okay, thanks'

'Right let's try this pond over here, follow me please.'

I watched him carefully tie the fly onto the line. Standing so close I could see the flecks of grey mixed within the light brown hair but he had plenty of it.

'Right, watch me'

He cast the rod gracefully over the water, carefully letting more line free with each cast. After a few attempts he stopped. I watched in awe as the remaining line flew out toward the middle of the pond.

'Okay, got the idea'

I nodded, not entirely confident of copying his example completely.

In an attempt to duplicate his experienced and most elegant cast, I slashed the line at the water; as I did so I noticed a few fish scarper down toward the bottom of the pond.

'Take it slower' he said. 'After two or three goes, let the line out full.'

Please go away, I thought, *leave me to practice on my own this is so embarrassing with you watching!*

'That's better just take your time. Will you be okay while I go and get the next chap started?'

Thank goodness 'Oh, fine, yes, and no problem. I'm fine. I'll practice. Don't let me stop you'

'But I'm here to help you. I'll come back when I've got him started okay? And don't forget, help yourself to a cup of tea'

I thanked him, glad in the knowledge he would not be present to mark my ridiculous attempts at lassoing a fish for a while. However, he had been gone no more than ten minutes when I managed to entice one to my line. I think I hooked the poor aquatic creature on the return of a slash, rather than tempted it to bite after spotting the fly resting in the water. I reeled it in giving the expression that I suffered from mild dyspraxia.

It weighed in, I guessed, at around a hefty 1lb; I hadn't baked cakes throughout my life to end up with little knowledge of weight, *bugger he was on his way back.*

'Oh! Well done! You've got one'

'Err, yes. About a pound I'd say'

'I think you're right. Let's tackle you up again then. You can catch up to three fish today'

'Righty ho then!' *Shit, did I just say "righty ho?" He'll think I'm a fruit cake.*

As I stood beside him, watching him select a fly from his own fly-box, I studied him a second time. He felt... *gentle.* Yes, that was it. Gentle. He was big but very gentle. And there was something else about him. What was it?

He looked up at me once he had finished attaching the fly. I noticed he had big, but soft brown eyes. I quickly averted mine; without realising I had almost been in a trance through staring at him.

'Now, you tie the fly on like I showed you before, okay?'

'Okay' why were my fingers shaking? 'Oops, I'm all fingers and thumbs today. Will you do it please?' *What lovely soft brown eyes he's got.*

'Right, there you go. Let's see you cast again'

Bugger! I wish you would go and leave me. I slashed at the water, embarrassed at my own performance.

'You're almost trying to whip it. Try to think of *casting* the line into the water, gracefully. You appear to be trying to punish it!'

I made a sober attempt to slow down and then got the feel of what he was on about. 'Bugger, the line's caught'

He laughed, 'Don't worry, I'll get it. But that was much better'

He walked over to where the line had caught at the edge of a wooded area.

'Just tug the line a bit so I can see where it went will you?'

I flicked the rod and, not only did the line miraculously free itself, but it returned accompanied by a piece of leaf that seemed determined to cling on, unfortunately as he raised his hand to catch hold of the line I shook the rod in an attempt to dislodge the unwelcome piece of fauna, my action proceeded to jerk the whole and the fly dug its barb into his finger.

'Yeea-awch!'

'Oops! Sorry!' I cringed.

He turned to look at me with mild exasperation furrowing his brow.

I felt a complete fool. *Bugger! Trust me. I have to admit, he is very good looking come to think of it.*

He started to grin.

I laughed, 'I'm really sorry' then giggled a bit more.

He looked into my eyes after carefully picking the fly out of his skin. A ripple shot across the inside of my body like a sand snake. *Flippin' heck he really was quite a stunner. He had to have a wife or girlfriend somewhere close by.*

After preparing myself once again, I took up the rod and he went off to leave me to my own devices, whipping whatever fish were foolish enough to swim toward my vicinity of the pond.

After a few hours alternately standing in the rain or making a cup of tea Id caught nothing else and thought it about time I called it a day. I could always pay another visit. The whole experience had gone well for me. My confidence in my own ability was returning and before long maybe I could almost forget what had happened to me, well, a little bit at least.

I gathered my equipment and turned to head back to the Clubhouse. He saw me from where he was standing, in the midst of helping what can only be described as a competent angler land a 5lb Trout. I felt envious.

'Hey, come and take a look at this one'

I walked over and congratulated the fisherman.

'Thanks and it's nice to see a woman fishing, there are not many about. Good for you'

I smiled and turned back to the Clubhouse.

'You're not going are you?'

'Well I think I've terrorised the fish enough for today'

'Look I'll be finished soon. Would you fancy having a bite to eat in the local pub?'

My heart literally stopped. I managed to stop my mouth falling open.

'Err, aren't you married or anything?'

'Oh, I have been in the past' He started to laugh. 'The stories I could tell you. I've been a bit of a lad in my time. Anyway, that was long ago. Would you like to have some dinner with me?'

After gaffing his finger on the hook while I wildly slashed my rod across the pond, like a cowboy rounding up cattle, he still appeared keen to ask me out to dinner. I can cope with that I thought and *he'll never know I'm different by just going out to dinner with him. What if he wants to sleep with you? What makes you think he would want to? Cross that bridge when I come to it.* I heard myself say, 'Yes, that would be nice, thank you'

*

I must admit I was a bit nervous but once we arrived in the pub, a roaring fire throwing out a welcoming heat on entry, I relaxed. A country girl at heart, I was brought up in the city. This urban female qualification, accompanied by good old primeval intuition, will always send an alert for a woman to be on the lookout when another is eyeing up your man. As I had not been in a similar situation for quite some years I was pleased to think that my senses were still in full working order as I detected the one or two women who looked in our direction with interest, as we entered, straight away.

I had never been out with such a handsome man before. We also had a lot in common. We both loved the country life and conversation was never slow. He also made me giggle but I could not understand why or where this girlie behaviour was coming from. Did it matter?

The evening went so well between us that we arranged another date. "Date!" We were both over fifty! It felt weird to use the same word, having the same meaning, to a teenager.

*

A couple of weeks later I returned, he greeted me like we had been friends for life.

'I booked us a table at the same pub, or would you like to go somewhere else'

'No, it was lovely there, I'd love to go there again, thanks' I giggled. But, during the afternoon, while I should have been concentrating on my fishing technique my thoughts tormented me.

Are you going to sleep with him? Will he want to when he knows? Look you only have to go to dinner. But he's gorgeous and I'd love to sleep with him.

Having only slightly worried a few fish, all had managed to avert my rod and line during the afternoon, I made a start on packing my gear and prepared to walk over to take a shower in the little, two room, cottage where he lived.

He came in as I was collecting my towel.

'You won't try to follow me in will you?' *What! Did I say that! What the hell for? He'll think you're a right idiot.*

He laughed, 'Don't worry your safe with me. Women normally walk in on me.' I lost his attention momentarily, he gave the impression he had returned to an event in his past. He returned quickly, sporting a grin and said 'Give me a shout when you've finished and I'll go in after you'

Once again the evening went well. We both got on, you could say, like a house on fire; we appeared to have so much in common. I also realised, with extreme clarity, that our desire to unite in bed was, very probably, a contributory factor to the inferno building within us both. He made it quite clear that if I wanted it, I could have it. Trouble was would his offer still stand once he caught sight of the, almost square, metal object sitting just under my skin above my left boob?

I certainly wanted it and this could be my last chance, so I chose "go get it".

Returning from the pub we started to kiss. I don't know how I got there but in just a few minutes I was stood by the bed. He gently put one hand on the right side of my face while the other attempted to pull my top sideways to expose my left shoulder, planting gentle kisses down the side of my neck as he did so, *bugger, Only a few inches lower and he'll see the unit.* I hoped he couldn't detect the feeling of despair raging through my heart, *Shit! Don't get your heart going. The pacemaker bit will be going overtime.* I froze.

'What's wrong darling? You look worried. Christ I'm not going to hurt you'
'Ha ha' I laughed nervously, it's me that could hurt you!'

'Eh! What!'

Shit! he'll think I'm a right nut case. Why did I have to die for goodness sake, only to come back fixed up with a piece of metal inside my body with the potential to deliver a shock like an electric eel?

Well, in all fairness the Consultant never said how hard a shock the unit would deliver; one doom filled assistant, mentioned the possibility of my being blown backwards across the room; so let's face it, it's not too romantic when you go to insert your key in the lock and instead of that nice warm feeling you give the bugger an electric shock instead. Oh, very sexy indeed. I imagined the outcome, *'How was it for you sweetie?' 'The shock was electric darling, electric', can we do it again soon?'*

Surely, the only males I would attract, sexually, in the future would have to possess kinky masochistic tendencies. I came back from my miserable fantasy only to gaze into the face of one of the most attractive and sexy men I had ever seen in my life. And, he did not reside within the covers of a glossy magazine, was not acting in a film or drama on the Telly and did not belong to anyone else; in short, he was very, very real and all mine to play with. *What the hell was up with me? I knew what to do; I didn't require the guidance of an instruction manual, surely?*

And, if the bully girls that had attended my school, all those years ago, could see me now! Eighteen stone's worth of ex-boxer, rugby player and, sex object. *He'll reject me once he's enlightened to the device.* The nurse had likened the ICD (Implantable cardioverter-defibrillator, try saying that when you're drunk...) to an angel. 'Just think of it as your own personal angel watching over you'

Manners bit back my planned retort of, 'Will she let me have sex without butting in?'

Life was so unfair, what a tease.

Over dinner Jack had, and it has to be said with slight embarrassment, explained how over the course of his life, he had at one stage been, literally, an unpaid gigolo; unqualified gynaecologist and, on one specific occasion, an uncertified marriage guidance counsellor.

If I slept with him, like I really wanted to, I would be the first woman he had ever slept with that nursed, not a viper, but a defibrillator inside her bosom; bringing a whole new meaning to the phrase "Did the Earth move for you?" At the most, or least, I wasn't sure; he might feel a bit of a tingle…apparently.

At least there was one dead cert going my way; at over fifty years old I had no worries about getting pregnant, only a handicap that could possibly deliver 5,000 volts to any person willing to have sex with me. *Now your exaggerating woman, pack it in, face up to the problem.*

I came back to my problem. Jack was now staring at me, a peculiar look on his face.

'Look, you don't have to do anything we can just have a coffee and talk. I'd like to see you again in any case. No woman I have ever met wanted to fish and we have such a lot in common'

As he started to turn for the kitchen, my one remaining hormone kicked in, sneaky little bugger, *'Go for it, you've nothing to lose, go for it!'* I knew I had to react quickly or he would forget the whole thing.

'Please don't move'

'Eh?'

'Please don't move. I want to sleep with you but, but .....'

'What? Please, can't you trust me? Please tell me what's wrong'

I blurted the words out quick in the hope he wouldn't hear.

'I've got a defibrillator-pacemaker fitted, it's above my left boob, see?' I pulled the neck of my cotton top to the side where you can just see the corner of my angel, sticking out from under my skin. 'I better tell you. I'm sorry, I understand if it will put you off.'

'Put me off! You're the sexiest looking woman I've come across in ages. Why the hell should a pacemaker put me off? I thought I noticed something strange sticking out at the side of your top when you brushed your hair back.'

'Well, thing is, if you get me TOO over excited my heart might get stressed and if it stops, with the excitement, the defibrillator will shock me to get my heart going again'

'Why should I worry about that as long as you're all right?'

'Well, if it shocks me you'll be attached to me so you'll feel it as well....I think...well, no one has actually discussed in great detail my having sex with the defibrillator fitted. I'm.., oh, I'm so sorry, I feel so awkward'

He looked bewildered.

Bugger! My one chance to get laid with the sexiest, most handsome man I had ever come across in my life and I've blown it.

He started to grin. The grin spread right across his face making him look real cheeky and even sexier, or was my one hormone full to capacity with overexcitement?

Carefully and quietly he held his hand out toward me.

'Come on baby, shock me!'

I drew in a deep breath, took off my cotton top and walked with him toward the bed. I glanced at my reflexion in the mirror hung on the wall. Making a study of me by way of return, I beheld a confident woman; she wore a sexy, black lace body, her seductive look was completed by the un-matching defibrillator peeking out over the top line of the garment, just above her heart.

My hormone screamed *'Go for it girl!'* What the hell, I knew there was a phone in the next room if I needed to get the ambulance for him and I felt like helping myself to some dessert. A giggle appeared from somewhere, circa 1971, my sense of responsibility and seriousness disintegrated. My hormone appeared to have collated a few more like minded friends.

I don't know why but I jumped toward the bed to land beside him. He burst out laughing at the catastrophe that followed.

Now I'm only nine and a half stone but whether nine and a half leaping, straight onto eighteen already laying is a bit of a force, I can't say, I never took much notice of Physics in school it not being my particular forte. Anyway, one can only assume the resulting combined weight, of twenty seven stone, or thereabouts, broke the bed and it collapsed on one side. We both burst out laughing.

My nerves started to settle a little and I tried to relax back into his arms. It's not easy because a defibrillator is around three inches wide and it's not made of rubber so it doesn't bend which means you have to arrange your shoulder and arms into a comfortable position sometimes. My negative thoughts broke through the locked gate to freedom, *He will get fed up with all this*, and it's not very romantic or sexy. I was just about to apologise again when he enquired in an altogether far too cheeky manner, 'Have you made yourself comfy now sexy, can I begin?'

I giggled, 'Sorry, it's not easy to relax'

'Don't be sorry, just let me love you'

I let him put his arms around me and away we went.

By the time he had performed one or two moves, that I had never before encountered, I really was nearly gasping in ecstasy. I could feel the orgasm building in my body; I started to moan, swamped as I was with a feeling of sheer pleasure. Inside my head, however, another negative section, the annoying Health and Safety, warned *'careful now, don't get too excited'*

Fuck off, I thought back in reply.

Oh my god! I gasped as I shot into space, half expecting the four inch metal manmade encore to stick its oar in and allow a shock to kick in, but my little angel obviously approved of sex.

I looked at him in wonder, still trying to catch my breath.

He grinned at me 'Are you okay? Was that good for you?'

I grinned back, allowing a sultry look to settle on my face, 'I'm fine, never felt better sweetie' a giggle escaped, I felt I had returned to my teenage years.

I felt my heart, it was beating steady. I wanted to congratulate the pacemaker section for pacing along nicely, as a good orchestra should, while I, the soloist, had lain back to experience the most profound plucking of my Stradivarius.

My hormones (there was now definitely more than one) were still on full alert and had liked what they had just experienced and were now demanding the full union of our bodies.

Did someone actually inform me I should take it steady when having sex with the ICD fitted? I couldn't remember and anyway I didn't care. I threw myself into the fun, completely forgot about the little metal box sat just below my collar bone, sat myself atop of him and rode my way into the sunset of ecstasy.

Rolling off, I relaxed and sank back into the bed, feeling complete and very alive. 'Fancy being my girlfriend sexy lady?'

'Do you only offer once you've tested them out for comfort?'

'You are one of the sexiest women I have ever come across and I've known many. I don't mean to brag either. It's just the way it was'

'You've had so many; I suppose I would have my uses', *where had my confidence gone?*

He grinned, 'Apart from being beautiful to look at, what particular use had you in mind?'

I studied him carefully; experience had left me wary of trusting men. I needed reassuring, especially since I had more or less become a, sort of, bionic woman. Why could I not be triumphant in the knowledge that the unit had not started to beep (alerting a need to change the battery) mid hump?

'Just what makes me so special? You've slept with umpteen beautiful women; literally offered up to you on a plate, according to your own admission', I laughed, 'Your own personal collection of Dolly's, like a bag of dolly mixtures!'

'Ah! But you're a very different Dolly to the others, you're the only one.'

'The only one, what? Do you mean like Tigger?'

He laughed again 'You could say that but you're the only woman I've known fitted with a defibrillator, you're my "Defibrillator Dollybird".'

I smiled, he made me seem very special but I was still full of realism. My life was slower in pace but I was still here to enjoy it. I studied his face but was lost for words with which to speak. But he carried on.

'Look, I've no money, I lost the lot, left it all behind in the houses I built, given to one woman or another, but you can have me and my love, exclusively; if you want it, it's all yours. Fancy growing old with me?'

I grinned, 'I'll think about it' *that grin of his was so fetching.*

'I think you're electrifying! Come here baby ...shock me.'

The End

Made in the USA
Charleston, SC
21 April 2015